DEVC

Please return/rene
Renew on te.
www.devonlibraries.org.uk

| SE 7/20 | | | | |
|---------|---|---|---|---|
|         |   |   |   |   |

Printed by Hedgerow Print, Crediton, Devon, EX17 1ES

Chudleigh Phoenix Publications

For the original Chibesa and WB;
Their fight goes on.

# ACKNOWLEDGMENTS

I have benefited greatly during the writing of this book from the support provided by my friends in thriving community of writers and readers in Devon and beyond, and I want to thank them all: Margaret Barnes for once more being my writing partner during the editing of our books; to my friends in Chudleigh Writers' Circle and Exeter Writers; to Sue, Clare and Helen, my MA buddies; and to Mary Anne McFarlane, Heather Morgan and Richard Morgan, Jenny Benjamin and Clare Lillington, my beta readers.

I am grateful to all my friends and colleagues in Africa who were so helpful and supportive during the COMESA project. In my research, I was particularly helped by three books: *In The Shade of the Mulberry Tree* by Catharine Withenay and *Don't Let's Go To The Dogs Tonight* by Alexandra Fuller helped fill in the gaps about life in Zambia and other countries in the region; and *An Evil Cradling* by Brian Keenan enabled me to write about a situation I will hopefully never experience myself.

Berni Stevens (@circleoflebanon) is responsible for the beautiful cover; Julia Gibbs (@ProofreadJulia) made sure the final text is as error-free as possible. My thanks go to both of them. I also owe a huge debt of gratitude to my sisters, Margaret Andow and Sheila Pearson, for their analytical reading skills, ongoing support and interminable phone calls. Finally, my thanks go, as always, to my husband Michael McCormick, my fiercest critic and strongest supporter, who keeps telling me 'just keep writing'.

# PROLOGUE: ZAMBIA; DEC 2003

Kabwe Mazoka walks up the hill, scuffing his feet in the rutted and baked red earth. It's been dry for months, but today thick clouds mask the sun and when the rains come, this will be a water course, pouring mud and stinking filth into the main street below. He turns through a broken-down gate and walks across the yard. A mangy dog, tied with rope to a ring on the fence, jumps to its feet yelping before sinking back on its haunches, eyeing him warily.

The building was painted white once. Pale flakes cluster around rusty lines where the reinforcing bars are breaking through the pitted concrete. In the single row of windows running below the flat roof, most of the panes of glass are missing.

A line of women sit in the dirt against the wall, taking advantage of the shade from the over-hanging roof. As Kabwe unlocks the shiny new padlock on the door, they rise and slowly follow him into the building. The first raindrops splash into the dust.

The downpour hits the corrugated iron roof like stones from an angry crowd. Kabwe uses a metal pole to stir the thick, creamy liquid in the cleaned-out oil drum.

The men were coming back today, bringing brightly

coloured labels and delivery instructions. They would be cross if the bottles weren't filled ready for labelling and packing. He didn't want them to be cross again.

They'd been cross when he suggested testing the ingredients before making the medicine. They showed him pieces of paper with green stickers and words in another language. They told him to 'just get on with it.' So he did.

When Kabwe ran out of the glycerol used to sweeten the cough medicines, they brought him drums in a battered lorry and told him to 'get them unloaded and stored in the lock-up.' The drums were different from the ones he'd had previously. These were red. Last time they were blue. The name was different too, longer. They told him it was just the chemical name for the same material. He pointed to the place where warning symbols and storage conditions were usually printed. The labels had been scratched and scraped; none of the words were legible. The men laughed at him and told him to 'just get on with it.' So he did.

Today, the men arrive just as the last of the brown bottles is being filled. They'd been pleased with Kabwe when he managed to source these from the local glass plant. For eleven months each year, the plant makes beer bottles, then the mechanics switch the moulds and they make medicine bottles, a year's supply in just four weeks. They need a lot more beer bottles than medicine bottles in Africa.

These bottles are rejects, slightly misshapen, no good for an automated bottling line. But Kabwe's filling team holds bottles under a tap, one at a time, operating the pump with a foot-pedal. He was able to negotiate a good price for them—and the bottling plant was able to hide the true reject rate, so everyone gained.

The perfect bottles would be sold to the reputable companies, the subsidiaries of multinationals or local companies working under licence to one of the well-known names. Kabwe's father's company had been one of those. For more than twenty years, they made cough syrups with someone else's name and logo on them. Once a year, auditors would fly in from London, talk to all the managers and some of the staff, check through a couple of batch documents—and confirm the renewal of their licence.

Then, five years ago, in a meeting far away, a decision was made and a takeover launched; two companies became one and thousands of lives were changed forever. With a super-sized factory in South Africa supplying the entire region, there was no need for licensees producing their cough syrups. Kabwe's father lost the contract and, with it, his factory. Within six months, he was dead and Kabwe was head of the family. Two months later, the men came to visit for the first time.

The new labels are pink and blue with white writing. The company name—this time an American one with an address in Milwaukee—is printed in small letters at the bottom. The picture of a mother and child looks comforting, although Kabwe wonders why they always use white people as models.

Just before the men drive away, they hand Kabwe an envelope, stuffed with stained and greasy banknotes. Now he'll be able to pay the filling team. Now he'll be able to buy supplies on the way home. Now his mother will be able to keep her appointment at the clinic.

The vans drive off into the night, heading for unprotected borders, to meet other vehicles driven by other desperate men trying to earn enough to feed their families. Kabwe sits slumped in his office, too tired to move, and tries to still the doubts flying around his head.

The men had told him the American company wouldn't mind. 'They sell medicines all over the world,' they said. 'They won't miss a few sales in Africa,' they said. 'You're helping people get hold of medicines they couldn't normally afford,' they said. 'It's a public service really,' they said.

Kabwe glances at the dispatch instructions for the latest batches of cough syrup. There are six names on the list: three government purchase houses; two regional hospitals; and a large distributor. They are spread across Angola, Malawi, Zimbabwe and Tanzania. He is relieved, as always, to see his own country missing from the list. Not his people, not this time. But one day, he knows, it will be their turn.

# PART I

# 1: SWAZILAND, SEPT 2004

'In conclusion, lack of controls on imports makes it inevitable that many of the medicines available in Africa today are counterfeit.' Suzanne Jones looked up from her notes. The light was dim. Moth-eaten gold velvet curtains had been closed to block out the midday sun, but she knew the hall contained representatives of every branch of healthcare in the region. There were regulators, mainly black Africans, from Kenya, Uganda, Tanzania, Mozambique, Zambia and Zimbabwe, hoping to learn from their South African colleagues, known to be even stricter than the American Food and Drug Administration. There were the Asian owners of local pharmaceutical factories, desperate for hints on how they could win vital government tenders. The very few white faces in the room belonged to the Afrikaans distributors or ex-pat managers of the handful of multinational companies still trying to maintain a presence in Southern Africa.

Suzanne took a deep breath and spoke directly to the hundred-plus delegates. 'The Intergovernmental Health Forum knows the problem is particularly bad here in Africa. We're doing everything we can to disrupt the supply chains at the factories. However, Africa must play its part by tightening controls.' She paused, smiling to take the sting out of her words. 'Thank you for your attention. Are there any questions?'

'I'm sorry, but I don't have the luxury of worrying about quality. My responsibility is to provide enough drugs for all the people. If a few bad ones get through, it's the price we have to pay.' The Honourable Walter Mukooyo, Kenyan Minister of Health, leaned back in his chair. He mopped his forehead with a large spotted handkerchief, and glared over his half-moon glasses at the crowded hall, as though challenging anyone in the audience to disagree with him. The minor civil servants who made up the Minister's entourage were sitting in the front row, nodding vigorously.

Suzanne bit back angry words. She tucked damp strands of long, straw-coloured hair behind her ears and tried to ignore the sweat trickling between her shoulder blades, down her back and soaking into the elastic of her knickers. She really didn't want to lose her temper in front of this group.

'That's an interesting viewpoint, Minister,' she said. 'I'd like to return to that during the panel discussion this afternoon. We're running a little behind on the agenda. Can I suggest we break for lunch now and pick up with Dr Businge's presentation in an hour's time?'

Someone switched the lights on and the delegates began filing out of the conference hall. Suzanne shoved her papers into her briefcase, muttering to herself. She looked around for the rest of her team.

'We did warn you he might be difficult,' said Chibesa Desai, who was lounging against the side of the stage. 'This is the guy who stood up in Parliament last week and announced he'd secured a huge consignment of drugs through his charity connections. The fact that they're out-of-date batches from China is irrelevant. He's the hero of the moment in this region.'

'I know, Chibesa,' Suzanne said through gritted teeth, 'I

should have listened to you and WB. But I so wanted my first conference to go well, especially as I'm standing in for the Director General.'

'Don't fret, you're doing fine,' said a voice from the back of the hall, where Wilberforce 'WB' Businge was sitting waiting for them. 'Most of the delegates arrived on time and I'm sure the rest will be here by the time we reconvene. Even the Minister was only ninety minutes late and with a bit of luck, he'll have left before we start the panel discussion.'

'Not if I have any say in it, he won't,' said Suzanne. 'He can't make an outrageous statement like that and then disappear without justifying it. I'm going to insist he stays for the debate.'

'Well, good luck with that,' said WB with a grin, 'The Honourable Minister won't take kindly to being bullied, especially by a woman!' He pulled himself out of his seat and brushed the shoulders of his already immaculate pin-striped, three-piece suit. 'Anyway, aren't you two coming for some food?' he continued. 'Come on—if we don't hurry it'll all be gone.'

Suzanne spent the lunch break thinking over what WB had said, and planning how she would handle the Minister. When he approached her after lunch, she was ready for him.

'Your campaign is admirable, Mrs Suzanne,' he said, grasping her hand in both of his. 'I salute what you are trying to do. You have my full support—just so long as it doesn't affect my budget.' He turned towards the door, where a uniformed driver was standing waiting, but Suzanne raised her voice so the delegates around her could hear her words.

'I'm sorry you have to leave so soon, Minister,' she said. 'I was hoping you could spare the time to tell us about your recent success in obtaining charitable donations. I'm sure we could all benefit from your experience.' She saw him pause and pushed home her advantage. 'And it would be great background for the Director General when he's drawing up recommendations for the next round of appointments within IHF.'

The International Health Forum had been set up the previous year as an inter-agency group to tackle the growing problem of counterfeit drugs, especially in the developing world. Supported by the World Health Organization, the European Union, the US government and a couple of philanthropic billionaires, it was well-funded and had in its gift a number of short-term ambassadorial appointments which were proving very popular.

The silence lengthened as Suzanne could almost see the thought processes going on in the Minister's head. Then he waved away his driver and turned back to her with a smile which didn't quite reach his eyes.

'Well, my plane's not due to leave until this evening, so I would be happy to stay a while longer.'

'That's great news, Minister; I'm sure the delegates will appreciate your continued participation.'

Back in the conference hall, WB talked of fighting counterfeiters in Kampala. Despite the heat and the fact that he was speaking during the 'graveyard slot', straight after a carbohydrate-rich lunch, most of the delegates managed to stay awake. However, Suzanne was very glad she'd chosen to sit in the auditorium rather than on the stage in full view of everyone. Her eyelids felt heavy and her legs stuck to the yellow leatherette seat. She wriggled to free herself and tried not to doze off.

But she was wide awake again when she took to the stage for the closing discussion. She'd asked WB to chair this session; the tall Ugandan knew many of the delegates and appeared to have their respect. She also wanted the opportunity to take part in the debate herself.

The Minister had declined to make a speech, saying he'd not been pre-warned and therefore had nothing prepared, but he agreed to sit on the stage with Suzanne to take questions.

'So, Minister,' she began, 'we're interested to hear about your recent success.'

'Well, Mrs Suzanne, it's not really my success. I was merely an intermediary.'

'Oh, I think you're being too modest, Minister. I read the report of the events last week and I understand you received a standing ovation from all members of the National Assembly when you announced the latest acquisition of aid.'

'My colleagues were being too kind.' He waved away her comments.

'Well, anyway, let's talk about the deal itself, Minister. I believe the donations came from China, is that correct?'

'Yes, that's right. Although it's not a full donation; my government is paying for the drugs, just at a hugely subsidised rate.'

'And can you tell us what types of drugs are being donated?'

'It's a mix of medicines including antibiotics, antivirals and antimalarials.'

'That's very impressive—and particularly important in view of the growth in the number of cases of Aids, TB and malaria in your country.'

'Well, not just in my country; it's the trinity of diseases the WHO is concentrating on at the moment. I believe you've even got some problems with them in Europe.'

'But it's true to say it's a major problem in Kenya, isn't it?'

'Correct.' He nodded.

'So being able to access significant quantities of medicines is a major coup.'

'Well, yes, I suppose it is, yes.'

'So we can see why you are such a hero at the moment.' She paused, allowing him time to bask in the praise, before continuing. 'Tell me Minister; is the additional testing going to cause problems for your government laboratories?'

'Testing, what testing?'

'The quality checks on all these drugs you're going to import.'

'Oh, no, we won't need to do that; they've all been tested on release in China.' .

'Really? That's very courageous of you.' Suzanne thought she detected a slight shift in the man's self-satisfied smirk.

'I'm not sure I understand your point, Mrs Suzanne.'

'Well, China's pharmaceutical companies are not exactly known for the effectiveness of their quality systems, now are they?'

'I'm sure the Chinese authorities wouldn't—'

'Wouldn't what, Minister? Allow poor quality drugs to be sold overseas? Allow local Chinese companies to export pirated drugs? Allow fake medicines to be sent to Africa?'

The Kenyan sat up straight and pounded his fist on the arm of his chair.

'This is outrageous! You have no basis for these accusations.'

Suzanne swallowed hard and forced a smile back onto her face.

'Minister, I'm not making any accusations. I'm merely asking how you can be sure that these things—which we know are happening elsewhere—aren't happening in this case. That's why I asked about your quality checks.'

'Mrs Suzanne, I can't be expected to have these sorts of details at my fingertips. I will go back to my Ministry and find the answers for you. I'm sure there is nothing for IHF to worry about.'

'Me too, Minister; me too. Incidentally, how did you manage to get the multinationals to agree to their products being included in the deal?'

'What multinationals? The agreement is purely with local Chinese companies.'

'I'm so sorry; I misunderstood you. When you talked

about antivirals, I assumed, as they're all fairly new products, you must have got the patent holders involved. Because you wouldn't be dealing with counterfeiters and pirates, now would you, Minister?'

There was a deathly silence in the hall as Mukooyo glared at Suzanne. She smiled back at him, although a little voice in the back of her mind was screaming that she might have gone too far.

The silence was broken as the Minister's aide, sitting in the front row, coughed discreetly and pointed to his watch. Mukooyo jumped up and held out his hand to Suzanne.

'I'm so sorry, I have to go! I'll be in touch—and again, I wish you luck with your programme.' As he walked through the hall, there was a smattering of applause, but Suzanne noticed not all the delegates were clapping.

## 2: SWAZILAND; SEPT 2004

It was early evening when Suzanne, Chibesa and WB left the conference hall. Along the street, trees were silhouetted against an orange sky. Although this was not her first visit to the region, Suzanne was still enthralled by this nightly spectacle, a brief display in an unfamiliar palette, before the light disappeared. There is no dusk in Africa.

'I don't really want to go back to the compound yet,' Suzanne said. 'Can we grab something to drink first?'

'Sure, why not?' Chibesa replied. 'Why don't we try the ice-cream parlour over there?'

'A beer would slip down really well,' WB said 'and look, they even sell Tusker.'

The day's heat lingered still. WB went inside to buy the drinks, while Suzanne and Chibesa took a small table on the dusty, crowded forecourt. Strings of lights stretched between trees above their heads. They flickered and faltered a couple of times then came on fully. Within seconds they were attracting beige moths that beat huge wings against the bulbs. In the doorway, the insectacutor buzzed and flashed continually as smaller insects were trapped and fried.

At the next table, a woman and three young girls were sharing the parlour's speciality, Rainbow Ice. They were dipping their spoons into a glass dish filled with myriad coloured ice-creams topped with cream, rolling their eyes extravagantly at each mouthful.

Suddenly the youngest girl looked across at the new arrivals. Her spoon fell on the table as she stared open-mouthed. Suzanne smiled at the child who slipped out of her seat and toddled up to the table. Reaching out a small, sticky hand, she gently stroked Suzanne's arm before running back, giggling, to her family and hiding her face in the woman's lap.

'Oh, bless her.' Suzanne waggled her fingers in a wave at the child, making her giggle even more.

'That's probably the first white skin she's ever seen,' said Chibesa.

'Here you go,' said WB, arriving with the tray of drinks, 'Tusker, Kenya's finest, for Chibesa and me; Sprite with no ice for you, Suzanne.' They sat sipping their drinks and watching the activities in the street, no less busy in the evening than it had been all day.

When the team had arrived in Swaziland two days earlier, they'd been told they wouldn't be staying at the country's only hotel as every room had been taken by the conference delegates. Chibesa, team secretary and logistics supremo, had been quick to reassure his companions.

'Apparently, we're going in the King's Villas, whatever they are,' he told them. They turned out to be a compound of four-bedroomed houses which Suzanne thought would be more at home in leafy Surrey suburbs than the African bush.

'There are twenty altogether. They were built to accommodate the overspill of dignitaries during an international conference last year,' WB told them after chatting to their driver on the way from the airport. To Suzanne's dismay, they put her alone in one villa while Chibesa and WB stayed next door. She ignored the leopard skin curtains and lion skin rugs of the twin King and Queen Suites on the ground floor, locking herself instead in one of the smaller Princess rooms upstairs. Even so, her first two nights were disturbed by unfamiliar creaks inside and rustlings outside. Now, as they headed back after their drinks, she was not sorry they would be leaving tomorrow.

As their cab drove away, a slight figure in the long, loose-fitting cotton dress of the local Muslim women stepped out of the shadows, her face shrouded by a headscarf.

'I must speak to you,' she whispered. As Suzanne and her colleagues stared at her she shook her head. 'But not out here; it's too dangerous. Please, can we go inside?'

Chibesa glanced at WB, who nodded, then pulled a key from his pocket and opened the door of the men's villa.

'Of course. Come on in—you too, Suzanne.'

In the lounge, the young woman stood, looking as though she might flee at any moment, peering anxiously through the plate glass windows into the darkness beyond. Only when WB closed the curtains did she relax. The hand holding the scarf across her face was darker than might be expected and, as the material slipped to her shoulders, Suzanne was not surprised to see the woman was African, not Asian.

'So, madam, what can we do for you?' asked WB gently, gesturing towards the zebra-printed sofa, on which the young woman now perched herself.

'I wanted to speak to you at the conference,' she replied, 'but I was afraid.'

'I remember seeing you there,' Suzanne said, 'you were talking with the Kenyan Minister.'

'Yes, I'm Sara Matsebula, chief pharmacist at the Swazi National Hospital. I've met Minister Mukooyo previously at conferences.'

'And do you agree with his viewpoint on counterfeits?' Suzanne tried to keep her voice steady, but the day's events were starting to catch up with her.

'Of course not,' Sara replied, 'although I don't believe he's necessarily corrupt or evil—he's just being pragmatic.'

'So what's with the cloak and dagger act?' Chibesa was blinking at her short-sightedly as he polished his glasses on the bottom of his embroidered shirt. 'Sara's not a Muslim name. Why the disguise? Did you think someone would report you to Mr Mukooyo?

'Oh, the danger doesn't come from the Minister,' Sara exclaimed. 'It comes from Banda!'

'Banda? What's that?' Suzanne asked.

'Not what; who! They're a group based somewhere in Southern Africa; no-one knows exactly where, but they pop up in most of the countries around here. They're behind eighty percent of the counterfeits in this region. Lots of people suspect they know who they are, but no-one will speak out against them, not openly anyway.'

'Go on.' Suzanne sank down into a giraffe-print armchair and waved her colleagues to sit as well.

'I want you to take this.' Sara pulled a large manila envelope from her bag. 'I've been gathering information for years. It's only bits and pieces, but I hope the IHF can do something with it.' She dropped the envelope on the glass coffee table, before rubbing the tips of her fingers as though to rid them of dirt or slime. Then she stood up and pulled the headscarf back over her head. As she turned towards the door, Suzanne spoke.

'Why, Sara?'

The young woman looked back.

'Why what?'

'Why did you risk coming here tonight? Why have you offered to help us when you obviously believe it puts you in danger?'

'For Ruth.' The words were barely audible. 'My sister Ruth. Our mother died seven years ago. There were only the two of us and Ruth was still at school. She couldn't wait to get on with her life; she wanted to be a hairdresser. But I promised Mother I'd make sure she finished her

17

studies first. She was very bright, but always getting into trouble for talking too much in class.

'A few months after Mother died, Ruth's teacher called me, saying she was worried. Ruth had changed, gone very quiet, and frequently complained of feeling sick. At first, I assumed she was still grieving for Mother, but when she started getting up several times each night to drink litres of water, I took her to the doctor. As I suspected, she'd developed juvenile diabetes and needed regular insulin injections from then on.'

'The poor girl! That's a terrible thing for any child to have to deal with, let alone one that's lost her mother.' WB tutted and shook his head. He took Sara's arm and guided her back to the sofa. Once more, she sat on the edge of the seat as she continued talking.

'I normally brought her insulin home from the hospital with me. But one day last year, I forgot to get the prescription filled out. We have a little pharmacy near our house, so I collected the insulin from there. Only, whatever was in the vial, it wasn't insulin. Ruth went into a coma and died two days later.' Tears ran down Sara's face as she finished her story and she rubbed them away with the back of her hand. Suzanne's hand was across her mouth and her eyes stung with unshed tears.

'I promised Mother I'd look after Ruth; but I failed. I can't help her, but I'll do what I can to make sure no-one else has to suffer like she did; no other relatives have to feel the way I do.'

# 3: ENGLAND; OCT 2004

The plane was delayed by two hours leaving Lusaka. The passengers sat in the brightly-lit new terminal, staring at the departure board and talking in the low murmur of anxiety Suzanne had seen so many times before at airports. It was an overnight flight due to take off at eleven pm, so all the shops and cafés had long closed; there was nowhere to get anything to eat. Suzanne was glad she'd remembered to buy some bottled water when they were still open. She gazed longingly at the sliding doors to the executive lounge, where she knew the more privileged passengers would be enjoying late-night snacks and complimentary drinks in comfy chairs.

One of the few aspects of her former corporate life which she missed was the option of travelling in some degree of comfort. When she'd transferred to the regulatory world, her expenses budget would only stretch to economy tickets although she had on occasion splashed out and upgraded her tickets herself. But she'd left even this option behind when she took on this new role. She could just see the headlines screaming from the front of the red tops: *Regulators travel in luxury while beneficiaries struggle to pay for drugs*. She wriggled on the unyielding plastic chair and stared at the departure board once more, praying for the 'delayed' to turn to 'boarding'.

Suzanne had worked on a large manufacturing site in the north-east of England for nine years before being recruited initially by the UK regulators and then by the European Medicines Agency. Five years down the line, she was seconded to the IHF's anti-counterfeiting programme. This trip, consisting of the conference in Swaziland and follow-up meetings with individual government officials and regulators in Zambia, had been the kick-off for the campaign in Africa. The organisers were delighted when the Kenyan Health Minister accepted their invitation to be Guest of Honour at the conference, but after his comments and their edgy public debate, Suzanne wasn't so sure.

At one-twenty am, they were called to the gate, where they found they would need to verify their luggage before boarding. Walking across the tarmac with the rest of the passengers, Suzanne picked out her suitcase from the untidy pile and wearily handed it to the airport official who grinned sympathetically at her as he checked her name off on his clipboard and slung the case on the conveyor belt rising upwards into the dark belly of the plane.

Once they had all boarded, there was the inevitable tussle to get all the hand luggage in the overhead locker: 'a real triumph of hope over experience' as someone had once described it to Suzanne. And then, within minutes, they were all seated, the emergency drill was explained, and they were off the runway and speeding northward, with all the lights switched off.

The delay to their flight meant they missed the early morning arrival slot and comparative calm of Heathrow. By the time they reached the immigration booths, they were competing with several other planeloads from America and the Far East. Suzanne hated having to queue to enter her own country, but at least it meant there was no wait in the baggage hall; the cases were already circulating on the conveyor when she arrived. At least, most of them were. Suzanne's was missing! She'd seen people in the past wait for bags that never arrived—and had felt sorry for them as the realisation dawned that something had gone awry but this was the first time it had happened to her. As the last of her fellow passengers wheeled away their luggage, she looked once more at the single bag still on the conveyor: it was the same colour as hers, but the make was different and there was some lettering on the side—someone's initials, she assumed.

'It looks like someone's taken my bag by mistake,' she said as the young girl on the lost property desk smiled sweetly at her. *Yes, you can afford to smile,* thought Suzanne; *you've just had a good night's sleep in your own bed!*

'Never mind, luv,' was the cheery reply; 'we'll sort it out. Now,' grabbing a form and a laminated card with pictures of cases of all sorts and sizes, 'can you just pick out what yours looks like and we can go from there.'

Mercifully, the journey on the Heathrow Express was painless and just after ten am, Suzanne emerged into the bright sunshine outside Paddington Station. As it was Sunday, the usual commuter crush was missing, and the queue for a taxi was quite short. As she sped through the streets of London, heading for the river and her sunny Vauxhall flat, she breathed a sigh of relief remembering she had changed the bed and tidied up before she left. She could take a quick shower, and then crawl into fresh bedclothes and sleep for the rest of the day.

When she reached her front door, the double lock was not engaged, although she knew she'd activated it before she'd left home. A friend had agreed to pop in and water her plants while she was away; obviously he'd forgotten to relock it. Didn't he know how dodgy it was, leaving your home unprotected these days? She'd have to say something when she went round to collect the keys later on.

But the next thing that hit her was the smell of cigarette

smoke, mixed with something else, and the fact that the lights were on in the hall and the kitchen. There were dirty cups and plates in the sink and on the draining board; an empty pizza box was on the table, together with an overflowing ashtray and several empty beer bottles.

Suzanne strode down the corridor to the spare room. Wrenching open the door, she glanced at the huddled shape under the duvet before yanking open the curtains. The tousled head on the pillow turned; a pair of bright green eyes opened slowly, drifted shut again—and then flew open once more. A rueful grin appeared on a face flushed with sleep.

'You're back then, sis; did you have a good trip?'

'No, I didn't have a good trip; I've had the trip from hell—and I was expecting to get back to my nice neat flat and have a good sleep.'

'Okay, you go and get your head down—and I'll see you later.' The eyes closed again and a freckled hand pulled the duvet up over a tanned shoulder. Suzanne grabbed the corner and tugged hard, pulling the bedclothes onto the ground. There was a howl of protest.

'What are you doing here, Charlie?' she asked. 'I thought you were still in Greece.'

'Um, we ran out of money; had to come home,' was the mumbled reply.

'But why are you *here*? Why aren't you at home with Annie?' There was a silence. 'She's thrown you out, hasn't she? Charlie, what have you done now?'

'Nothing really, sis,' came the muffled reply as the recumbent figure struggled to regain control of the duvet. 'There was this waitress I used to work with, in the bar—but it was nothing really, just a bit of a laugh.'

'Yes, well, Annie never did have much of a sense of humour when it came to you and other women.'

The green eyes were open once more and gazing up at her appealingly.

'I thought you wouldn't mind if I kipped here while

22

you were away—and I was going to clear up this morning—had a bit of a late night of it.'

'You and me both, Charlie,' retorted Suzanne, 'you and me both.' She stared at the figure in the bed, trying to hold on to the anger that had flooded her head when she'd realised her privacy and order had been breached, but it was too late—and she was too tired. 'Right,' she said, 'I'm going to bed. When I get up I expect this place to be spotless and every sign of tobacco (or whatever else you've been smoking) to be gone; and then we'll talk about what's happened and where you're going to be sleeping tonight.' She waited for a response, but all she got was a gentle snore. Pulling the door closed behind her, she dragged herself across the hallway to her own room and threw herself on the bed, fully clothed, as exhaustion finally overcame her. Waking a couple of hours later, she undressed, took the shower she had been promising herself since the previous night in the airport, and crawled between the fresh cool sheets. She lay awake for a few moments, acknowledging the fact that there was no sound coming from the rest of the flat. Her last thought before falling into a deep dreamless sleep was that once again, she was going to have to play the responsible sibling role. Charlie, or Charlotte Agnes Jones as their parents had christened her, might be two years older than Suzanne, but she had always been happy to turn to her younger sister for help whenever things went wrong. And with Charlie, things seemed to go wrong with alarming regularity.

# 4: ENGLAND; OCT 2004

By the time Suzanne woke, it was mid-afternoon and an empty stillness told her she was the only occupant of the flat. Dreading what she might find, she tightened the belt around her kimono and headed for the kitchen.

There wasn't a dirty cup or plate in sight, the table was spotless and a scent of lavender hung in the air. In the spare room, the bed was made. It was as though her visitor had never been there.

Just then, she heard a key in the lock—and the front door opened. It was Charlie, carrying a bag of shopping in one hand and a big bunch of lilies in the other.

'Hi, sis. Did you sleep okay?' She dumped the bag on the kitchen table and thrust the flowers at Suzanne. 'Here—I wanted to say sorry. Now, are you hungry?'

Thinking back, Suzanne realised she hadn't eaten since the supper on the plane. No wonder her stomach was feeling hollow.

'Yes, I'm starving.'

'Well, I didn't think you'd fancy cooking this evening, so I've brought you some stuff to be going on with and I thought we could go down to the Indian by the park later on, if you're not too tired.' Suzanne watched with amusement as her sister pulled from the bag a couple of packets of bacon, a tin of beans, a large melon, an unsliced brown loaf—and a pack of watercress. 'They didn't have any fresh at the greengrocer's, but I managed to get a bag of the packed stuff in the supermarket.'

Touched that her sister remembered her favourite first meal after a trip—watercress and brown bread sandwiches—Suzanne filled the kettle and pulled the teabags from the cupboard while Charlie grabbed the bread knife.

'And the bacon?' she asked.

'Well, I didn't have anything in for breakfast...'

It was as they were finishing their sandwiches, sitting at the table in the bright little kitchen, that Suzanne remembered something her sister had said earlier that morning.

'You said you ran out of money in Greece. You shouldn't be buying food.' and reaching for her purse, 'How much do I owe you?' Charlie coloured to the roots of her jet black hair.

'Er, it's okay, I took the money from your purse while you were asleep.' Suzanne looked at the vase of lilies sitting on the draining board and Charlie shook her head. 'No, they really are a present. I just borrowed the money to pay for them. I'll pay you back as soon as my giro arrives.' Suzanne was just gearing up to have a go about taking other people's money and spending it freely, when the doorbell rang.

'That'll be the man from the airport;' said Charlie, 'do you want me to go?'

'What man from the airport?'

'I left you a note. Didn't you see it? He rang this morning to say he had your suitcase.' Charlie pushed an old envelope across the table.

'No, I didn't see it.' The doorbell rang again—a longer, more impatient peal this time. 'Well, you'll have to go. I can't answer it dressed like this.' And grabbing her mug of tea, she dashed into the bedroom as Charlie ambled towards the hall. Pulling the bedroom door to after her, she put her ear to the crack and listened.

'Good afternoon,' the voice was deep and Eastern European. 'Are you Suzanne Jones?' *Say yes, Charlie,* she thought, *just say yes!*

'No, I'm her sister. We spoke on the phone. You are Mr...?'

'Mladov, Nico Mladov. I bring your sister's case. She is in?' *Say no, Charlie, just say no.* But once again, her sister failed to read her mind.

'Well, she's in, but not available right now. I can take it for her.'

'No, I need the signature of the owner. It's airport procedure.'

'Oh, right; well, you'd better come in then. She won't be long.'

Suzanne sighed as she heard Charlie take the man into the lounge. She pulled on jeans and a fresh T-shirt.

When she entered the lounge, Mladov was perched on the edge of the sofa, with the suitcase in front of him, holding on to the handle as though he thought Charlie might steal it away from him. He was a huge man, broad-shouldered, wearing black leather and Ray-Bans. The lounge suddenly seemed much smaller. Charlie smiled as her sister walked in.

'Suzanne, Mr Mladov has brought your case—but he needs a signature for the airport.' Suzanne held out her hand.

'Mr Mladov, it's good of you to come all this way.' His hand felt icy to her touch and he pulled away after the briefest of handshakes.

'Miss Jones, on behalf of Heathrow airport, I apologise for the delay in returning your case and any inconvenience caused.' Romanian, Suzanne guessed, or maybe Polish? But his English was very good. He'd obviously been here for some time.

'Well, it wasn't your fault,' she said, 'someone took the

wrong case, didn't they?' He looked surprised.

'No, I believe your case slipped off the conveyor behind the baggage hall and was only found after you'd left the airport.

'Oh, but I thought when I saw the other bag...' He was looking at her blankly. 'Oh well, I guess it doesn't matter. Has Charlie offered you a cup of tea, Mr Mladov?' Her sister nodded.

'Yes, of course. The kettle's just boiling. Tea, black, two sugars, wasn't it?' The man inclined his head and Charlie disappeared towards the kitchen.

'Did you enjoy your trip to Africa?' Mladov said. Suzanne gave a start.

'How did you know...?' He pointed to the baggage tags.

'You took the overnight flight from Lusaka. Was it business or pleasure?' He grimaced. 'Although, I'm not sure many people go to that part of the world on holiday.'

She ignored the disdain in his voice.

'Yes, business.'

'And was it successful?'

'Very, thank you.' She was beginning to find his questions and the sharp stare he gave her unsettling, and looked up in relief as her sister came back into the room with three mugs of tea precariously balanced on a tiny tray.

As Mladov drank his tea, the sisters attempted to talk to him about how long he'd been in England and how he liked working for the airport, but he seemed distracted and answered their questions briefly, his eyes continually roving around the room. Then draining his mug, he jumped up.

'Well, ladies, I must go,' he said, heading for the hall.

'I thought you needed my sister's signature,' Charlie said quietly. He gave a start and then laughed.

'Of course! Thanks for reminding me.' He pulled a typed sheet out of his pocket, together with a cheap biro which he handed to Suzanne.

'I do hope you won't get stuck in traffic going back to

Hounslow at this time" she said as she handed the signed paper back to him.

'Oh, I'm sure it will be fine,' he said. 'There was no problem on the way here—and the way back looked clear as well.'

'What a strange man,' said Suzanne as she closed the door. Charlie gave a theatrical shiver.

'Creepy, I'd say. I'm glad I wasn't here on my own when he came.'

"That's funny,' Suzanne said, as she opened her case, ready to throw the dirty clothes in the washing basket.

'Hmm?' Charlie was sitting cross-legged on the floor in the corner, scrolling through the menus on her laptop.

'Well, I'm sure I put this dress at the bottom of the case. But now it's on the top.'

'How on earth can you remember what order you did your packing in?'

'I put all the dirty stuff on the bottom, tuck my caftan around it, and then put any unworn clothes on the top.'

'Well maybe you didn't wear that dress after all?'

'Oh I did, definitely, because WB was teasing me about it glowing in the dark when we went out to dinner on the last evening. And then someone knocked over a glass of wine and it went all down my skirt.' She pulled a few more things out of the case. 'And my toiletries don't look right—the toothpaste's out of the box.'

'Only you would keep your toothpaste tube in a box, sis. You've really got to lighten up a bit.' Charlie grinned up at Suzanne, taking the sting out of her words, before returning to studying the screen.

'But the lock's not been tampered with,' Suzanne continued, checking the padlock. 'How very strange. I reckon someone's been through this case. Good job I never keep anything of value in there, isn't it?'

'Well, anyone who's going to trawl through your dirty underwear must be dedicated to their job,' was the muttered response. As Suzanne looked around for something soft to throw at her sister, Charlie suddenly sat up straight and looked sharply at her.

'Didn't Mladov say the journey from Heathrow was a smooth one?' she asked.

'Yes, you know he did; only took him forty minutes, he reckoned. Why?'

'Well, he must have come by helicopter, then,' said Charlie, 'or teleported. There's been a serious accident on the Great West Road. It says here the M4's been closed since early this morning and all the other roads are gridlocked.'

'Which means—'

'Wherever your Mr Mladov came from this afternoon, it certainly wasn't Heathrow!'

## 5: ENGLAND; OCT 2004

When Suzanne arrived at the office on Monday morning, she was still concerned about the incident with the suitcase and the mysterious Mr Mladov. But the pile of papers, phone messages and faxes on her desk soon pushed the events of the weekend to the back of her mind. She was halfway through drafting a reply to a query about import regulation requirements between two countries in the Horn of Africa when Sir Frederick Michaels knocked on the doorjamb and peered into the room. Suzanne always thought Fred's habit of knocking was ironic—after all, who was going to refuse entry to the IHF Director General when he wanted to talk to them—but she appreciated the gesture. She pushed her chair back from her desk with a smile of welcome.

'Sir Frederick, good morning. Come on in.'

'Suzanne, my dear, I didn't want to intrude; I can see you are swamped. But I just wanted to see how you got on last week.' Suzanne's mind flew back to her delayed case, but she doubted if Sir Frederick was really interested in her domestic travel problems.

'Well, yes, I think it went well,' she said, waving her boss to a seat, 'but you can never tell with these things, can you?'

'Get any push-back from the locals, did you?'

'Well, everyone agreed the problem of counterfeiting is terrible, but there was no consensus on what should be done about it. The industrialists think the governments should do more. The regulators want the factories to improve so they don't have to import so many drugs, and the distributors say they've seen it all before and campaigns like this never work.'

'So we still have a way to go, then?'

'And the Kenyan Health Minister was a bit hostile, which didn't help.'

'Yes, well, Walter always was a bit of a stroppy bugger, but I think his heart's probably in the right place.' Suzanne looked questioningly at Sir Frederick. 'Didn't I tell you the Honourable Walter Mukooyo and I were at Kings at the same time?' Suzanne shook her head, 'Yes, we used to go shooting together in the long vacation; crack shot he was too—always bagged more birds than I could.'

Suzanne didn't have time to adjust her perception of the Kenyan Health Minister, or of her boss for that matter, as her phone started to ring. Sir Frederick jumped up.

'Look, I'll leave you to it,' he said, 'but we've got a briefing session booked for eleven hundred hours tomorrow. Nothing elaborate, just an initial report back for now.' And with a wave of his hand, he was gone.

Picking up the phone, Suzanne thought ruefully that she was going to have a long day—and night—in front of her if she was going to have her report ready for the next morning. Sir Frederick might be affable on the outside, but inside he was a hard task master.

'Miss Jones?' The voice broke into her thoughts. 'Are you there, Miss Jones?' She gave a start.

'Yes, this is Suzanne Jones.'

'Miss Jones, this is Melanie? From Heathrow Airport? You reported a suitcase missing on Saturday morning?' Suzanne vaguely remembered a tiny badge on a large bust and a cheery cockney laugh.

'Oh yes, Melanie, thanks for ringing. I was going to call you later today, to thank you for sorting out the problem so quickly—and finding someone who was willing to come out to Vauxhall on a Saturday too.'

'But, Miss Jones—'

'Although I did wonder if the case had gone through customs before it came to me.'

'Sorry, Miss Jones?'

'The contents seem to have been disturbed, and I wondered if that happened at your end or before it left Zambia.'

'But, Miss Jones.' The voice sounded a little more shrill with each interruption. "Miss Jones, I was ringing to say we haven't been able to find your case.'

'But your Mr Mladov brought it round at the weekend.'

'Mr Mladov? No, the name doesn't ring a bell. But this is a big place, Miss Jones, and the left hand often doesn't know what the right hand's been nicking, as the saying goes.' Suzanne was pretty sure that wasn't how the saying went, but the girl was talking again. 'It was probably the baggage handlers, doing it off their own bat, as it were. Did he say where they found it?'

'He said it had slipped off the conveyor...'

Well, there you are, then. Probably thought there was a reward in it.' The voice sharpened. 'You didn't give him a reward, did you?'

'Only a cup of tea.'

'Well, I don't think we'll begrudge him that, will we?' There was a burst of laughter. 'Okay, so I'll mark this one as resolved then.'

'But how would he know—'

'Well, I'm glad it's all been sorted out. Cheery bye, Miss Jones.'

'No, wait a minute—' but the buzz at the end of the phone told Suzanne she was talking to herself. She stared into space, trying to work out how Mladov had got her address, then gave a smile as the penny dropped.

'You idiot, Suzanne, there's an address label on the case, isn't there?' And with a shake of her head, she turned back to her work.

Five hours, several cups of coffee and a cheese and celery sandwich later, she'd got her notes for the presentation in a reasonable order and was just about to start work on the PowerPoint slides when the phone rang. The display showed a familiar number; her own.

'Charlie, what do you want? I'm right in the middle of a report and haven't got time to chat.' There was a silence at the other end of the line. 'Charlie? Are you there, Charlie?' The voice, when it came was a cross between a whisper and a croak.

'Suzanne, I'm sorry, I only went out for a few minutes.' There was a pause. 'I thought I'd left the door open, so I came straight in. He was still here.'

'Charlie, what are you talking about?'

'There was a man, here, in the flat. You've been burgled.'

'Good grief, Charlie, are you okay? Is he still there?'

'No, he ran away when I arrived. I'm so sorry, Susu.' It was a long time since her big sister had called her that. Now Suzanne was really scared.

'Charlie, I'm on my way. Stay right there. I'll be ten minutes.'

The main attraction of the Vauxhall flat for Suzanne was its close proximity to St Thomas', the sprawling hospital complex on the embankment opposite the Palace of Westminster, where IHF rented offices. In good weather, she walked to work in less than twenty minutes. Today, she grabbed the first taxi she saw on the embankment and made it home in just under ten.

The door of the flat was ajar and the hallway was dim. Suzanne didn't see her sister until she switched on the light. Charlie was on the floor, slumped against the wall, eyes closed and phone still in her hand. The phone was emitting a high-pitched whine. Suzanne dropped to her knees beside her and put her hand on her sister's shoulder. Charlie groaned and opened her eyes. A thin trickle of dried blood ran down the side of her face.

'You should see the other guy,' she mumbled with a lop-sided grin that turned into a grimace. She touched her fingertips to her head and sucked in air sharply. Then she tried to stand up but Suzanne pushed her gently back against the wall.

'You stay right there, sweetie. I'm going to get you checked out before you move. Let me have the phone.' Charlie held the handset out, but her fingers were still tightly wrapped around it.

'I can't seem to...' She started to shiver violently and a whimper escaped from her mouth before she clamped her lips together. Suzanne carefully uncurled her sister's fingers, one by one. Taking the phone gently and placing it briefly on the cradle to get the dialling tone, she hit the bottom right hand button three times.

'Hello, yes, police please—and an ambulance, my sister's been attacked.'

While the paramedics were checking out Charlie, Suzanne surveyed the damage to her home. The lock had obviously been forced—so Charlie didn't need to feel guilty about leaving the door open. The drawers and cupboards in the kitchen were all open. In her bedroom, the contents of her dressing table had been tipped onto the bed. She gazed ruefully at the untidy pile of knickers and bras, thick winter tights and summer T-shirts plus colourful chiffon scarves bought for her every year by a maiden aunt who didn't realise Suzanne didn't wear a scarf unless it was an angora wool one in winter.

But the worst mess was in the lounge. Every book had been pulled off the shelves and thrown on the floor. They were all lying open and looked like they'd been shaken before being discarded. Papers, which she kept neatly catalogued in pigeon holes in the dresser were scattered on the patterned carpet, together with the contents of her box files which seemed to have been upended haphazardly. Every painting on the wall was askew. Her collection of LPs—she still preferred listening to vinyl, even though most of her friends favoured CDs these days—were scattered across the room.

'Well someone's gone to a great deal of trouble searching for something, haven't they? What do you think they were looking for, Miss Jones?' The voice took her by surprise in the quiet of the flat and she jumped nervously. A uniformed police officer was standing in the doorway looking at her. 'Sorry, Miss Jones, I didn't mean to startle you. Can we go into the kitchen and have a chat?' And as she followed the man into the hallway, Suzanne was asking herself the same question. What was the burglar looking for? Was this just a random piece of bad luck or something more?

## 6: ENGLAND; OCT 2004

By the time the policeman had finished talking to Suzanne, the Scenes of Crime Officer had dusted every surface of the flat for prints, and the local locksmith had repaired the door, it was early evening. The paramedics had confirmed Charlie didn't seem to be suffering from concussion.

'He didn't hit me on the head or anything like that,' she kept insisting. 'I was standing in the hall and he shoved me out of the way as he came out of the bedroom. I fell against the corner of the telephone table and ended up on the floor, winding myself. By the time I got my breath back, he was gone.'

'So you'd have got a good look at him, miss, would you?' the young PC asked for the third time—and for the third time, Charlie shook her head and pulled a face.

'I told you, it was dim in here and I didn't have time to put the light on. He had dark clothes on and wore a hat pulled down over his face.'

'Like a ski mask, would you say, miss?'

'Er, yes, I guess so.'

Suzanne was surprised at her sister, who was usually the more observant of the two, but put it down to shock and didn't push the point. She hoped more details would come back to Charlie after a good night's sleep.

'I suppose the chances of you finding the guy who did this are very slim, aren't they, Constable?' said Suzanne as the PC tucked his notebook back into his pocket and pulled on his gloves. He went pink and seemed to be searching for the right words.

'Well, officially, our clear-up rate is higher in this borough than in most other parts of London—and I'm supposed to reassure you that we will do everything we can to find the perpetrator and restore your stolen goods—'

'—but in practice, when you have as little to go on as you have here... ' Charlie broke in,

'and when, as far as I can tell, nothing's actually been stolen... ' continued Suzanne,

'then the chances are high that we will never know who did this and it will be closed and filed as an unsolved case,' concluded the PC, 'although you didn't hear that from me, okay?'

'Of course not,' Suzanne said with a smile. 'Let me see you out.'

She double-locked the front door and also closed the doors to the kitchen and the bedroom. She knew she would have to do some tiding up later on, but for now she and Charlie just needed a few minutes peace and quiet. When she returned to the lounge, her sister was staring out of the window into the darkness, chewing on her thumb. Suzanne knew that look; she'd seen it many times as they'd grown up—always just before Charlie confessed to her parents something which she had hoped to keep hidden, but was about to come out anyway. She took her sister by the arm and pulled her gently over to the sofa.

'Okay, sis, sit down and relax. It's all over now.' Charlie tried to resist her steering.

'I was going to start tidying up the kitchen...' but Suzanne pushed her back onto the seat and then sat beside her, holding her hand.

'What is it, Charlie?' she asked. 'What is it you're not telling me?' Charlie stared at her silently and Suzanne thought she wasn't going to get an answer, then her sister's shoulders dropped and she let out a sigh.

'It's my fault,' she said, and Suzanne was startled to see tears welling in her sister's eyes. Charlie never cried. This must be really serious. She waited for her to go on, stroking her hand. 'I didn't tell you everything that happened in Greece. And I wasn't completely honest about why I'm here and not with Annie.'

'I'm listening.'

'The guy who ran the bar, Sandro, was a real piece of work. Oh, he was nice enough when we arrived, but that soon changed. Once we were working there, he kept upping the number of hours, delaying payment of our wages—and threatening to sack us if we didn't do what he asked. He could be really mean, too. He made Annie cry one day. I wanted to have it out with him, but she begged me not to, saying it would only make things worse.' Suzanne stared at her sister in horror.

'Why on earth didn't you just walk out?'

'We had no money and nowhere else to go—and besides, he had our passports.'

'What? How many times have I told you—?'

'Yes, I know, sis, but when we first arrived, he said we needed to register with the local police as temporary workers, and offered to do it for us; but once we'd given him our passports, we never saw them again.'

'So how...?'

'Well, one day he had to go over to the mainland for a funeral. He told us he wouldn't be back until the next morning and gave us a long list of things we needed to get done while he was away. Most of us were so subdued by then, we just did what he asked.'

'One of the things I had to do was clean out his office. He was usually in there when I did it—and he would really gross me out, sitting and staring—or creeping up behind me and fondling my boobs. But, of course, this time, I was on my own. So I had a good look around, checked out the drawers on his desk, things like that.'

'They were all unlocked?'

'Well, yes, all except this tiny little one hidden underneath. I wouldn't have seen it but I knocked a box of pencils off the top of the desk and had to crawl around picking them all up. It was behind a little flap to one side. So I grabbed a couple of paperclips and with a bit of jiggling, I soon had that mother open.'

'Charlie, I don't know where you get all these phrases from!'

'Annie's brother actually.'

'Isn't he in—'

'Yeah, that's right—he's also the one who taught me the trick with the paper clips. Anyway, it was really disappointing to start with—it seemed completely empty. But when I ran my hand around the inside, I found a big old key sellotaped to the inside.'

'That's a bit of a cliché, isn't it?'

'Well, to be honest, the whole thing was very Sam Spade. Sandro had this little pencil moustache and slicked back black hair—looked like he came straight out of a black and white movie.'

'So, this key...?'

'Well, I guessed straight away what it was for. Sandro had this big old-fashioned safe hidden behind the drinks cabinet. I heard him tell Missy once that he didn't hold with all this new-fangled electronics and would rather trust a good old-fashioned lock and key any day.'

'Who's Missy?'

'His pet snake, who do you think?'

'I beg your pardon? Did you say snake?'

'God, you are so gullible, sis,' Charlie said with a grin. Suzanne realised she must be feeling better. 'Actually, he did have a pet snake, but her name was Gloria. Missy is his mother. Looks after him like he's a little child; doesn't seem to realise he's virtually a slave owner (or if she does, she doesn't care).'

'So you opened the safe?' Suzanne's head was beginning to buzz.

'And found all the passports—plus a load of Euros. I rounded up the others—there were seven of us at that time—we packed in about two minutes flat and then hightailed it down to the port. The beauty of the Greek Islands is there's always a ferry passing by.'

'So you got away from the island without detection?'

'I think so. By the time Sandro got back the next morning, most of us were out of Greece; in fact Annie and I were on a train, halfway back to France.'

'But, I don't understand why Annie is so cross with you, then. After all, you saved everyone.'

'Well, yes, but you see, we weren't alone on the train. There was this young Irish girl called Kitty who sort of latched on to us, well, to me really. Annie had been jealous of her all along and wanted me to dump her once we got back to the mainland—but she was so sweet and innocent, I just couldn't do that. There wasn't anything going on, but Annie didn't believe us and when we got back to London, she suggested we had a bit of time apart—to consider our futures, as she put it.'

'And where's Kitty now?'

'Goodness knows. Probably gone back to Wexford—or maybe heading back to the Mediterranean and another unsuitable boss. I really don't care.' There was a note of cold in her sister's voice that Suzanne wasn't used to hearing. She decided to leave that side of the story for now, although she suspected there was more to it than her sister was willing to admit.

'Okay, Charlie, so I get the bit about you grabbing the passports—and I can understand that this Sandro might be unhappy about the money, but surely he's not going to send someone all the way across Europe just because of that?'

'True, but he might do that for the book.'

'Book? What book?'

'There was this little leather-bound notebook at the bottom of the safe. I grabbed it by mistake really when I picked up the bundle of money. It wasn't until we were on the train that I had a chance to look at it. It was all Greek to me,' her cheeky grin was back again, 'but it's full of names, dates and numbers. I found my name and Annie's too. I think it's a record of all his girls. It's also got other names and what look like phone numbers in it.'

'So you think someone's come looking for this little book? Where is it, by the way?' There was a pause.

'I threw it away,' Charlie said eventually. 'But yes, Suzanne, I do think someone's looking for it. And the question is, would it be Sandro—or someone else— someone even more dangerous? And as they didn't find it this time, are they going to come back for another look?'

# 7: ENGLAND; OCT 2004

Despite the activity of the previous evening, Suzanne was awake before six am the following day. There was no sign of movement from Charlie's room as she tiptoed around the flat. Although the audience was going to be much smaller today than the one she'd addressed in Swaziland, there would be some senior people there. Logically, she knew that her choice of clothing would have no effect at all if she was unable to answer any of Sir Frederick's trademark searching questions, but she still dressed with even more than her usual care.

There had been a nip in the air for the past couple of days; the Indian summer appeared to be over, so Suzanne pulled from her wardrobe a slightly heavier than normal pair of black wool trousers and a black top.

'Always create a column of colour' a friend of hers had told her when she was setting up an image consultancy and had given Suzanne a free consultation. 'You'll be one of my guinea pigs,' she'd said. Much of what she'd heard had gone in one ear and out of the other, but she had remembered the bit about the column of colour—and she always chose black, ever since her mother told her it was 'very slimming, my dear.' Looking at her rack of brightly coloured jackets, she rejected the red one—too intimidating for the audience which would mainly be men—and the pale yellow one—too insipid, too 'little woman'. She finally opted for the short sleeved black and white check. Then after grabbing a coffee and a piece of wholemeal toast while scribbling a quick note to Charlie, she let herself quietly out of the flat.

It was just gone seven when she arrived at the hospital administrative block and no-one was around apart from the night watchman who was sitting with his legs up on the reception desk, flicking through the *Daily Mirror* and humming tunelessly along to the music on his Walkman. He jumped up when Suzanne walked through the automatic doors.

'Morning, Miss Jones; you're very early today.'

'Morning, Pete. Had a good night, have you?'

'Can't complain; just the usual—there was a drunk around midnight who tried to get in, but I'd locked up by then so he didn't have any luck. Oh and there was a car hanging around earlier on. It kept driving around the block slowly, then it parked over there under the tree for ages. I walked over to the door and flashed my torch a couple of times, and then it sped off. Big thing, it was, a Hummer, I think. Apart from that, it's been as quiet as the grave.' He pushed his Walkman into his canvas haversack and picked up a mug from the desk. 'I'm just going to put the kettle on—do you want a coffee?'

'No thanks, Pete,' Suzanne said, heading for the lift, 'I've got a big presentation later on and I want to get my slides finished before everyone arrives.

'Well, I'm afraid you're going to have to walk this morning. The lift's been playing up, so I've shut it down and I'm waiting for maintenance to come and look at it.'

'Good job I'm only on the third floor, then, isn't it,' she said and with a wave of her hand, she turned and headed for the imposing glass staircase in the centre of the foyer.

By the time eleven o'clock arrived, Suzanne had

prepared all her PowerPoint slides and reread her notes three times. Although Sir Frederick had said this was just an informal feedback session, she'd checked with his secretary and he'd invited all the staff of IHF to attend, and the conference room was already filling up when she arrived ten minutes early. She was taken aback, however, when her boss strolled in exactly one minute before she was due to start—accompanied by a short stocky woman who was leaning forward to hear what he was saying, hands clasped, royal consort fashion, behind her back.

Francine Matheson was a familiar figure to most people; she appeared on the news frequently, and in at least half the weekend broadsheets each Sunday, especially since she'd taken on the role of Parliamentary Undersecretary in the Department for International Development following the last government reshuffle. She was known as a no-nonsense hardliner who didn't suffer fools gladly—and her appointment had been greeted with some very public groans of dismay from the major overseas aid agencies. But Suzanne knew there was a softer side to this up-and-coming politician, if only one could find it.

Once the last attendees were seated, Suzanne took to the stage and introduced her presentation with a few words of background and an overview of the team she'd been working with. She saw the guest roll her eyes and glance at her watch during this preamble, but she ignored this. Francine had always been impatient.

'So, as you can see, it was a bit of a mixed bag,' she concluded twenty minutes later. 'The people on the ground really get it and know they need help. But we're going to have problems with the politicians.'

'Well, that won't be a first,' came a voice from the back of the room, to general laughter. Francine Matheson looked like she'd been sucking on a lemon.

Sir Frederick stood up and addressed the room.

'I'm sure we're all grateful for the presentation Miss

Jones has put together at such short notice. Does anyone have any questions?'

A forest of hands went up and for the next fifteen minutes, there was a lively question and answer session. It was one quiet question right at the end that reminded Suzanne of something she'd not mentioned so far.

'It seems to me that this is going to be a hearts and minds job. We're going to have to win people over with emotion, rather than just facts.' It was Simon, responsible for public relations at IHF. 'Did you actually meet anyone who's been affected by the counterfeit drugs? Do we have any case studies we can use in our publicity material?'

'Well, yes, I did,' Suzanne said slowly, 'but I'm not sure we can use what she told us in publicity. It would be too dangerous for her.' She went on to relate to the hushed audience the story of Sara Matsebula and her sister Ruth.' She took a big chance talking to us,' she concluded, 'and I wouldn't want her to come to harm because of anything we said or did.'

Suzanne looked across at the front row where Francine Matheson was talking urgently to Sir Frederick, gesticulating wildly with her hand and shaking her head. He was nodding solemnly in agreement. Then he rose to his feet once more.

'I think we've probably got as far as we can today,' he said. 'I'd like to once again thank Miss Jones, Suzanne, for her diligent work both during the trip and in preparing this presentation. We'll wait until her final report is ready—middle of next week, did you say, Suzanne?—and then we'll reconvene for a more detailed discussion.

Suzanne hadn't given any timescale for finishing the report and had hoped for a bit longer, as she'd got a huge pile of outstanding texts and emails to deal with—not to mention the clearing up still waiting for her back at the flat—but she recognised Sir Frederick's question had been rhetorical, so she smiled and nodded her head.

As everyone filed out of the conference room, Suzanne

collected her papers together and she was the last to leave. She found Sir Frederick waiting for her by the lift—which appeared to be working once more.

'Ah, Suzanne, Francine Matheson had to leave for another appointment, but she asked me to thank you for your presentation and to say sorry she didn't have time to stop and chat.' He looked at her over the top of his glasses. 'I didn't realise you knew our aspiring leader?' Suzanne nodded.

'Yes, we were at school together,' she said, 'and we were quite friendly, after a bit of a rocky start, but we lost touch some years ago and I don't think I've had a chat with Francine since we were in the sixth form!'

'Even so, it doesn't hurt to have a personal relationship with someone in her position.' At that point the lift arrived and he stood back to usher her in. 'If you've got a few minutes, come up and have coffee with me.'

Suzanne rarely got inside Sir Frederick's office—his secretary guarded him more jealously than any harem guard ever protected an Arabian princess—and she'd not been invited to take coffee with him since the day she was interviewed for this secondment more than twelve months ago. She sat staring out of the huge glass windows across the river to the Houses of Parliament, as he flicked through a pile of papers on his desk and his secretary poured the coffee. Then he sat with her and they chatted for a while, him asking questions about her early life and career path to date.

'I like to get to know my people on a more personal level, if I can,' he said. 'We're always so busy these days, the personal often gets lost in the public, don't you agree?' Then he looked at his watch. 'However, I'm sorry, my dear, but we're going to have to call this to a close. I've got a lunchtime appointment at the Club.'

'Yes, of course. Thanks for the coffee.' Suzanne jumped up at once. But as she headed for the door, he spoke again.

'Er, Miss Jones, Suzanne, I wouldn't take this woman's story about her sister too seriously, if I were you. There's always someone willing to take advantage, you know.'

'Oh I think she was genuine enough,' Suzanne blurted out. 'Dr Businge certainly believed her story and felt we should try to help her.' Chibesa, on the other hand, had argued vigorously that they should be cautious, not knowing whether Sara was speaking the truth or not. But Suzanne decided it would not be politic to mention this fact to Sir Frederick.

'Yes, I'm sure she was genuine, my dear; but it doesn't do to get personally involved, you know. Take it from one who's been in this game for a long time.'

Then with a smile, he waved her goodbye and started riffling through the papers on his desk once more.

# 8: ENGLAND; OCT 2004

When Suzanne arrived home that evening, the flat was in darkness and she assumed Charlie was out. Switching on the hall light and dropping her briefcase and the bag of shopping she'd picked up on the way home in the kitchen, she pushed open the door to the lounge.

'Shut the door! I don't want them to see any lights,' hissed a voice. Suzanne peered into the darkness.

'Charlie, what on earth are you doing in the dark?' With the light from the hall spilling over her shoulder, she could just see her sister, pressed against the wall, peering through the edge of the curtains. Then she turned, rapidly crossed the room and pushed Suzanne out into the hall, pulling the door closed behind her. 'What's going on, Charlie?' Suzanne didn't even try to keep the irritation from her voice. 'I've had a long, tiring day and the last thing I want to do is play silly games.'

'I'm being watched,' Charlie said, striding up and down the hall and chewing her thumbnail. 'I went out for a walk earlier on and noticed a van across the road. It was parked just inside the alleyway, blocking the back entrance to the curry house, which is why I particularly noticed it.'

'So what makes you think you're being watched?'

'Well, as soon as I came out of the front door and looked across at it, it drove off.'

'So what makes you think…?'

'But then it came back. I spotted it down the road when I walked back across the bridge and when I arrived up here in the flat and looked out of the window, it was parked back in the alleyway again. And it's been there ever since.'

'Well,' Suzanne said, taking her sister's arm and steering her back towards the lounge, 'if they *are* watching you— and I'm not for one minute saying I think they are—they know you're in here, don't they? They saw you walk down the steps from the bridge and come through the front door? So what's the point of hiding here in the dark?'

She clicked on the lights and walked across to the window, having a good look around as she flung her arms wide to draw the curtains across. The alleyway opposite was empty, as was the road as far as she could see in either direction.

'There's nobody there now, sis. Are you sure you're not imagining it? We've had a pretty stressful few days, after all.' But Charlie shook her head stubbornly.

'I know what I saw,' she said.

'Well, if we see them again, we can give that nice young PC a ring with the registration number.' Charlie groaned and Suzanne looked at her sharply. 'You did make a note of the registration number, didn't you?'

'I must be mad! I never thought to do that. I was too busy hiding behind the curtain.' Suzanne patted her sister on the arm and smiled.

'Never mind; we're not all trained detectives,' she said. 'Now, more importantly, what are we going to eat? I'm starving. How about popping across the road for a curry?'

'But, what if…?

'…they come back? No problem. Unless they're planning to prise open the fire exit, there's only one way into this building—through the front door. I'll ask Sanjay to give us the table in the window, so we can keep an eye on the place at the same time. And we'll leave the curtains open, so we can see if anyone comes into the flat.'

'Wow, that was a great curry,' Charlie said a couple of hours later, pushing her chair back and rubbing her stomach, 'I'm stuffed.'

'So you won't want any dessert?' Suzanne asked. 'They do a mean julabjumen here.' But her sister just pulled a face and shook her head. Then she put her hand to her mouth.

'I'm so sorry, I forgot to ask how your presentation went.'

'I think it went quite well, although there was a surprise guest that rather threw me. The boss brought Francine Matheson with him.' Charlie gave a laugh.

'What, Little Piggy Matheson? And was she still stuffing herself like she did at school?'

'The Parliamentary Undersecretary was looking very good,' said Suzanne primly. 'She was elegantly dressed and really looked the part. Mind you, she was too busy to stop and say hello to me. She left a nice message with the boss instead.'

It had been the spring term of the first year at the grammar school on the outskirts of Exeter. Suzanne had settled in well, helped by the fact that her sister was a couple of years ahead of her in the school. The new girl, transferring from Liverpool Institute High School, had seemed standoffish and talked in an accent which would have made her very popular two decades before, but was now just seen by Suzanne and her friends as 'weird'. The two girls had gradually learned to tolerate each other and even to enjoy each other's company over the following seven years as they vied for the top spot in every exam they took. They'd lost touch with each other when they moved on to university—Suzanne to Oxford and Francine to the School of Oriental and African Studies in London—

but Suzanne had watched with interest the rising fortunes of her erstwhile school friend.

'That's nice; although I never really warmed to her the way you did.' Charlie took a swig of her beer and pointed at Suzanne. 'By the way, I meant to tell you, I've remembered something about the vehicle that was, I mean might have been, watching me.'

'And that is…?

'The registration began with an X?'

'Not much to go on, is it?'

'Well there aren't many Hummers around in this city; maybe your PC would be able to narrow it down for us.'

'He's not *my* PC, Charlie, don't be silly; he was just being—' She stopped suddenly and stared at her sister. 'Hummer; what Hummer?'

'The Hummer that's stalking me.'

'You didn't tell me it was a Hummer!'

'Didn't I? Sorry. Is it important? I thought you didn't believe in it—so why should it matter what type of vehicle it was?'

'Because there was a Hummer acting suspiciously outside the hospital last night. Bit of a coincidence, isn't it?'

'But why would they be outside the hospital? I've got no connection with that place, apart from via you—and I never mention your place of work to anyone. You've drummed that into me often enough.'

'Charlie.' Suzanne reached across and took her sister's hand, 'I don't think they're after you. I think they're after me.'

'You?'

'Think about it.' She started ticking off a list on her fingers as she spoke. 'There was the loss of my suitcase; the strange way it was returned to me, the fact that the contents had been rifled—at least I'm fairly sure they had; the break-in at the flat—and now the same, or a similar vehicle hanging around both the flat and the office.

Besides which, how would anyone know where you are staying anyway? No, I definitely think they're after me.' Charlie stared at her sister with a look of uncertainty on her face, and then her shoulders dropped as the tension went out of them.

'Oh, thank goodness for that. I was so sure Sandro had found me and was coming after his little black book.'

'Well, I'm glad that's taken a weight off your mind,' said Suzanne dryly. Charlie bit her lip and opened her eyes wide.

'Shit, I didn't mean it like that, Suzanne; you know I didn't.' She looked so guilty, Suzanne couldn't keep a straight face any longer. Charlie screwed up her napkin and threw it across the table. 'But do you have any idea who might be doing this to you—and what they're looking for?'

'Well,' Suzanne said, 'I've got an idea, but I don't want to talk about it here, especially if we're not sure who's listening. Look, I'll settle up with Sanjay while you pop next door to the off-licence and grab a bottle of red. Then we'll go home and I can tell you what happened while I was away.

'So,' Charlie said, after Suzanne had finished telling the tale of Sara and Ruth for the second time that day, 'you think all this might be connected with that brave woman and her poor sister?'

'I'm rather afraid it is,' she replied, 'and I'm only glad I didn't leave the papers in the flat yesterday. She risked a lot, talking to us like that—she was terrified and kept telling us to be careful. I'd hate to think I was responsible for blowing her cover.'

'So where are the papers?'

'The originals are with WB in Kampala. He's hidden them somewhere—wouldn't even tell us where *in case we were compromised* as he put it.'

Charlie barked a laugh.

'That's a bit "cloak and dagger" for you public servants,

isn't it?' Suzanne smiled ruefully and nodded.

'Yes, I wondered at the time if he was being a bit paranoid, but now I'm beginning to think he might have been right.'

'And the copies?'

'They're on my phone—and Chibesa's laptop. We scanned them in before giving them to WB.'

'So what happens, now?'

'I'm not sure; I need to think about it and talk to the rest of the team. But one thing's for sure.'

'What?'

'I think it might be a bit late for Sir Frederick's warning about not getting too involved.'

'Hmm, and are you going to tell him about all this?'

'Well, he knows about the break-in, but that's all for now. I didn't mention my suitcase, as I thought it was just a mix-up in communication and I could hardly tell him I thought my knickers were arranged in a different order, now could I? Pete might have mentioned the Hummer from last night, but unless it was a red alert report, it won't have reached the boss's office anyway. And no-one knows about it being outside the flat apart from the two of us.'

'So you could keep it all to yourself, then?'

'Yes, and I will for the time being—apart from talking to the guys in Africa, that is.' Then a thought struck her and she slapped her hand over her mouth. 'Oh no; my presentation!'

'What about it?'

'Everyone was there—the whole of IHF; plus a senior politician. And I told them about Sara and Ruth. Not by name, obviously, but there was enough information in there that she could be uncovered quite quickly by someone who was really trying.'

'But who's going to want to do that?'

'Who knows, Charlie? That's the trouble; we don't know who we can trust and who we should be wary of. And the default position is always to err on the side of caution. If you don't know who to trust—trust no-one, no-one at all.'

## 9: ZAMBIA; NOV 2004

'Oh for goodness sake, not again!' On Chibesa's computer screen, a small egg-timer was spinning gently. A high-pitched buzzing was just audible above the sound of the ceiling fan that languidly moved damp, hot air from one part of the room to another.

The buzzing stopped and the egg-timer disappeared, to be replaced, not for the first time that morning, by a small white box bearing a message in blue writing: *A NetBIOS error has occurred. Dial-up discontinued.*

'Right, that's it—I give up!' Chibesa glanced at the clock on the wall; the hands standing at a few minutes before noon. Grabbing his sunglasses from the desk, he headed for the door. They were the most expensive pair he'd ever bought, costing him ten dollars in the market, but the Dolce & Gabbana logo made them worth the money. They certainly managed to fool most of his friends.

He ran down the outside stairs from his third floor office and turned right out of the gate, waving to the two security guards in their little yellow hut. The noise and dust of midday Lusaka hit him like a brick wall. The street had been quiet and empty when he'd arrived at seven-thirty, but a bustling market had sprung up during the morning while he dealt with paperwork and fought with his computer connection.

Nestled against the red-brick walls of the complex, and sheltering from the sun under the overhanging jacaranda trees, was a row of food stalls. Chibesa could smell a pungent mixture of frying onions, melons and overripe bananas. His stomach rumbled; he'd not eaten for hours.

The rest of the stalls were ranged along the edge of the pavement in full sunlight. Stallholders perched on small plastic stools, protecting themselves from the strong rays with umbrellas. The shoe-seller had his usual pile of sandals, plimsolls and flip-flops on the old tarpaulin stretched across the pavement. There was no order to the stock, and no two adjacent shoes made up a pair. Potential buyers scrabbled through the pile, trying to find two shoes that matched.

Next were the clothes stalls. There were racks of tie-dyed caftans in purples and greens; cotton blouses in blacks, creams and oranges, decorated with gold embroidery; and the maroon and lemon patterned shirts that were Chibesa's trademark. He often whiled away his lunchtimes looking at these stalls. But today he was heading to the government pharmacy on the other side of the street.

'Hey, Uncle Chibesa, wait for me!' He turned, hearing his name called. A young boy was trotting along the pavement, pushing his way past shoppers and waving vigorously. He wore a tight shirt of yellow gingham that rode up, exposing a thin sharp-ribbed torso. By contrast, his orange shorts were a couple of sizes too big and he'd threaded an old silk tie through the belt-loops to try and keep them in place. He kept yanking at them to stop them slipping down. Panting when he reached Chibesa, he gave his uncle a huge smile.

'Hey there, Joey,' Chibesa patted the boy's head. 'How's Samuel?'

Chibesa was the sole wage-earner supporting his eight-year-old brother, Samuel, and a growing number of cousins, second cousins, nephews and nieces, all Aids orphans. For the past three weeks, they'd all been concerned about Samuel whose latest chest infection seemed to be lingering longer than usual.

'Better today, but still coughing,' Joey replied. 'You know he finished his medicine last night?'

'Yes, I saw the empty bottle on the table this morning. I'm just going to buy some more and you can take it home to him. Do you want to wait here or come in with me?'

'Er...' The boy put his finger in his mouth and looked longingly up the street at the food stalls. Chibesa grinned and pulled a couple of coins out of his pocket.

'How about you go get us some lunch,' he said, 'and we'll eat it in the garden before you take Samuel's medicine to him.'

As Joey grabbed the money and ran back up the street, Chibesa pushed open the door to the pharmacy. It was cool inside, cooler than his office and much cooler than the street. He wondered what it would be like to work in a place like this. He felt lucky that his job in the Health Ministry, and especially the secondment to IHF, gave him access to this government facility. Otherwise, he'd have to buy his medicines from the market and you never knew what you were getting there.

His visit to the pharmacy was short and within a few minutes, he was sitting on a bench in the Ministry grounds sharing a slice of water melon with his young cousin. As they ate, they watched the ants massing around the pool of juice dripping from their hands onto the path in front of them. Joey picked up the medicine bottle and rubbed his thumb along the slight bulge on the neck below the cap.

'I'm going to ask Samuel if I can have this bottle for my strange-shapes collection when he's drunk all the medicine,' he said.

Lunch finished, Chibesa took Joey back onto the busy street and flagged down a passing minibus. It was packed, but the boy managed to find a place on the back seat, squashed between two elderly ladies loaded down with parcels. He held Samuel's medicine carefully in one hand as he waved to Chibesa with the other.

When Chibesa got back to his office, there was a post-it note stuck to his computer screen. It said: *Phone Suzanne Jones* and a telephone number beginning +44. Chibesa punched in the numbers and smiled as he heard the quiet English tones on the recorded message.

'Hi, this is Suzanne Jones. I'm not at my desk right now, but please don't hang up. Leave a message and I'll get back to you as soon as I return.'

'Suzanne, this is Chibesa returning your call. I'll be here —' but a voice broke in before he could finish his sentence.

'Hi, Chibesa, I'm here.'

'Suzanne, hello. It's great to hear your voice. What can I do for you?'

'I wanted to see how you were getting on with the recall. Terrible, isn't it?'

'Recall, what recall?'

'Didn't you see the email?'

'No, I've not seen anything—mind you, I've not been able to dial in all morning.'

'Oh good grief, Chibesa, I never thought of that. Look, I'll fax it over to you now. The guys in Uganda found diethylene glycol in samples of cough syrup from a local pharmacy. It's supposed to be an import from the States, but they think the labels are fakes. The stuff probably came from somewhere in Eastern Europe—or from a local factory.'

'Diethylene glycol; that's antifreeze, isn't it?' Chibesa asked.

'Yes—but occasionally it gets used in place of glycerol—it's cheaper and easier to get; but it's highly toxic! There were loads of children who died in Haiti in 1996 and the same thing happened in China a couple of years back. We're hoping we've caught it in time in Uganda, but we're recalling the product across the region in case some of the batches have gone to other countries.'

'Hang on,' Chibesa said, 'the fax is just coming through.' He reached across the desk and tore off the strip of thin paper. 'Okay, I've got it.'

'Great,' Suzanne said. 'Can you get a message out to all the distributors and hospitals straight away?' But Chibesa wasn't listening. He was staring at words screaming off the page at him. The paper slipped from his fingers and fell to the ground.

'Suzanne—I've got to go—I'll get back to you,' he yelled, slamming down the phone and racing for the door. Taking the stairs three at a time, he ran to the basement garage. The two official Land Rovers were parked in their usual places, but the little room where the drivers waited for orders was empty. So were the hooks where the car keys normally hung. Chibesa ran over to the two vehicles. He couldn't get into the first one, but the second was unlocked. Jumping into the cab, he wrenched open the glove-box and rifled through the papers and old sweet packets. 'Come on, come on,' he muttered, 'I know you leave the spares in here.' He checked behind the sun visor. Then he ran his hand under the driver's seat. Finally, his fingers felt the jagged metal of a key.

The guards looked up in surprise as the Land Rover sped past them. Chibesa forced his way around the traffic island and onto the main road. He pushed the accelerator hard to the floor, not caring that he was well over the speed limit.

'Let him be okay. Please let him be okay. I'll do anything,' he muttered. A quarter mile from home, Chibesa saw the traffic ahead of him slow to a standstill. A lorry carrying crates of chickens had overturned and the street was littered with shards of wood, broken crates and fluffy yellow birds wandering around aimlessly. Pulling the Land Rover onto the grass verge, he jumped out and started running. He could see his home in the distance but, dream-like, it seemed to take hours before he reached it.

The two-metre-high wooden gates were wide open. Chibesa raced across the yard and stopped just inside the front door. Bending double, with his hands on his knees, he fought for breath. The bungalow was silent and he ran from room to room, searching for his brother or the cousins. Finally, he ran through to the back garden. Grandmother Hannah was sitting in the shade of an acacia tree shelling peas and chatting to her husband, Silas, as he weeded a row of sweet corn. The couple had moved into the family home when their daughter Mary, Chibesa's mother, had died giving birth to Samuel; it was a comfort to Chibesa that there was someone trustworthy to look after the children when he was away from home on business.

'Where is everyone—where's Samuel?' Chibesa gasped.

'Well, let me see,' Silas drawled, 'most of them have gone fishing with the youngsters from across the street. Samuel's gone with Joey to visit that friend of his who's so ill.'

'Did Samuel take his medicine before he went?'

'No, he didn't,' Hannah replied, 'and I told him he was an ungrateful little boy, after you bought it and Joey went all the way to town to bring it home. But he said he was feeling much better and he'd take it later. He stuck it in his bag and took it with him.'

Just then, Joey came out into the garden, followed by Samuel, who was coughing and spluttering. When he saw his brother, he stopped short and looked down at his toes.

'Did you take it? The medicine—did you take it?' Chibesa cried. Samuel continued looking at his feet and shook his head. Chibesa caught the boy in a tight hug. 'Thank God,' he said, 'if anything had happened to you, I'd never have forgiven myself.' The boy lifted his head, the look on his face showing he was relieved not to be in trouble after all. He cleared his throat.

'Chibesa,' he said, 'please don't be mad at me. My cough was a lot better today and George is so ill. His mother has no money for medicine. So I gave him mine. She was really grateful, gave him a big spoonful straight away.' Chibesa stared in horror at his brother, but Samuel didn't notice. Grinning, he grabbed a handful of peas from the bowl on Hannah's lap; and as he dodged to avoid her playful slap, he continued speaking. 'I think George is going to be okay, now. We said we'd go and visit him again tomorrow.'

## 10: ENGLAND, NOV 2004

Suzanne was stirring her first coffee of the morning when Chibesa's call came in. The line wasn't good and she had to ask him to repeat himself before she understood what he was saying.

'It's my fault,' he gasped, 'I should have been more careful!'

'Chibesa,' Suzanne raised her voice slightly over the man's sobs, 'you did everything right. You didn't buy the medicine from one of the roadside stalls; you went to the government pharmacy. You had no way of knowing.'

'But George is dead...'

'And that's tragic, I know; but you can't blame yourself. That won't bring him back.'

'And I keep thinking it could have been Samuel—being thankful he's okay—and then feeling guilty for feeling glad.' He gave another sob. 'Oh, Suzanne, you have to stop them—we have to stop them!'

'Believe me, Chibesa, I know. But we don't know who they are.'

'But what about the stuff Sara—'

'We're not going to talk about that,' she broke in, 'not on the phone.'

'But…' Suzanne could hear the disappointment in his voice, even with the poor connection.'

'I'm bringing my next trip forward,' she went on. 'I've had some positive responses to the work we did in Swaziland; the Ugandans and Kenyans want some help, so I'll be flying down to Lusaka in a couple of weeks' time. Can you make the same arrangements as last time?'

'A driver to meet you from the airport and a room in the same hotel? Of course. Are we going travelling again? Do you want me to contact WB?'

'I expect so, but let's decide when I get there, shall we? I want to talk to some of the people in the Ministry of Health and the government purchasing officers in Zambia first.'

Sir Frederick raised his eyebrows a little when Suzanne told him she wanted to go back to Africa so quickly. He'd heard about the diethylene glycol contamination and had even phoned Chibesa himself to commiserate about George's death.

'But you mustn't let a one-off incident, no matter how tragic or close to home, cloud your judgement,' he said when she took her travel plans to him for approval. 'The political climate in that region is sensitive to say the least. And we have to remember we have no authority in these countries, only influence. And we can lose that influence overnight if we upset the wrong people.'

Suzanne knew that when he said 'we', he really meant her. But when she explained she'd had requests from three Health Ministries to help draft their import regulations, he nodded and signed her travel warrant.

'Just make sure your project status report is finished before you go, won't you?' he said. She had delivered her Swaziland report, as promised, the week after making her presentation, but the status update was a much bigger document. 'I've had Francine Matheson on the phone and she wants to use it at some meeting or other later in the month.'

Suzanne nodded, although she wasn't really sure if having her report used as political ammunition by a member of the government was a good thing or not.

It was later the same week that Charlie pointed out a news item she'd picked up on the BBC News website.

'It was hidden right down the bottom,' she said. 'I wouldn't have spotted it if I hadn't put in a special search for anything relating to Africa, cross referenced with pharmaceuticals.'

It was only a brief item, but there was enough detail in the couple of paragraphs to make Suzanne go cold. Fire had broken out in an industrial complex on the outskirts of Kampala. A garage, two shops and a pharmaceutical factory had been completely gutted. There was no mention of injuries or fatalities, but the owner of the factory hadn't been seen since. It wasn't clear from the news report whether he was suspected of setting the fire himself, but his wife, Mrs Constance Businge, was quoted as saying that 'my husband would never do anything dishonest. My WB is a good man.' The report continued that Constance and her children were all very concerned for his safety.

Suzanne paced up and down the lounge while Charlie stared at her from her usual seat by the window.

'You don't think he did it...? Charlie asked.

'No, of course I don't,' her sister snapped, 'if you knew WB, you wouldn't have to ask such a stupid question!' Then she stopped pacing, took a deep breath and sat on the sofa, smiling ruefully at her sister. 'Sorry, sis, that was uncalled for.' Charlie waved her apology away with a grin. 'But I would like to know where he is, and if he's okay.'

'And where Sara's documents are?'

'That's right. He said he was going to hide them somewhere safe. I'm just hoping it wasn't in the factory.'

The next few days disappeared in a blur for Suzanne.

Getting her status update finished didn't take too long; but sending it out to Chibesa for comment was a nightmare. In the end, she emailed each chapter individually. The link to Lusaka was still difficult and it took the best part of a day to get everything through. For speed, Chibesa, who read the document overnight, phoned his comments back: there were a couple of name corrections and a phrase that he suggested she rewrite—ever the diplomat, he reminded her that even if she didn't approve of what some people had said, she still needed to retain their support.

'I know Walter Mukooyo is a difficult person,' Chibesa told her, 'but he's very influential in the region. We need him, Suzanne.'

Reluctantly accepting the point, Suzanne made the suggested corrections, finalised the document and circulated it. As usual, she printed and bound one copy for Sir Frederick.

'The Director General of the IHF doesn't have the luxury of using his office to read,' he'd once said to her. 'I use the back of my car—on the way to meetings in Whitehall. So I need everything hard copy.' There was a rumour among IHF staff that Sir Frederick couldn't actually use his computer at all, which was the real reason for his request, but whatever the truth, everyone complied. And to give him his due, the report would often come back a few days later with detailed questions and comments in the margins, so at least they knew he read everything that was given to him.

Suzanne also had to clear her desk of other issues. Although Africa was her major project, she also had an ongoing investigation in Latin America. She knew at some point she'd have to go out there too, and was looking forward to her first visit to the continent.

'Are you sure you're going to be alright?' she asked Charlie on their last evening together. They'd popped across to the curry house once more for an early evening meal. Suzanne was heading off to the airport at five-thirty the next morning.

'Why shouldn't I be?' Charlie mumbled through a mouthful of Peshwari Nan and Chicken Vindaloo.

'Well, what with everything that's been going on over the last couple of months…' But Charlie shrugged and dipped her bread into the sauce once more.

'They've already searched the flat and got nothing. We've established that it's you they're after, not me. Why do I need to worry? It's you who needs to be careful.'

'Oh, I'll be fine; I'll have Chibesa to take care of me.' She searched around for a change of subject, as she was not really as calm as she was pretending to be, but didn't want to alarm her sister. 'Have you made contact with Annie yet? Do you think there's any chance…?' But her sister was already shaking her head.

'I think I may have really burnt my boats there,' she said. 'To be honest, things weren't wonderful when we were in Greece, even before it all kicked off with Sandro. In fact, if we hadn't been having such a bad time on the island, I suspect she might have refused to come with me.'

'Oh that's a pity, Charlie. I liked Annie—and, apart from anything else, it would have been somewhere for you to go if anyone started watching the flat again.'

Charlie shrugged her shoulders again and grimaced.

'I guess you're stuck with me for now.' She suddenly looked up, an uncertainty flitting across her face. 'That's okay, isn't it? I could always go and look for somewhere— .' But Suzanne reached over and laid a hand on her arm to stop her.

'Charlie, you're my big sister. My home is your home— for as long as you need it.' She smiled as she helped herself to more curry. 'Just remember to do the washing up occasionally, will you? And no smoking inside!'

# 11: SWAZILAND, NOV 2004

Sara Matsebula trudged along the path towards her house at the end of another long day running the pharmacy at the Swazi National Hospital. Her shoulders ached from pushing the trolley laden with drugs around the ward all day. Her assistant was off sick again and she'd had to do everything herself. She rather suspected she wouldn't be seeing the poor boy for much longer and would have to look for a new apprentice to help her. Her head bowed, she sighed and concentrated on putting one foot in front of the other. She would think about staffing tomorrow or the next day—when the situation arose, in fact. One thing was for sure—there would be no shortage of candidates. Jobs, especially good jobs in the hospital, were few and far between in Swaziland and there were always dozens of people queuing to be considered every time a position was advertised. Sometimes, the grapevine was enough and there was no need to even put out an advert at all.

The sun had already gone down, but Sara was used to walking home in the dark, and felt her way by instinct, even on a night like tonight when the moon was new and little more than a nail paring in the sky. Since Ruth died, Sara often imagined her sister's shade was out there in the darkness, keeping her company. Sometimes she talked to her, telling her what had happened during the day; who was recently admitted—so many these days—who had got better, or who had gone to meet their Maker. 'Take care of her,' she would say, referring to whichever of their neighbours had passed this time, 'she's going to need help to find her way around to start with.' There seemed to be more deaths every day. The scientist in Sara knew Ruth wasn't really there, just as she knew the recently deceased wouldn't be wandering around in Heaven trying to orientate themselves, but the other Sara, the Sara who had gone to church with her parents throughout her childhood—and still attended when she was not on duty—that Sara found comfort in talking to her sister on the long walks home.

But tonight it seemed a longer way, a darker path, and she felt shivers running down her spine as she crossed the final piece of open ground and passed through the broken-down old gate to the patch of earth she called her front garden. She felt a prickle on her shoulders as though eyes were boring into them and looked back along the path as she groped in her bag for her key. But the darkness stared back at her impassively and she shook herself, tutted at her imagination, and opened her front door.

She flicked the light switch several times, clicking her teeth with her tongue in exasperation. The electricity had failed once again. Groping for the candle and matches she kept by the door for just this occasion, which happened far too often these days, she used the flickering flame to light her way to the kitchen. She was too tired to cook, and didn't want to try and light the calor gas stove in the dark anyway. She'd eaten lunch at the hospital, although that was many hours ago now. She took a few biscuits out of the old tin her grandmother had given her one Christmas, and poured a glass of water from the bottle in the tiny pantry. It was still warm from the day's heat, but she'd filled the bottle herself at the hospital, so at least she knew it was clean and safe to drink.

She was just about to go to bed when she heard the crack of a dry stick breaking outside the back door. It was never completely silent in this area, just on the edge of town, but there was something about that sound that made her think it wasn't just a normal night noise. A cat, maybe, although most of the cats in the neighbourhood were too skinny to break anything by stepping on it. Or maybe a wild dog? Something larger? It was rare for any of the animals to come down from the hills and into town, although occasionally there were sightings of zebra or buffalo. But something told Sara if there was an animal outside her door, it was more likely to be walking on two legs than four.

She groaned gently; she'd always known they would find her one day. Ever since she'd talked to the English woman, she'd been waiting for a knock on the door. She briefly considered hiding, but there was nowhere to hide—and besides, if they'd been watching the house, they would know she was in there. And if she didn't come out, they might just burn the place down. House fires were quite common—a gas cooker malfunction would be blamed and that would be all that was said about it. They'd find another pharmacist for the hospital—and Sara, tragic Sara who lost her sister the other year, would be forgotten.

The quiet step on the veranda was followed, not by the pounding knock she was expecting, but by a gentle scratching noise. She bit her lip and opened the door. A huge figure stood facing her, standing to one side, so the light from Sara's candle barely illuminated him. A figure that looked slightly familiar, although she couldn't quite place him.

'Miss Sara, we need to talk,' he said, 'please let me in.' And without waiting for an answer, he gently pushed past her and closed the door.

'I know you, don't I?' Sara whispered. The man smiled and held out his hand, taking the candle from her. To her surprise, he blew it out and then taking her by her shoulders, pushed her gently back into one of the two old armchairs in front of the empty fireplace. He took the other chair himself, easing his huge body carefully onto its creaking frame.

'We met at the IHF conference in September,' he reminded her, 'and afterwards at my accommodation.'

'Dr Businge?' she said.

'Call me WB, Miss Sara; everyone does.'

'But, someone was talking about you in the hospital the other day—the fire—your disappearance—they're saying you did it yourself...' She stopped as he shook his head.

'No dear lady, I didn't do it myself. In fact when it happened, I was no longer in Kampala. I got a warning that I was in danger, and decided a tactical disappearance was the better part of valour, as it were.' He paused and shook his head once more. 'Such a pity about the factory, though; we worked so hard to build it—and all those people will now be out of work.' He sighed and looked across at her. She could see his features in the faint moonlight and realised he was smiling at her. 'But at least no-one was hurt in the fire. It wasn't people they were after, thanks be to God.'

'But why are you here? Do you want to hide?'

'No, no, dear lady.' WB chuckled gently and shook his head. 'I don't think hiding in the home of a respectable unmarried lady in Swaziland would be very effective for very long, do you?'

Sara thought of the neighbours she'd lived among for such a long time—wonderful people who had been so sympathetic when she lost Ruth—but no denying, the biggest gossips in the kingdom.

'No, you're right. So, I don't understand...'

'I've come to fetch you, Sara,' he said gently. 'They know who you are; they're on their way here. You're not safe.' She jumped up and looked wildly towards the window. Although she'd known it was only a matter of time, having her thoughts confirmed by someone else was heart-stopping. 'Sit down,' he went on, 'my sources tell me we've got a few hours' start on them.'

'Your sources?' she asked.

'I'm lucky enough to have a very wide network of contacts and friends across the continent,' he said. 'Most of them are left over from my days in government, before I 'went over to the enemy', but they're still willing to give the nod to an old friend. Even if there are very few of them brave enough to do what you did, dear lady.'

'I don't feel very brave,' she whispered, shivering violently as the impact of WB's words gradually sank in. 'They're really coming to get me, are they?'

'But you won't be here, will you?' he said. Then he stood up and rubbed his hands together. 'Now, I think the time for talking is over. Go quickly, Miss Sara, and pack a few things. Anything you can't live without. I doubt if you will be back here—at least, not for a while.'

'And my papers, my passport?'

'Yes, anything like that will be useful—although I've got some others you can use for tonight.' He handed her the candle. 'Use this if you have to, but keep it away from the windows.'

'But you said they aren't coming tonight.'

'And they're not. But I suspect you are being watched. Banda has watching eyes everywhere. And I would prefer any spies who are still up to think you are safely in bed at this time of night.'

In less than thirty minutes, Sara was ready. In her mother's old carpet bag she had a couple of changes of clothes, her documents, and a picture of Ruth. It wasn't much, but she found it was all she really wanted to take with her.

WB put his finger to his lips and opened the back door. She slipped out onto the veranda behind him and he quietly pulled the door shut. Then, taking her hand in his, he headed across the garden, down the bank to the little

71

dried-up river bed marking the border of her property. They set off across the scrub land, keeping in the shadow of trees wherever possible. When Sara looked back a few minutes later, her house and, she suspected, her life in Swaziland had disappeared from sight.

# PART II

# 12: ZAMBIA; DEC 2004

Suzanne was surprised and touched to find her sister waiting for her in the kitchen when she crept in with her bags at five am.

'Well, I couldn't let you go without saying goodbye, now could I?' Charlie said. 'Sit down and I'll pour you a coffee. I take it you'll eat when you're checked in?' Then half an hour later, the taxi arrived bang on time. Charlie gave Suzanne a tight squeeze as she headed for the front door. 'Take care of yourself, sis—and let me know how you're getting on, won't you?'

'I'll text you when I get to Kenya this evening. I'm stopping overnight and meeting with someone from the Health Ministry in the morning, so I'm not due to land in Lusaka until mid-afternoon tomorrow.'

At that time of day, the traffic heading westwards out of London was light and Suzanne was checked in and sitting in the departure lounge by just after seven o'clock. She had plenty of time for a croissant and yet more coffee before the flight was due to board. Then wiping the butter off her hands, she pulled her report out of her bag and started to reread it.

'Passengers flying to Nairobi on BA flight number

0065 should proceed immediately to gate 31 where boarding is about to commence.' The tannoy announcement made her jump. She'd been lost in plans for the next stage of the project and hadn't realised how time had flown by.

As the plane taxied along the runway, the crew made the usual announcements about emergency exits and what to do in the event of a landing on water. Like most seasoned travellers, Suzanne paid very little attention to the words, but she did, as always, take note of the nearest emergency exit—and checked that her life jacket really was attached to the bottom of the seat.

'Please ensure that all mobile phones are switched off and remember they must stay off for the duration of the flight.' As the steward completed his announcements, Suzanne reached automatically into her handbag for her mobile. She usually switched it off while still in the departure lounge, but she'd been so engrossed in her report that she'd forgotten to do it this time.

She felt around in the pocket where it was usually kept, but it was empty. So were all the other pockets and compartments. She grabbed her briefcase from beneath the seat and rummaged around in there too. But the phone was nowhere to be found. There were no pockets in her coat, so it couldn't be there. As the steward walked down the aisle for one final check, she pushed her briefcase and handbag back under the seat in front of her and threw her head back against the headrest in frustration. It looked like her phone was gone. Lost or stolen, she would probably never know. But one thing she did know, was that her copies of the papers given to her by Sara Matsebula and scanned onto her phone for safety before she left Africa last time were no longer in her possession. She just hoped Chibesa had done a better job of looking after his copy than she had with hers. And that whoever now had her phone would not understand the significance of the documents.

Suzanne scanned the sea of faces and the name signs being waved around in the arrivals hall. All around her were smiling, laughing people, greeting friends and relatives at the end of long flights. At first she thought no-one was there to meet her, and was considering taking a taxi, when she spotted a tall, lithe figure leaning against a pillar at the back of the crowd. She pushed her way through the hugging, noisy groups and, dropping her bags on the floor, opened her arms wide.

'Chibesa, I'm so glad to see you.' His face lit up as he pulled her to him and gave her a tight squeeze.

'Suzanne, it's great to see you. How are you?' Suzanne was surprised to feel her eyes pricking with tears as she stood hugging this man she hadn't realised she was becoming so fond of. She'd only met him once, during her previous trip, but they'd been in constant contact over the past few weeks, both by phone and email—and of course, they had so much shared history, with the conference, Sara Matsebula's story and the counterfeit medicine he'd bought after she'd returned to England. At the thought of this incident and its terrible consequences, she pulled herself out of his embrace and looked at him steadily.

'How is Samuel?' she asked. Chibesa's smile faded and his shoulders slumped.

'He's not doing too well, I'm afraid. He blames himself for George's death—and it doesn't matter how many times I tell him it's not his fault. He's started coughing again over the past few days and he doesn't seem to want to get better. It's almost as though he's trying to make up for the loss of his friend by making himself ill—or worse—as well.' Then Chibesa shook his head and smiled at Suzanne once more. 'But you'll see him later this week. You made me see it wasn't my fault; maybe you can do the same for him. Now, come on, let's get out of here.' And grabbing her bags, he strode out of the airport, heading for the car park.

Twenty minutes later, as they were driving westwards along the T4 towards the city, Chibesa turned towards Suzanne.

'I hope you're not too tired?' he said. 'I want to make a quick detour on the way to the hotel. I've got a surprise for you.' Suzanne tried to get him to tell her more, but he just shook his head with a smile and said, 'wait and see.'

The car pulled into a driveway lined with jacaranda trees, their heavy mauve blossoms waving in the warm breeze and dipping towards the car, as though bidding Suzanne welcome.

'Where is this place?' she asked, but Chibesa just took her arm and helped her out of the car, telling the driver he could go around to the kitchen and get himself a drink while he was waiting for them. Then, still holding her arm, he escorted her up the steps to the colonial-style veranda. The large oak doors swung open in front of them and a young boy in a white suit with large brass buttons waved them into the cool, dark interior.

'Chibesa, where are we going?' Suzanne pulled against his guiding hand and stopped just inside the doorway. 'I'm tired and I'm hot and sweaty after my flight. I'm not in the mood for silly games. I insist you tell me what this place is.'

'Suzanne, don't be like that. I've come a long way to see you.' The voice floating down from the landing at the top of the curving staircase was deep and contained a smile. Suzanne peered up through the dim light, not believing her ears. 'Come on up and we can talk—if you're not too tired, that is,' the voice continued.

But Suzanne was already halfway up the stairs, her tiredness forgotten. She threw herself at the huge man standing waiting for her.

'WB! You're alive! I knew it,' she said before bursting into tears. The two men stood and laughed at her, especially when she stamped her foot in temper at them. 'Stop it! I've been really worried about you.' Then she too burst out laughing, and wiped her tears away with the back of her hand. WB pointed to a door off the landing.

'Come on in here; we'll be more comfortable and we can have a drink while we're talking.'

'So I decided that, as the Bard says, "discretion is the better part of valour," and headed for the airport,' WB finished his story a little while later, as they sat drinking sweet milky tea and nibbling shortbread biscuits. He'd told them about the strange calls he'd had in the middle of the night, silent calls that came through with disturbing frequency; he'd talked about the vehicles he saw around Kampala too regularly to be coincidence, which had to be watching him—and he'd gone on to discuss the early morning warning he'd had from an old friend, that Banda was planning to visit the factory. 'I wasn't frightened for me,' he said, 'I'm big enough and ugly enough to look after myself, but I didn't want to risk any harm coming to my wife and daughters.'

'So you staged your disappearing act,' Suzanne said. 'And your beautiful factory—all gone. Such a pity.' WB shrugged.

'I needed to cast suspicion on myself, so my family would be safe. And I wanted to confuse Banda; make them stop and find out whether any of their rivals was also after me. It gave me the breathing space I needed to get away.'

'You're not saying you fired it yourself, are you?' gasped Suzanne. 'I've been telling everyone there's no way you would do something like that.' But WB shook his head.

'Of course not!' He smiled and patted her arm, 'Let's just say I made a few unwise comments in the wrong places.'

Suzanne stared at WB with her mouth open, unable to take in everything she'd been told. Just then, there was a gentle tap on the door. Not the door off the landing, but a second one, behind a screen, that Suzanne had not noticed before. Chibesa jumped up and opened it, standing back to let a slim young woman slip into the room. Suzanne was sure she'd seen her before, but couldn't place her at first.

'Ah, the fourth member of our little band,' said WB. 'Will you take some tea, my dear?'

As the newcomer nodded to WB, she smiled shyly at Suzanne and lifted a slim hand to brush her hair out of her eyes. The gesture took Suzanne back to a villa in Swaziland ten weeks before and she gave a gasp.

'Sara; Sara Matsebula!'

'I thought Miss Sara would be safer out of Swaziland,' said WB, 'so I made a bit of a detour on my way to Lusaka and picked her up.'

'That's quite some detour. And how did you manage to get across the borders undetected?' Suzanne asked. WB shrugged.

'Well, there are always back roads that are less well controlled; there are trains; and of course,' he pulled a face, 'neither of us was actually using our real names.' As Suzanne opened her mouth to ask yet more questions, he held up his hand and then put his finger to his lips. 'Trust me, Suzanne, you don't want to know!'

'I'm very grateful to Dr Businge,' Sara said, shaking Suzanne's hand and then sitting with her cup of tea in one of the large chintzy armchairs. She looked much more relaxed than the previous time they'd met and, from the looks she was stealing across at the big Ugandan, Suzanne wondered if she was developing a bit of a crush on her rescuer.

'Sara's not been in contact with anyone since she left Swaziland,' said Chibesa, 'it's too dangerous to let anyone know where she is.'

'And there's no-one left in the family to worry about me anyway,' Sara added softly.

'But my contacts tell me we got out just in time,' WB continued. 'I understand there's been another incident of arson. It seems to be Banda's weapon of choice.'

'Oh, Sara, I'm so sorry to hear that,' said Suzanne, but the girl just smiled sadly.

'There's nothing they can do to me that's any worse than what they've already done. I just hope the papers I gave you can help put an end to this terrible trade.'

Suzanne's heart plummeted and she looked at WB.

'Please tell me you didn't keep the papers in the factory,' she said, 'I'm afraid my copy's gone. My phone disappeared when I was in Heathrow waiting to take off.' Chibesa's head shot up and he looked at her, askance. But WB gave a chuckle.

'No, it's okay. The papers weren't in the factory. They were never in the factory. In fact, they were never in Uganda.'

'Well, where were they?' Suzanne asked.

'Have you ever heard the saying about hiding something in plain sight?' he said. 'Well that's what I've done—and I think we can be sure the papers are still safe. Although I'll keep the details to myself, if you don't mind. The fewer people who know, the better.' And with a grin, he tapped his long forefinger against his nose. 'Let's just say, I may need to visit Lusaka University Library over the next few days. Now, I think there's just time for another pot of tea and more of these wonderful biscuits and then Chibesa will escort you to your hotel, Suzanne.'

## 13: ZAMBIA; DEC 2004

At the hotel, Suzanne refused Chibesa's offer of help with the luggage and once he had handed her over to a porter, he left. As she watched him sending the official driver back to headquarters and strolling across the hotel car park towards the bus stop, she felt a pang—of loneliness, of fear, she wasn't quite sure which—but pulling herself together, she followed the porter inside and checked in. The three days of travelling, and the revelations of the past couple of hours were starting to catch up with her and she was dozing as she walked. Within minutes of reaching her room, she had undressed and crawled inside the bedclothes, asleep almost before she'd had time to register that the sun was just going down and the orange sky was filtering through the black silhouettes of the trees.

She woke with a start to complete darkness, and the whine of a mosquito in her ear. She groaned as she realised she'd forgotten to put on her insect repellent! She thought she could feel the insect's progress up her arm and neck, although she knew in reality that any bites she might have picked up would take a few hours to start itching. Bleary-eyed, she untied the mosquito net from the wall above her head, pulled it out and secured it to each corner of the bed.

Then, ignoring the rumbling in her stomach reminding her it was hours since she'd eaten, she closed her eyes and attempted to go back to sleep. But it was no good. There was a party going on in the grounds of the hotel and the smell of barbecued lamb and the sounds of drumming and laughter reached her even through the closed windows. Clicking on the light at the side of the bed, she checked the clock. It was not yet half eight; she'd only been asleep for a couple of hours. It would be ages before the noise outside subsided. Her stomach gave another rumble and she admitted defeat.

Pulling on her crumpled travel clothes once more, she went down to the bar and ordered a toasted sandwich and a rock shandy, no ice. Looking around at the few fellow guests who were still inside, rather than out in the garden party, she wondered if there was anyone she might chat to; maybe pass a couple of hours before attempting sleep once more. But a group of businessmen were engrossed in a noisy discussion about the relative merits of soccer versus American football; the young couple in the corner looked like newly-weds and only had eyes for each other; while the only other single woman in the room was talking quietly into her mobile phone, and seemed to be taking no notice of anyone else. From her position near the bar, Suzanne could watch the woman's reflection in the mirror. Her long, bushy red hair was topped by an Adidas baseball cap and her eyes were hidden behind huge reflective sunglasses, which she kept on even in the dim lighting. She didn't look like she wanted company, so Suzanne picked up a newspaper instead. When she'd finished her supper and waved good night to the barman, she glanced in the mirror once more, but the table was empty and the woman had gone.

When the lift arrived on the seventh floor, Suzanne turned left along the threadbare carpet and stopped outside room number 721. She was just about to open the door when she got the distinct feeling she was being watched. Turning, she thought she caught a glimpse of movement from one of the rooms further down the corridor. There was a click as though of a door being quietly closed—and then nothing. Suzanne stared at the empty corridor, then turned the key, and entered her own room. Within minutes she was back in bed and this time, she had no trouble falling asleep.

The following morning, Suzanne awoke bright and early, refreshed despite her broken sleep and raring to go. She was keen to get on with the official business of the trip: to talk to government ministers and civil servants about how to level the playing field for drugs made in Africa, against the more expensive imports from Europe and the United States. And she wanted to make time for the unofficial business: finding out what she could about the activities of Banda and what could be done to shut them down. She was not naive enough to think she could solve all the problems of counterfeiting singlehandedly—or even with her little team of collaborators—but meeting Sara and hearing Ruth's heart-wrenching story, not to mention the tragedy of Samuel's friend George, had personalised the whole issue for her and, despite her boss's misgivings, she was determined to do something to prevent other families going through the same heartache.

The corridor was empty as she left her room for breakfast, but once again, she had the feeling she was being watched. She peered down the corridor, dim in the early morning light, and tried to decide which door it had been that she heard being closed the previous night. She thought it was 726, across the hallway and a couple of rooms down, but she couldn't really be sure. Maybe it was the one on the other side, or even on the same side as her own room. She'd been convinced she heard something when she reached her room the night before, but now she was beginning to doubt her own memory and senses.

Suzanne was seated at a table on the veranda, enjoying

mango, paw-paw and coconut from the hotel's own gardens, when the woman from the previous evening strolled into the dining room. This time, she was wearing a large floppy straw hat, but her hair and sunglasses made her instantly recognisable. She waved away the table next to Suzanne, which the waiter offered her, and disappeared instead into one of the darker recesses of the room. Sitting outside and dazzled by the sunshine, Suzanne could no longer see her, but she had the distinct impression the woman was watching her; she felt her shoulder blades prickle.

'Pull yourself together,' Suzanne told herself, 'you're being ridiculous. She's a total stranger who just happens to be staying at the same hotel. Why would she be staring at you?'

Finishing her coffee, Suzanne set off through the foyer to meet her driver for the short journey to Chibesa's office. The two spent the whole morning on plans for the rest of the trip, including meetings in the Copper Belt and in Lusaka, plus a couple of short visits to South Africa and Kenya. Suzanne had told Sir Frederick she wasn't sure how long this latest trip would last, but she'd cleared her diary of all other commitments in London for the next three weeks.

'And that will take us up to Christmas,' she told Chibesa, 'I need to get home in time to spend the holiday with Charlie.'

By lunchtime, the plan was more or less complete and Chibesa had a long list of logistical tasks to work on.

'Let's grab a quick bite to eat,' he said, 'and then you can go and see WB and Sara while I get on with this lot.' They'd all agreed that for the time being the two fugitives should stay hidden. Suzanne had learnt the previous day that the large house she'd visited was the home of a former Zambian Ambassador to Uganda, who had become friendly with WB during the early days of his mission. Now retired, he was living well for a government official, and although Chibesa wasn't completely certain where his money had come from, WB was willing to vouch for the man, and it was certainly a good place for the pair to hide.

As on her previous trip, Chibesa took Suzanne across the road to his favourite fried chicken stall for their lunch. As Suzanne bit into the spicy coating and wiped the juice from her chin with a serviette, she gazed idly around the crowded street.

'I don't believe it!' she exclaimed, dropping the chicken leg back on her plate and wiping her fingers.'

'What's the matter, said Chibesa; isn't it properly cooked?'

'What? Oh no, it's fine; great in fact. No, I've just seen a woman from the hotel staring at me from across the road, that's all.

'Well, it's a public place, in a fairly small city,' he said with a smile. 'You're bound to see someone you know, aren't you?'

'I suppose so,' she said, picking up her chicken again. 'It's just that I keep seeing her wherever I go—and sometimes I feel she's watching me.'

'Maybe she recognises you from the hotel. Maybe she's lonely. Is she travelling alone?'

'Well, yes, I think so, but if she sees me in the hotel, I get the impression she's trying to avoid eye contact with me.

'Suzanne, you can't have it both ways,' Chibesa said, grinning. 'Either she's watching you—or she has no interest in you. It can't be both.

Privately, Suzanne disagreed. The woman wouldn't catch her eye when Suzanne looked directly at her; but if she looked away, she immediately got the feeling the woman's eyes were boring into her back. However, she didn't argue the point and when she looked across to the same place again, the woman was gone. Maybe she was imagining things. As Chibesa said, this was a small city. It was inevitable she was going to bump into the same people from time to time. And another white woman in the middle of Lusaka was difficult to miss.

*Nevertheless*, she thought as she left Chibesa to return to work and got into the car for the trip to the safe house, *if I see her in the hotel this evening, I'm going to find some way to strike up a conversation. Maybe I can find out a bit more about her.* There was something about the woman that made Suzanne think she should know her. *I'll find out her room number from the receptionist,* she decided, *and invite her to have dinner with me this evening.*

## 14: ZAMBIA; DEC 2004

Back at the hotel, Suzanne chatted to a friendly receptionist and discovered that the red-headed woman was staying in room 726. As she stood in the elevator ascending slowly to the seventh floor, two thoughts hit her: that was the room from which she thought she had been spied upon; and if she could get room numbers so easily from the hotel staff, anyone else could probably do the same. *Maybe I ought to think about moving rooms, or even hotels,* she thought. This time, as she walked along the corridor, she kept a close eye on room 726. And sure enough, she saw the door was slightly ajar. Without waiting to think through the consequences, she stopped and slapped her hand hard against the panel, just below the spy hole. The door swung back and there was a thud, followed by a muffled yell and a string of colourful words, some of which Suzanne had never heard before.

'You might as well come out; I know you're watching me,' she said. The door slowly swung open, revealing her 'stalker', who was holding her hand over her right eye.

'Shit, that bloody well hurt.'

'Well it serves you right!' Suzanne said. 'Don't you think you'd better tell me who you are and why you're following me?' The woman slipped her sunglasses back on and stepped out of the way, waving her hand to indicate Suzanne should enter the room.

As Suzanne walked into the mirror image of her own room across the hall, the woman spoke once more.

'I'm going to have a beautiful shiner in the morning!' The voice was younger than Suzanne had noticed before—and suddenly very familiar. She spun around, shock running through her.

'Charlie?' She couldn't believe she'd been fooled by a red wig, huge glasses and a couple of hats. No wonder the 'stalker' hadn't wanted to sit close to her at breakfast.

'Well, it's taken long enough for the penny to drop, sis.'

'Charlie, when did you arrive and what on earth are you doing here? And why the silly disguise?'

'I flew down the day you did your stop-over in Nairobi. Got here the day before you did. And why do you think I'm here, you daft cow; to keep an eye on you, of course.'

'On me? Why?'

'Well, let me think: you've recently been burgled; your luggage has been interfered with; your close colleague has apparently disappeared; at least two children have died—and you're out here playing Sherlock Holmes to stop a dangerous group of criminals singlehandedly. Can't think why you might need some protection, can you?'

'Oh, Charlie, that's sweet of you...'

'Besides, we'd run out of milk and this seemed more fun than popping down the shops.' Charlie was laughing now and, against her will, Suzanne joined in. When they finally calmed down, she pointed to the long curly wig now lying discarded on the bed.

'But why the disguise?'

'Well, if I'd suggested coming with you, what would you have said?'

'Absolutely not!'

'Precisely. And I thought it might be easier to keep close to you without any of the bad guys realising who I was, if I tried out some of my old acting roles.'

'Yes, you were never happier than when you were rehearsing for the end of term plays, were you? A regular little Julia Roberts.'

'I reckon it was only my acting skills that kept me from being expelled on more than one occasion.'

'Although I'm not sure about the choice of role this time. You're hardly inconspicuous.'

'It's called hiding in plain sight, sis. No-one's going to suspect a flamboyant young woman of being a spy, now are they?'

Suzanne was struck by the phrase her sister had used: *hiding in plain sight.* She'd heard someone else use the same phrase just recently, but she couldn't remember whom. She dismissed the stray thought and nodded at Charlie.

'Very true. I noticed you, couldn't fail to really, but never for one minute suspected…' Suzanne shrugged and smiled ruefully. 'But the question is, how are we going to get you home again?' Charlie looked startled.

'Home? I'm not going home, Suzanne. I'm staying right here to look after you.'

'But I don't need looking after.'

'Are you sure about that, sis?'

'Completely.'

'So tell me: when did you realise I was Charlie and not some stranger who was following you around for nefarious purposes.'

'When you talked about the shiner, and used your own voice, of course.'

'Which was after you'd come into my room?'

'You know it was.'

'So don't you think someone who's willing to enter a stranger's bedroom, completely alone, without warning anyone where they're going, might need all the protection they can get? I'm going nowhere, Suzanne, so you'd better get used to it.'

Suzanne glared at Charlie, unable to think of a suitable

reply. Then she finally broke into a huge smile and hugged her sister.

'Okay, you win; welcome to the team. But you're going to have to work on your surveillance skills.'

If the waiters in the hotel's restaurant were surprised by the new friendship between the two English women, they were too well-trained to say anything. Suzanne and Charlie, back in character, had breakfast together the next morning. Then Suzanne was collected by the Ministry car while Charlie took another to the local game park, which she'd declared loudly in the foyer she wanted to see.

A few hours later, Suzanne and Chibesa were just walking up the steps to the front door of the safe house when a taxi drew up and an elegant young woman with long dark hair stepped out, carrying a large hold-all. When they'd made their arrangements earlier, Charlie had said she was looking forward to spending some time as herself, and would change at the game park. She joined the other two at the top of the steps and together they entered the cool entrance hall.

It was while Suzanne was introducing her sister to the rest of the team that she remembered where she'd heard the phrase about hiding in plain sight. WB had used it when he talked about Sara's papers he'd been given for safekeeping. It was this memory, as much as the fact that none of her co-conspirators seemed at all surprised to hear Charlie was in Zambia, that made Suzanne realise her sister hadn't been the only one making plans behind her back. She made a note to herself to ask Chibesa who was funding this trip. She didn't think Sir Frederick would be at all impressed if any of it came out of his budget. Introductions made, tea and biscuits ordered, the five sat around the large oak table and looked at one another.

'Okay,' said Chibesa, 'where do we start?' Charlie gave a little cough.

'Well, I've been doing a little searching on the internet,'

she said. Her colour was higher than Suzanne was used to seeing and she seemed to be very nervous, fidgeting in her seat and twisting her fingers together. 'Using Sara's papers and what we know about Banda's customers, I thought I'd see if I could track the money.'

'Sara's papers? But when did you…?'

'I uploaded the files from your phone when you were asleep the night before you flew out,' she said biting her lip and looking apprehensive. 'It was after I'd spoken to Chibesa and arranged to fly out here once you'd left for Kenya.' Suzanne just sighed and shook her head.

'How are Banda's customers going to help?' asked Chibesa. 'Surely all their transactions will be in cash?'

'Most of them, yes. But we know they supplied the government pharmacy here in Lusaka where you bought Samuel's medicine.'

'And that won't have been a cash transaction!'

'Exactly! And there must be other examples you'll be able to get from your Ministry contacts, that we can use to cross reference. But in the meantime, I'm working my way through the first set of records.'

'And have you found anything?' asked WB.

'Well, the trail is very convoluted and I lost it at the moment in the Cayman Islands, but I'll keep working on it.'

'And can you put a name to the account?'

'Not yet, but I'm sure I will.'

'Charlie, I've had an idea.' Chibesa took off his glasses and rubbed them on the bottom of his shirt. 'How good are you at hacking into phone records?' The question sounded so innocuous; it almost passed Suzanne by. Almost, but not quite.

'Hacking? Charlie's not a hacker,' she said indignantly. Chibesa and WB just smiled at her while Charlie pulled a wry face.

'How do you think I was able to find the money, sis?' she asked. Then she turned back to Chibesa. 'I'm not sure, but I'll have a go. It depends which network you want me to get into.'

As the rest of the team chatted about the next steps in their investigation, Suzanne walked to the window and leaned her forehead against the cool glass. There was obviously quite a lot she didn't know about her sister. She wondered what other secrets she was hiding—and whether she would ever be completely honest. Suzanne still suspected there might be more to Charlie's flight from Greece than she was willing to share—but this obviously wasn't the time or the place to go into that.

## 15: ZAMBIA; DEC 2004

Suzanne flipped through the papers Chibesa had printed out for her. They'd been working all day on the outline for the pilot study and it was coming together well. She would visit some of the factories manufacturing drugs in Southern Africa, get an overview of the situation across the local industries, and then pick one or two from each country that they could work with. Then she would set up training courses and mock audits, all aimed at bringing the chosen companies up to a standard that would allow them to make products under licence from the multinationals. That way they could compete both with expensive imports and cheap counterfeits. And once the pilot companies had reached the right standard, it would be easier to roll out better controls across the region.

'Which ones would you suggest I visit here in Zambia?' she asked, running her finger down the list of companies. 'They don't necessarily have to be the best; but they do need to have a management team committed to making the project work.'

'There's only a few,' Chibesa replied. 'You're going to have to look at all of them, I'm afraid.'

'But some of them won't be suitable...'

'Yes, I know that, and you can explain that once you've done your audit, but this is as much a hearts and minds exercise as anything else. This is a small industry and there are some very proud owners around—and if you don't leverage your trip and spend at least a couple of hours with each of them, you'll alienate all the ones you miss out and reduce the possibility of your objectives ever being achieved.'

Suzanne sighed, wishing Chibesa didn't always reduce everything to management-speak. He'd be talking about low-hanging fruit and pushing the envelope next. But she also knew he was right.

'Okay, let's do this,' she said. It would be good to get at least one country's industry audited and the pilot companies into the plan this time around. 'Can we put together a timetable and work out how long it's going to take?'

As Chibesa had said, there was only a handful of Zambian companies and most were in Lusaka or within a short distance so she decided to get those visits done first.

'If necessary, I'll do the long distance ones next time I come out here,' she said.

'Well, there's only really one that requires much travel,' Chibesa said, 'and even that can be done in a day if you don't mind getting the early flight.'

'And by early flight, you mean...?'

'Eight-thirty,' he said with a grin. 'You're in Africa, remember; nothing happens much before then.'

'And where will I be going?'

'To the Copper Belt. It's a little company called Mazokapharm, located just outside Ndola. Used to be a contractor for one of the big boys out of Switzerland.'

'Used to be? What happened?'

'Not sure why, but they lost the contract a while back. I don't think there was anything wrong with what they were doing. Just a question of commerce, I think. I've met Kabwe Mazoka but only once. Ask WB; I think he knew

Mazoka senior, the guy who set the place up. He'll give you some background.'

'Okay, I'll do that next time I go to the safe house. Right, let's see if we can knock the rest of this schedule into shape, shall we?

'Ah, yes' said WB later that week when Suzanne went to visit him and Sara. 'Mazokapharm. Nice little factory, that was. So sad.'

'What happened?'

'Well, it was built by Joshua Mazoka back in the 1970s, I think. Yes, that's about right; it was just after TAZARA was opened.'

'TAZARA?'

'The Tanzania-Zambia Railway. My late father, God rest him, was an engineer on the project and actually travelled on the first train to make the journey from Dodoma to Lusaka. I was working as a pharmacist in South Africa at the time and came up here to meet him. I'd not been home for a few years you see and my mother...'

WB stared off into the distance, rubbing the tiny scar on the inside of his right wrist with his left thumb. Suzanne cleared her throat and he gave a start, as though he'd forgotten she was there.

'I'm sorry, Suzanne,' he went on, 'I was just thinking about ...' But then he shook his head and smiled at her. 'Now where was I?'

'Mazokapharm?'

'Yes, of course. Well, as I was here, I thought I'd make some contacts—you never know when they might come in handy.'

'Well, you certainly seem well-connected,' she said—and he inclined his head in acknowledgement before continuing.

'Joshua was in town at the same time and we were introduced by a mutual acquaintance. He was a few years older than me, but we struck up a friendship and kept in touch after we'd both left Lusaka. His factory was working as a contractor for a European company, although I can't remember which one.'

'Chibesa said he thought the contract was with a Swiss firm.'

'Hmm, yes, that rings a bell. Anyway, I saw him from time to time over the years, although we didn't write so much as we got older and our lives were busier—and then about five years ago, I heard he'd died. I wrote to his widow to offer my condolences, but never got a reply.'

'And they lost the contract after his death?' Suzanne asked. But WB shook his head.

'No, I think that happened the year before. I don't believe there was a quality problem or anything. The Swiss company got bought out in one of the industry mergers, I think. It's been happening all over the region. Multinationals merging; too many factories making the same products; rationalisation, it's called.'

'That must have been devastating after all those years?'

'True; in fact I wouldn't be at all surprised if that didn't contribute to Joshua's death.'

'So who's running the company now?'

'Well, he had a couple of older sons, but I don't think they're still around. There was a much younger boy as well; I suppose it would be him. Name began with a K; Kwame? No that doesn't sound right. Kabwe, that's it! Kabwe Mazoka. Bright little lad he was, according to Joshua, when I first knew them; but that was before the accident. A fork-lift truck ran into one of the stacks in the warehouse and knocked a drum of chemicals off the top shelf. It landed on the boy; he was lucky he wasn't killed, really, but it made a proper mess of his arm. He changed after that; became quieter, more self-conscious.'

Suzanne knew she was a soft touch, but the story of Mazokapharm, Joshua and Kabwe had convinced her. She would find the time to visit Ndola before this trip finished.

'And if they've got years of experience working under

97

contract already, they should be in a reasonable state,' she said. 'Who knows, maybe the project is further advanced than we realise.' WB smiled at her and nodded.

'Yes, that's true—and it would be really good if we could do something for Joshua's son. Maybe I'll risk breaking cover and come with you. It would be nice to finally see the factory I've heard so much about over the years—and pay my respects in person to Joshua's widow.'

# 16: ZAMBIA; DEC 2004

When Suzanne arrived at Mazokapharm the following Monday, Kabwe Mazoka took her to his office and gave her sweet milky tea, made with evaporated milk, while she explained the purpose of her visit and what she hoped to achieve.

'So you see,' she said, 'we're trying to identify a few companies that will act as pilots in the study we want to carry out. If we can strengthen the legitimate industry, we have more chance of stamping out the illegal trade and putting the counterfeiters out of business.' She also told Kabwe it was WB who had recommended involving Mazokapharm in the pilot study.

'He has fond memories of your father,' she said. 'He tells me Joshua Mazoka ran a very tight ship; otherwise, the principal contractor would have pulled the plug years ago. WB knows you've been in charge now for a few years; he's keen to hear how you're getting on.'

WB had wanted to come with her on this trip, but they'd decided it wasn't safe. While they'd managed to get word to his wife, to the rest of the world they were still maintaining the fiction that he'd disappeared, and they agreed it wasn't sensible for him to start travelling around

Africa again, using his passport.

And for some reason, Chibesa had been reluctant to accompany her on this trip. He'd pleaded concern about Samuel's health and although Suzanne suspected that wasn't the only reason, she didn't push him. It was only a day trip, after all. So Suzanne had travelled alone. She was used to doing solo trips but now, dealing with Kabwe, she wished one of her African colleagues was with her. They would certainly have been able to work out what was wrong. And something was definitely wrong.

Suzanne watched Kabwe as he led her around the factory. What on earth was wrong with the man? There was sweat rolling down his face and soaking into the collar of his white coat. She found it hot, and had spent far longer inspecting the interior of the cold room than was strictly necessary, but she thought a local would be used to the heat. Kabwe had a folded handkerchief in his undamaged left hand which he used constantly to mop his face. His voice kept breaking and he frequently had to cough and start a sentence again. She didn't understand it. He'd been fine earlier on, happy to chat about his father and the history of the company. He'd treated her to a large lunch; an old trick she had seen during many inspections— the longer you can keep an inspector in the canteen, the less time they have to actually inspect the premises and therefore the less chance there is of finding something going wrong.

Then, at some point during the afternoon, something had changed and Kabwe Mazoka was obviously concerned, even frightened; although she couldn't understand why. The factory was a little old-fashioned, some of the rooms were not as pristine as they might have been, and they really should have replaced the glass in the broken windows but, despite its history, it was still a tiny company in the middle of nowhere, up a dirt track. She wasn't expecting miracles.

'Okay, Mr Mazoka,' she said now, thinking it was time

to let him off the hook, 'I've seen enough of the manufacturing facility. Let's go back to the office and chat about where we go from here.' He swallowed hard, nodded and led the way back through the packing hall and across the yard to the administration block, a tiny brick building nestling against the wall of the compound. He looked like he was about to burst into tears. *What is wrong with this man?* she thought again.

'Well, you could do with a bit of refurbishment, but generally, everything seems to be fine out in the factory,' she said as they brought her yet another cup of tea, 'and some of those contracts you've got are quite impressive.' She'd spotted a label for one of the biggest American companies on a shelf in the warehouse. 'I'll need to check with some of the principals that they are okay with us using you as an example, but I can't see any problem.' She consulted her notes once more. 'Just one thing before I get out of your hair,' then, realising he looked confused at this peculiarly British phrase, she went on, 'I mean, before I head back to the airport and leave you in peace; I'd like to see a couple of examples of batch documents—and if you can give me the names of your contacts at a couple of the contractors, that would be great.' Kabwe looked startled, then slowly, he shook his head.

'I'm very sorry, Mrs Suzanne, but the documents are all locked in the laboratory and my quality control manager has gone home.'

'And you don't have a spare key?'

'Regretfully, no. We take the separation of production and quality control very seriously here.' Suzanne thought this a commendable sentiment, although, if she was honest, she found it hard to believe and suspected the spare key had merely been lost.

'And the contact names…' she asked, without much hope.

'My business manager has them, but she's already—'

'—don't tell me—she's gone home too.' There was a

note of asperity in Suzanne's voice that she knew shouldn't be there, but she was disappointed at the sudden lack of co-operation from Kabwe. She looked at her watch. It was approaching six-thirty. 'Goodness, I'm sorry; I've kept you much longer than expected,' she went on.

'I can send you the details tomorrow, by express courier,' Kabwe said. 'Now, Mrs Suzanne, if you are to get to the airport in time, you need to leave now. Your taxi is here.'

As he led the way out of the building, the short African dusk was fading and a deep cloak of darkness descended over the factory grounds. A broken-down Ford was sitting in the yard, its engine running. The driver lounged against the bonnet, chatting to one of the women Suzanne had seen in the packing hall, but as his passenger approached, he jumped to attention and the woman melted away into the darkness without a word. Suzanne stopped dead.

'But what's happened to the airport car; the one that brought me here? I arranged for him to pick me up at six forty-five to take me back.' Kabwe shrugged and shook his head.

'Very sorry, Mrs Suzanne,' he said. Your driver called to say he had a puncture and wouldn't be able to get here in time. Joe Simons here,' indicating the driver who was now standing so straight he looked like he was on the parade ground, 'he does some driving for us occasionally. He's agreed to take you.'

'Oh, very well,' Suzanne said, looking with distaste at the dusty, dilapidated vehicle and regretting the cream suit she was wearing. 'Let's get on. I don't want to miss my plane.'

She and Kabwe shook hands; he was still sweating and his skin was cold and clammy to the touch. She really must work on her empathetic skills, she thought, if she could have this sort of effect on someone, especially when she wasn't giving them a hard time at all. Just imagine what he'd have been like if this had been an official inspection resulting from a complaint, rather than an informal audit.

As the taxi pulled out of the site, Suzanne looked back at Kabwe. He was staring after the car with a horrified expression on his face. *Gosh, I really must work on my technique*, she thought. *The poor fellow looks traumatised.*

They reached the bottom of the steep lane and turned onto the main road. As the driver put his foot down and the car started to speed towards the airport, another vehicle passed them, going in the other direction. It was silver and large. Suzanne sat up straight and looked around.

'That looks like my car,' she called out, tapping the driver on the shoulder. His eyes met hers in the mirror and he shook his head.

'No, lady, you mistaken,' he said, as the car sped even faster along the road.

Suzanne sat back, irritated, but not sure what she could do. 'I'll probably have to pay for both cars now,' she muttered,' 'although if the other one said he wasn't coming, I guess they cancelled, not me.'

Abruptly, the car slowed, and then ground to a halt.

'What's happening now?' she asked. The driver pointed out of the windscreen.

'Roadblock,' he said. Suzanne peered into the gloom and could just make out dark figures standing in front of a makeshift barrier of tyres and packing cases. To one side of the road, a fire flickered in an old oil drum and Suzanne could see the flames reflected in the metal of the guns held in the hands of the men manning the barricade. One of them strolled over to the car and rapped on the driver's window. Glancing over his shoulder at her with an uncertain look on his face, he rolled down the window.

The conversation was incomprehensible to Suzanne, but she could tell it was not a friendly one. The man with the gun, who seemed to be wearing some sort of military uniform, shouted questions at the driver who answered them quickly and quietly to begin with, but gradually got louder. In the end the two men were both yelling at the same time. Then, abruptly, the noise stopped and the soldier turned and started walking around the car. Suzanne held her breath, but he walked straight past the rear door and round to the back. He popped open the trunk, stood for a short while looking inside, then slammed it shut again. He shouted a single word to his compatriots at the barricade who pulled some of the boxes to one side and waved them forward. As the car eased its way through, the soldiers saluted, with what looked to Suzanne more like irony than genuine respect.

'What on earth was all that about?' she asked.

'They're looking for weapons. They think they're smuggled into the country on this road.'

'Well, thank goodness they allowed us through.' As they continued to drive into the darkness, Suzanne wondered why the road block would be looking for smugglers driving towards the airport, rather than away from it, but she didn't bother to raise the question with the driver.

They'd been driving for nearly half an hour since they left the factory, which puzzled Suzanne. She was sure it had only taken half that time to make the journey in the other direction that morning.

'Are we nearly there?' she said, tapping the driver on the shoulder. But he just glanced at her through the driver's mirror and put his foot down even more. 'I said, are we nearly there?' she repeated. 'We've been driving for ages. Are you sure this is the right way? It was much shorter this morning.'

'Different road,' he threw over his shoulder. 'Other one closed. Traffic accident.' Suzanne knew this was a common occurrence, especially on the unlit roads on the outskirts of towns.

Suddenly, the driver wrenched the steering wheel sideways and took a tight left turn. The darkness, if possible, thickened even more and as they drove between trees on a narrow track. Suzanne held her breath and stared out of the window. Then she spotted a light on the road ahead of them. The driver slammed his foot on the brake and Suzanne was thrown forward as the car came to a skidding stop. The back door flew open and she was dazzled as a blinding light shone directly in her face.

'Get out,' a rough voice hissed at her.

'I will not—' but strong arms seized her and dragged her out onto the ground. With the light still shining in her eyes, she couldn't see who was there, or how many. Someone stepped up behind her, and pinned her arms by her side, then a coarse canvas bag was pulled over her head.

'Stand up,' said the same voice. She was yanked to her feet and half walked, half dragged across the track. Then the sound of their feet changed from muffled to hollow and it felt firmer under foot; they appeared to be entering a building. She was pushed across the room until her legs hit the frame of a bed. Losing her balance, she fell across it, feeling rough wool under her hands and smelling the musty odour of blankets stored too long without air. As the hands left her, she ripped the bag from her head and rolled over to see her assailants. But she was too late. The door banged shut, a bolt crashed home, running feet moved away from the building and then, the worst sound of all, she heard laughter and slamming car doors, before the vehicle drove off into the night.

Silence descended. And she realised her handbag and briefcase were still in the car. She had no means of communication. Suzanne was alone, in the dark. She had no idea where she was. And neither did anyone else.

# 17: ZAMBIA; DEC 2004

Suzanne sat motionless in the pitch black hut, waiting. Waiting for the car to return; waiting for the men to tell her she was free to go; waiting for someone, anyone to drive her back to the airport and let her continue with her journey. She would not let herself believe this was really happening. It was all a mistake. It had to be.

Eventually, she forced herself to stand—on legs so cold and cramped, they buckled beneath her, throwing her back onto the bed. She tried again—and again, until finally she was able to remain upright. She began to explore the hut with her hands. Apart from the bed, there was a table, rough wood that caught at her fingers as she stroked its surface, a single chair and a bucket in the corner. She pushed that away in disgust. She wouldn't be here long enough to use that.

A jug stood on the table. Picking it up, she heard the contents slosh around inside and guessed it was about half-full. It was warm to her touch and gave off a slight metallic odour. She was parched and her tongue stuck to the roof of her mouth; but she didn't dare risk drinking this unseen liquid.

Finally she threw herself onto the bed, shivering in the

night air. Wrapping the noxious blanket around her she lay shuddering, listening to the sounds of the African bush around her. Did the world of nature herald even more danger than the terrible human world she had stumbled upon? Her mind told her stories of snakes, long sinuous shapes that could slip through spaces too small for humans to see, and insects—especially insects. There was a persistent whine of mosquitoes. She pulled the blanket over her head, but the stench made her gag and she pushed it away, gasping for air. Instead, she tried to block out the sound by stuffing her fingers in her ears. She tried not to think about what other creatures might be with her in the hut, the bed or the blanket. The rising panic kept her awake for a long time and when she did drift off to sleep, it was to recurring dreams of being eaten alive by giant insects.

The sound of a car in the distance woke her to a room no longer pitch black. She waited with dread to hear whether it was coming towards the hut, and yet, wondered what she would do if it didn't stop. But it did stop. A door opened and slammed shut; footsteps approached the building and she heard the bolt on the outside sliding back. As the door opened, a shaft of bright sunshine illuminated the hut and temporarily blinded her.

When she could see again, she was no longer alone. A tall figure in black, wearing a knitted ski mask, was standing in the doorway, staring at her. The absurdity of his apparel struck her and she gave an involuntary giggle, which she stifled with a grubby trembling hand to her mouth.

'Why have you brought me here?' she asked quietly and calmly.

'Don't worry, you are safe, we will not hurt you,' was the muffled response.

'But why am I here?' she repeated.

'Are you hungry?'

'Yes, I'm hungry. I'm hungry, thirsty, tired, cold, and

dirty,' she said, clinging to her calm as though by her fingertips. 'Who are you and why am I here?'

The man merely shook his head and dropped a bag on the table, which was right by the door. He placed a bottle of water next to the bag.

'Drink, it is safe,' he said. Then he turned to leave.

'Noooo,' Suzanne screeched, her calm shattering. 'You can't leave me. You must tell me why I'm here.'

'It won't be for long, I promise,' said the voice. And before she could say anything else, the door shut and the bolt slammed home again

Suzanne threw herself across the room and hammered on the door with both fists. She heard the retreating footsteps pause and held her breath, praying the man would come back. But the steps resumed, the car door slammed and the vehicle drove away. She slumped to the ground, pressed her back against the wooden planks and hugged her knees. Then the tears she had managed to hold back since the shock of being kidnapped finally came.

Time passed. She had no idea how long. Her watch was gone, probably lost as she was manhandled from the car to the hut. At some point, she ran out of tears, but still she sat, head on her knees, waiting once more. Finally, she wiped the back of her hand across her nose, rubbed the drying tears from her cheeks and pushed herself upright. There were small unglazed windows at the top of the wall, giving a dim light to the room. It was sufficient for her to see the bag on the table contained food. There was bread, a little hard, but still smelling fresh—well fresh enough to eat, anyway—some rancid-smelling dried meat, and a couple of apples. She pulled a chunk off the loaf, stuffing it into her mouth and chewing eagerly. But then she caught sight of the bucket in the corner and the taste of the food died in her mouth. She pushed the bag away from her. She could live with the hunger for now, and the man had said it wouldn't be for long. But she couldn't stand the thirst. She grabbed the bottle, broke the seal and greedily sucked in the cool liquid. After her first few mouthfuls, caution returned and she left the rest, screwing the top back on tightly to keep out insects. A glance at the jug on the table showed she had been right to avoid it; it was indeed water, but it was faintly green and dead flies floated on the surface.

'Okay, Suzanne', she said out loud, 'let's put those famous analytical skills of yours to work.' Her voice croaked and she glanced at the bottle of water, before resolutely turning her back on it. 'What do we know so far?' She began ticking off on her fingers. 'Firstly, the purpose of all this is not to kill me. They could've just done that last night and left my body out in the bush somewhere.' This thought made her shiver and a single tear rolled down her cheek, but she gave herself a mental slap on the hand and carried on. 'So, if they don't want me dead, they either want me to do something, or they want someone else to do something in order to rescue me'—and then another possibility occurred to her—'or they want to stop me from doing something.'

She paced up and down the hut. For some reason, which she couldn't explain, she trusted her captor when he said, 'we won't hurt you.' That proved he wasn't working alone, although she already knew that. There had been at least two people manhandling her when she was grabbed, plus the driver, who was obviously in on it—whatever it was.

'So, on the plus side, they don't want to kill me,' at least not yet, a small voice at the back of her head tried to whisper, but she resolutely ignored it, 'and they've given me some food and water, so they want me to be reasonably comfortable. No-one knows where I am—even I don't know where I am—but the rest of the team know I came to the Copper Belt to inspect Kabwe's factory, so they will have somewhere to start searching from. The driver was Kabwe's friend, so maybe he can be persuaded to help—' and then with blinding clarity, it hit her! The driver was Kabwe's friend. Kabwe was nervous the whole time she was inspecting the factory. The real car arrived at the factory just after they left. 'It's Kabwe! Kabwe is in on this! No, it can't be!' The idea seemed such an unlikely one, but the more she thought about it, the more obvious it became. 'Well, I've seen some extreme reactions to inspections, but this tops the lot,' she said. She gave a giggle, which turned into a laugh. And once she started, she couldn't stop until tears flowed down her cheeks, and her laughter turned to sobs once more.

Much later, she decided the possibility of Kabwe's involvement reassured her. The gentle factory owner had been very nervous although without justification; she had found few problems in the factory. And he had been unwilling to answer all her questions. But despite this, she didn't believe him capable of doing anything really bad. *So long as Kabwe's calling the shots, I should be okay*, she thought. She wondered if Kabwe was the man in the ski mask. She thought the height and build was about right, although he'd been standing in the doorway, with the sun behind him and she hadn't been able to see him clearly. The voice was muffled but she believed it was African. Then she remembered Kabwe's right arm. Damaged in the childhood accident WB had told her about, it was twisted and shrunken. He held it awkwardly and frequently put it out of sight behind his back. She would look more closely at her captor next time he returned.

Tired from pacing around the hut and dizzy with hunger, she tore another chunk from the loaf and chewed it slowly, sinking back on the bed. Her stomach churned and she glanced with loathing at the bucket in the corner. She would NOT use it. To occupy her thoughts, she began to go back over every second of her visit to Mazokapharm. It wasn't actually true to say Kabwe was nervous the whole time she was there. He had been fine to start with, if a little shy. He had been positively affable at lunchtime. The problem only started when they walked around the factory.

When she picked up the labels in the warehouse; and then later when she wanted to get in touch with his contractors. But why should that be a problem? Then she groaned as the truth finally became clear. 'Because the contracts don't exist,' she said, the words echoing around the hut and disappearing into the silence. 'It looks like we were closer to Banda than we realised.'

'I have to get out of here. How do I get out of here?' The panic rose in waves, threatening to choke her. 'And when they come, I can't let Kabwe—or whoever it is— know I've worked out the connection between the factory, Banda and this kidnapping.' Of course, she had no idea how long it would be before anyone came. She just hoped it would be sometime today. She didn't want to spend a whole day and night without seeing anyone else, even an anonymous captor in a ski mask.

The temperature in the hut rose steadily. Suzanne stripped off her suit and blouse, wrapping herself in the grubby tablecloth.

The dim light in the hut was starting to fade when she heard the car once again. There had been no other vehicles passing during the day and no sound of pedestrians. Wherever they were keeping her, they had chosen well (*what am I thinking?* she asked herself—*I'm not inspecting these premises*—but old habits die hard.) Now she heard the familiar sounds: car, doors opening and closing—more than one door, so probably more than one person— footsteps approaching the hut. She pulled her crumpled clothes back on and seated herself calmly on the bed, staring intently at the door. She would use logic and quiet persuasion to get her captors to release her and take her to a telephone—the rest of her team must be going frantic at her continued absence.

The bolt shot back and the door swung open. The figure this time was of a woman—possibly only a young girl—with no mask on her face. Maybe they weren't concerned about the young girl being recognised. She

111

stopped in the doorway, as the man had that morning, and dropped more food and a bottle of water on the table.

At some point during the interminable hours, Suzanne's resolve had finally been broken and she had been forced to give up what she saw as the last shreds of her dignity. The bucket had become malodourous in the heat and when the girl pointed to it and then pointed to outside, Suzanne nodded, glad they were willing to relieve some of her discomfort. The girl sidled across the room, keeping a close eye on Suzanne, then picked up the bucket, replaced it with a clean one and carried the soiled one out of the hut.

'Is Kabwe coming tonight?' Suzanne said quietly. The young girl spun around and looked at Suzanne with startled eyes. Then she looked across the veranda and Suzanne realised there was someone else standing outside, hidden from the doorway. 'Kabwe, is that you, Kabwe?' she called, jumping up and running towards the doorway. But it was too late. With a bang, the door was slammed shut and bolted. 'Come back, please come back,' she called, hammering on the door. Suzanne could hear the man talking before the pair ran to the car, starting the engine and driving rapidly away. 'What have I done?' she sobbed. She threw herself across the bed and lay, shuddering, as the darkness and the silence descended slowly into the hut and cloaked her once more.

And once more, with the darkness came the insects, the rustlings, the imagining. The bites she had managed to ignore during the day throbbed and itched now. She rubbed, she stroked and finally she scratched, tearing at her skin to ease the pain. It was many hours before exhaustion overcame her. In her dreams, the giant insects came again—and in the morning her arms and legs were a blood-streaked mess of aching lumps.

When the dawn finally came, Suzanne pulled herself off the bed and used some of the dirty water in the jug to try and clean her face. It wasn't very refreshing and without a mirror, she had no way of telling how successful she'd been, but it made her feel better that she'd tried. She ate a mouthful of bread and allowed herself a tiny ration of water. And then she sat at the table gathering her thoughts ready for the next meeting with her captors. She had to find a way to engage with them and get them to talk; to set up some sort of relationship with them. But how?

After a couple of hours that seemed more like days, Suzanne finally heard the car drive down the track. Just one door opened this time and the footsteps that approached were quieter than she was used to. She was not surprised, when the door opened, to find the young girl from yesterday standing on the threshold looking in at her.

## 18: ZAMBIA; DEC 2004

The two stared at each other in silence. The young girl looked to be about fifteen years old. She wore a faded cotton dress that must once have been very colourful, but now barely showed smudges of pattern against the cream background. Her feet, which were very dusty, were shoved into a pair of bright orange flip flops. But the most unusual thing about her was her hair, braided into elaborate plaits running across and around her head. The ends of each plait were held in place with blue and white clay beads which clicked quietly as she moved her head.

Suzanne watched a mixture of emotions flit across the young girl's face. Regret was one she thought she recognised; another was sympathy. But the one that most surprised her, while at the same time giving her hope, was fear. *Good gracious*, she thought, *the poor thing's terrified of me. Aren't I supposed to be the one who's frightened?* For the first time since she was brought to this deserted spot, Suzanne thought there was a distinct possibility of getting free.

The girl put yet another bag of food down on the table, together with two bottles of water. The bag of food was larger than on the previous two occasions. Why was that? Were they starting to feel sorry for her and wanted to give her a little more comfort? Was it because the young girl, rather than the tall man with the ski mask and the muffled voice, was in charge of bringing the rations today? Whatever the reason, she was grateful, especially for the extra water. Grateful? What was she thinking? If it wasn't for these people, she wouldn't be in this situation in the first place.

Next the girl collected the bucket from the corner of the room and replaced it with a clean one. But there was something different about this too. When Suzanne looked closely, she realised there were three buckets in total, all stacked together.

'Will you talk to me?' Suzanne said gently, desperately trying not to make her 'captor' more scared than she plainly was already. 'Please, I need to understand why I'm here and what's going to happen to me.' The girl just looked at her with sad eyes and shook her head. Suzanne tried again. 'You're frightened, aren't you?' The girl stared at her and slowly nodded her head. 'Well. You can't be frightened of me; so it must be of them, whoever 'they' are. Is that it?' The girl nodded again, more hesitantly. Suzanne smiled to herself, realising she was finally getting somewhere. 'That's why they don't bother to cover your face, isn't it? They're not worried about you getting caught.' Once more the girl nodded. 'Look, I know you're only doing what they tell you to. I promise you won't get into trouble if you help me.' Suzanne didn't really know whether she could make good on that promise. She had no idea about police procedures in Zambia, but she suspected they might be a little harsher than back home. And of course 'they' might harm the girl if they found out she had helped their prisoner, but at this point, after nearly three days in a filthy dirty hut, with no washing facilities, little food and only rudimentary comfort, quite frankly, she didn't care. She crossed her fingers behind her back and carried on talking in the same quiet voice.

'I can see you're scared, so let's take this gently, shall

we? Can you tell me your name?' The girl shook her head once more and pointed to her mouth. 'You aren't able to talk?' Suzanne asked, 'Is that it?' The girl nodded. 'Can you read and write?' The head shook more vigorously this time and the little beads clicked noisily. Suzanne finally realised exactly why there had been no attempt to disguise this young girl. They probably didn't care about her safety; but more importantly, unable to either speak or write, she would be incapable of informing on anyone—and she certainly wasn't going to be able to give evidence against any of 'them' even if they were caught and brought to trial. Suzanne wondered how this young girl had come to be involved with Banda, and hoped vehemently that she was related to one of the men that had kidnapped her. Any other explanation just didn't bear thinking about. She scratched her head and looked with a rueful grin at the young girl.

'So, we have a bit of a problem,' she said. 'You can't speak and you can't write, so it's going to be very difficult to communicate. Can we try doing it with questions?' The girl looked puzzled and shrugged her shoulders. Suzanne patted the bed beside her. 'Look, why don't you sit down for a bit?' The girl bit her lip and cast a look out of the doorway towards the waiting car. Just then, the horn blared and Suzanne realised with a jolt that the young girl hadn't come on her own. She reached out and tried to take the girl's hand. But she flinched at the touch and pulled away. Then she walked to the door and reached out onto the veranda. She picked up another bag, this time a large black sack and dropped it on the table. Then, with a backwards look filled with regret and sympathy, but from which the fear had somehow disappeared, she pulled the door shut and slid the bolt into place. Her fading footsteps were rapid and no sooner had she climbed into the car and slammed the door shut than the engine started up and the vehicle drove away.

Suzanne let her whole body slump and she gave a little

sob. She'd thought she was getting somewhere with the young girl. If only she'd had more time; if only the girl had come on her own—but that wasn't likely—there would always be at least one of the gang there with her.

Then she straightened her shoulders and pushed herself to her feet. She checked through the bags and confirmed, as she'd suspected, that they had left her twice as much food as before, as well as twice the amount of water. 'How very strange,' she said out loud. 'Maybe they're not coming this evening for some reason.' Then she examined the buckets in the corner and confirmed that indeed, there were three clean ones, all stacked neatly together. Finally, she pulled open the black bag, tipping the contents carefully on to the floor, wary of closed containers in countries where much of the wildlife is small, agile and potentially lethal.

But in this instance, there was nothing to worry about. There were two objects that fell out of the sack: her briefcase and her handbag. 'Oh, thank God,' she gasped. 'They've had a change of heart.' Opening her handbag, she rummaged around and pulled out her mobile phone, the new one she'd purchased just a few days ago—was it really only a week or so since she'd had her previous one stolen in Heathrow airport? She clicked it on, praying there would be battery left; there was—she'd charged it up before leaving Lusaka and it had been switched off since she arrived at Mazokapharm. She clicked the numbers for her sister's mobile and put the phone to her ear. Silence. Absolutely nothing! She tried again. Same result. Maybe there was no signal out here? But then she noticed the words across the top of the screen: *Insert SIM card.* She wrenched the back off the phone and pulled out the battery. Sure enough, the SIM card was missing. She threw the pieces of the phone across the room with a cry of despair and lay back against the pillows staring at the roof. So, no change of heart, then—or at least not a complete one. Why would they have given her back her things like that? They were no use to her stuck out here. *But if they're with me, they don't create evidence against the gang*, she thought suddenly. The suspicion that the bags had been returned to her as a matter of expediency rather than as a humanitarian action was an uncomfortable one, but one she found impossible to shake off.

As she started putting other parts of the puzzle together, an icy certainty grew in her mind: It wasn't that they weren't coming back this evening; they weren't coming back at all! They had abandoned her, alone in an isolated hut in the middle of nowhere and there wasn't even the possibility that her captors were coming to see her twice a day. No young girl with sympathy in her eyes and fear in her heart; no tall man with a ski mask and a muffled voice. No-one was coming to see her at all. She was alone and no-one was going to be able to find her.

Her final vestige of hope died and she began to scream. Since she'd arrived, she'd been relatively calm, but to no avail. She ran to the door, hammered on the rough boards, yelling, 'let me out; please help me; let me out,' over and over again until she was hoarse. Then she slid down the door and lay on the floor, her cheek pressed against the dirt, her fingers digging into the ground, sobbing.

When there were no tears left, she found herself watching, as though from a distance, the prone woman on the ground. This wouldn't do! She was stronger than this. She made herself stand up. How long had she been here? She couldn't remember—and suddenly it was very important. A calendar—she needed a calendar, so she could record the passing of time. She'd been here two days—or was it three? She'd better have two calendars, so she would know one of them was accurate. She looked around for a stick, something she could draw lines with. She would make a mark for each passing day. But then she remembered her briefcase and laughed out loud. 'You silly woman, you've got paper and pens in there!' She pulled out her notebook and tore a blank page from the middle, then, sitting at the table, biting her lip, she started drawing two neat grids. For some reason, she knew they needed to be neat. And would she fill it in each morning when she woke or in the evening before dark descended? She shook her head. She was too tired to think about that now; she could decide that later. 'It's not as though I've got anything else to think about,' she said with a laugh.

When the calendars were finished, she smoothed out the paper and arranged it carefully in the centre of the table, with a water bottle top and bottom to anchor it. Then she sat on the bed and stared at the door, willing it to open. But it remained resolutely shut and as darkness fell, she could no longer see it.

Bruce Willis was driving and she was holding on for dear life to the dashboard, while ancient vehicles driven by men in ski masks tore along the road behind them and tried to outflank them. Over the sound of squealing tyres and rapid gun fire, someone called her name. She woke with a start. She could see the door again; dim light filtered through the tiny window below the roof. She was curled under the blanket and straightening her legs, she groaned as cramped muscles protested—then she heard the call again. It sounded like her sister.

'Charlie,' her first attempt was feeble and her throat was raw from all the shouting and screaming. 'Charlie, I'm over here, Charlie.' This time her voice was stronger. She couldn't believe this was happening and she just hoped it wasn't a trick by Banda—or that they hadn't captured her sister as well. She jumped from the bed, but her cramped legs gave way and she fell to the ground. She heard feet running up the path and across the veranda, then the bolt shot back and the door flew open.

'Suzanne, oh sweetie, it's okay, we're here, we've found you.' Strong arms helped her to her feet and led her gently to the bed. Her sister sat down beside her and put her arms around her. 'Some bodyguard I've turned out to be.

We've been going frantic looking for you.' The sisters were both crying now and hugging each other tightly. There was a discreet cough from the doorway.

'Ladies, I think we should get away from here sooner rather than later.' It was WB, looking unaccustomedly tentative and quiet. 'Charlie, we need to get Suzanne checked out by a doctor and, besides, I'd rather not hang around in case someone comes to check on their 'guest'.' Charlie jumped up at once.

'Of course, you're right; would you mind getting the car and I'll look after Suzanne.' She held out her hand. 'Come on, sis—let's take you somewhere more comfortable.' WB picked up the briefcase and handbag from the table and walked out of the hut. He headed off down the track and Suzanne looked questioningly at her sister. 'We parked a little way back; we didn't know whether you would be alone or not and we didn't want to warn anyone of our arrival. But when we saw there were no vehicles here, we guessed you'd be on your own.' She put her arm around Suzanne's shoulders and the two sisters walked slowly out of the hut and across to the track without a backward glance.

Suzanne didn't really believe she was being rescued until they were in the car, off the track and bowling down the highway towards the main town. They had to pass the airport and she was shocked to see how close she had been to her destination when her driver had taken the turn along the track and her nightmare had begun.

Once past the airport, they saw the signs to the city centre. Suzanne assumed they would be going that way. However, WB drove straight past the turning and kept going at high speed. Suzanne grabbed Charlie's arm.

'Where are we going? Why aren't we stopping?' Waves of panic rose up inside her, threatening to choke her. She thought of WB as a friend, but when all was said and done, she'd only met him twice. He'd arrived at Chibesa's office one morning at the start of the project and introduced himself as the Ugandan representative, saying he wanted to help 'rid Africa of this dreadful scourge'. But what did they really know of this man, who had somehow managed to leave his own country undetected, steal Sara Matsebula out of Swaziland, right under the noses of the Banda members who had been sent to 'deal with her'—and had now managed to locate a deserted hut in the middle of nowhere? He was just too good to be true. Could she trust him?

Charlie was making hushing sounds and stroking the hair off her face with one hand while the other held her close. Come to think of it, could she trust her sister? The story about her leaving England and arriving in Zambia in disguise was a very far-fetched one; maybe she was part of the plot—whatever that plot might be. Was she really safe, or had she just exchanged one prison for another one? She struggled to free herself from Charlie's arms and tried to reach the door handle.

'I have to get out!' she cried. 'Stop the car and let me out now!' Charlie held her arms tight against her sides and her smile faded, to be replaced by a snarl.

'Put your foot down, WB,' she said, 'I can't hold her much longer.' WB glanced over his shoulder—but it wasn't WB—it was Kabwe and he was grinning in a mocking way. Suzanne screamed, tore herself free of Charlie's grasp and lunged at him with fists raised—and then the lights went out.

# 19: ZAMBIA; DEC 2004

When Suzanne woke, she was lying on a deep, leather sofa, with soft cushions under her head and a warm blanket tucked around her. It was dark outside the windows, but in the moonlight, she could see the tops of acacia trees, telling her she was not on the ground floor. The soft light from the lamps around the room showed her she was in a large, luxurious bedroom. The king-sized bed in the centre was empty. Its golden yellow counterpane fell to the floor in sumptuous waves, which were reflected in curtains of the same material. Brown, white and lemon cushions were piled on the bed. There was a European style dressing table and matching wardrobes. The floor was covered in brown and white tiles. Whoever lived here had good taste—and the money to indulge it.

Suzanne wondered briefly why she was on the sofa, rather than in the bed, but then she noticed her arm lying on top of the blanket, streaked with dirt and covered in angry red lumps. Raising her hand to her hair, she felt lank greasy locks that definitely hadn't been under a shower for quite a while. She could understand why the owner of this beautiful room wouldn't want her messing up the pristine bed. The door opened and Charlie poked her head into the room.

'Oh good, you're awake. How do you feel?'

In a flash, it all came back to her: the kidnapping, her days alone in the hut, her rescue—and the terrible moment when her sister turned into an enemy and WB became Kabwe. The fear must have shown on her face, as Charlie ran across the room and dropped to her knees in front of her.

'It's okay, Suzanne, it's really okay. You're safe. No-one can hurt you now.'

'But in the car…'

'Yes, you gave us a bit of a fright back there,' Charlie said, smiling ruefully. 'Poor WB nearly drove off the road when you tried to attack him. Not too kind after we'd come to rescue you.' But her smile showed she was only joking. 'Apparently, it's quite common for people who've gone through the sort of experience you had to hallucinate like that. And the doctor says you were probably malnourished too, which is why you passed out when you did.'

'So, where are we—and how long have I been asleep?'

'We're at one of the rose farms; WB knows the son of the owner and asked him if we could stay here for a while. You've been asleep for about four hours. The doctor thought it was better to let you sleep it off before she does a full examination.'

'Ugh, I'm going to need a shower before then,' Suzanne said, wrinkling her nose, 'and some food would be good too.' Her stomach rumbled, reminding both women she'd not eaten anything for hours and it had been many days since she'd had a proper meal. Charlie jumped up and held out her hand.

'You wish is my command, madam; walk this way.' She led Suzanne, who felt light-headed but able to walk unaided, across the room and through the door into an en suite bathroom decorated in cool blues and greens. She pointed to the walk-in shower, the bottles of shower gel and shampoo, the pile of fluffy blue bath towels. 'Everything you need is all there. Would you like me to stay and help you…' she held her hands up at Suzanne's indignant look, 'just asking, sis, that's all. You take your time and I'll wait for you in the bedroom.' She pointed to hangers on the back of the bathroom door. 'I brought some clean stuff for you from Lusaka; just jeans and a few T-shirts. Leave your dirty stuff in a pile on the floor. I'm guessing you won't want to wear that suit again?' And with a wave, she was gone. Then she popped back in again. 'And don't be long; dinner's nearly ready and there are people waiting downstairs for you.' Suzanne wasn't sure she was ready to meet 'people' yet, but it was too late to say anything; her sister had gone again.

She stood and let the hot water cascade over her head and shoulders, turning the heat up gradually until it was almost too hot to bear. Then she turned it back down to tepid to cool herself off. She'd only been held captive for a few days, but she was finding it difficult to come to terms with being free once more. Her thoughts went back to her days at university; how they had watched the reports on television of kidnappings in Beirut. She couldn't imagine what it would be like to be held for weeks or months— even years in some cases.

Once she was clean, dry and dressed in fresh clothes, she went back into the bedroom and Charlie took her downstairs. The staircase was oak, highly polished and curved around and down into the centre of a magnificent entrance hall. There was an oak table at the bottom of the stairs, almost completely covered by a massive arrangement of highly scented roses. Suzanne stopped and buried her nose in the blooms, inhaling deeply.

'That's one of the advantages of having a rose farm—a constant supply of flowers for the house.' Suzanne spun at the sound of a quiet male voice from the doorway behind the staircase. A tall, slim man with skin whose colour suggested roots both in Africa and Europe, was lounging against the door jamb, a lazy smile playing around his lips. Now, he pushed himself upright and strolled across to meet her. 'I'm Nathan Harawa, Miss Jones; so pleased to meet you—although I'm sorry it's under such terrible circumstances.'

'Suzanne, please call me Suzanne,' she said in a quiet voice, holding out her hand, which he took in his. A cool, firm grasp from a hand hardened and roughened by manual work. Nathan Harawa would appear to be someone who worked on the farm, rather than just running it.

'Suzanne,' he said as he inclined his head, 'and you must call me Nathan.' Then he tucked her arm through his. 'Now, the others are waiting; come this way, you must be starving. Let's get some supper inside you.' As Suzanne accompanied her young host into the dining room and towards the enticing aroma of chicken soup, WB and Charlie rose from their seats and began to applaud. Suzanne felt herself go pink, but smiled back at them and finally started to relax.

The other person in the room was the doctor, who, to Suzanne's surprise and delight, turned out to be female. She was also Nathan's mother, Annette Harawa. After supper, Annette took Suzanne back up to her room and examined her thoroughly. She was declared physically fit, considering the ordeal she'd been through, and prescribed rest and good food for a few days. Mentally, she was told there was a possibility of bad dreams and anxiety attacks. Annette offered Suzanne something to help her sleep and she accepted the tablets 'just in case' but certainly, this first night out of captivity, she had no difficulty falling asleep and, as far as she could remember, her sleep was dreamless.

The following morning, Suzanne, Charlie and WB sat with their host on the terrace eating fresh fruit and home baked bread for breakfast. And now, at last, Suzanne started to ask questions: when did they realise she was

125

missing; and how did they finally find her? And what contact, if any, had been made with the IHF Headquarters in London?

'Well, we didn't realise anything was wrong to start with,' WB said. 'Charlie got the text from you, saying you were going to extend the inspection and to wait until we heard from you before doing anything else.'

'Text? I didn't send any text!'

'We did wonder how you were going to manage without a change of clothes,' Charlie said, spearing another chunk of pineapple from the dish in the centre of the table, 'but I assumed you knew what you were doing.'

'And that's why we didn't come looking for you before,' WB carried on. 'We were starting to get a bit concerned yesterday morning, especially when you didn't answer your mobile.'

'And then we got the phone call, saying you needed help,' Charlie said. 'So WB chartered a plane and we flew straight up here.'

'Phone call? What phone call?' Suzanne asked. 'You didn't mention any phone call last night.'

'We were just concerned about you yesterday, sis; we didn't want to go through any of the details until we knew you were okay.'

'Who made the call?' Suzanne asked quietly, expecting to hear the answer and dreading it nevertheless.

'He didn't give his name, I'm afraid. And the line was very poor. It came through to Chibesa's office, so it was someone who knew who you are working with.'

'He just said you were in trouble and needed help. He gave us an idea of where you were and then rang off.'

'Tell me,' Nathan said, putting down his coffee cup, 'how did you manage to locate the hut? It's a pretty isolated area up there.'

Charlie went pink and glanced across at Suzanne with a look of trepidation on her face.

'Er, that would be me; I put a tracker in Suzanne's

briefcase. It was only short range, but it worked once we were in the general area.'

Suzanne got up from the table, walked over to her sister and stood with her hands on her hips, staring down at her.

'You mean to tell me you used a surveillance device on me—without telling me?' Charlie bit her lip and nodded her head slowly. 'Suzanne grinned and bent to hug her sister.

'Well, thank goodness you did—otherwise I'd still be alone out there. Although I'd like to know where you got one of those from.'

'Er, no, sis; actually, you wouldn't,' was the enigmatic reply.

'Hmm, we'll talk about that later,' Suzanne said. Then turning to WB, she took his hands in hers. 'And I am especially grateful to you for coming to find me,' she said. 'Are you sure 'breaking cover' was a sensible thing to do?' The Ugandan shrugged and squeezed her hand.

'What else was I going to do; leave Charlie to come and get you on her own? Besides, I have reason to believe my secret's out of the bag already. We had a reporter at the house the other day, asking if he could have an interview with me! Not much point in hiding when your face and current address are all over the front of the *Lusaka Times*!'

Everybody laughed and Nathan handed around the coffee pot once more.

'And what about the IHF headquarters?' Suzanne asked once more, 'have you told them anything yet?' WB shook his head.

'We thought we'd wait and see what was going on before we contacted them. Once we found you, I phoned Chibesa; he's waiting for your instructions.'

'Well,' Suzanne said slowly, pursing her lips, 'I don't think there's any point in telling anyone now you've found me—and I'm still not sure who I can trust back there.' She nodded her head, having come to a decision. 'We'll say nothing for now, and I'll brief Sir Frederick in person when I get back.'

'Okay, you're the boss,' said WB, rubbing his hands together. 'Right, where do we go from here?'

'Surely we should go to the local police?' asked Charlie. WB looked at Nathan with a raised eyebrow.

'What do you think, Nathan? Are they trustworthy around here?'

'The jury's still out on that one,' their host replied, looking uncertain. 'How much evidence do you actually have against Kabwe Mazoka?' Suzanne had told them her suspicions during supper the previous evening.

'None at all,' said Suzanne, 'although the kidnappers acted strangely when I mentioned his name.

'Well, I think that has to be our starting point,' said Charlie. 'We need to go and confront him and see what he has to say...' Her voice trailed off as she noticed WB was shaking his head.

'Not we; not this time, I'm afraid, Charlie.' She opened her mouth in protest, but he held up his hand for quiet and his authoritative manner worked. She closed her mouth again, although she still looked fiercely at him.

'This is a very delicate situation; and having two women, white women at that, steaming in and making accusations, is not going to help matters. I'll go and see him myself. I knew his father; I even met him once when he was little, so I have a legitimate reason for visiting him.'

'I would like to go with you,' Nathan said. 'I was at school with Kabwe, so he's not going to refuse to see me.' WB smiled and nodded his head.

'Excellent; let's go this morning, take him by surprise.'

'And ladies,' Nathan looked over at Suzanne and Charlie, 'maybe you would like a tour of the roses while we're out. My mother's coming back to check up on you, Suzanne, and she's staying for lunch. I'm sure she'll be happy to show you around.'

## 20: ZAMBIA; DEC 2004

Annette Harawa was wearing her doctor's hat again when she arrived at the farm just after the men set off to confront Kabwe. Suzanne and Charlie were still sitting on the terrace, staring out over the farm to the distant hills, enjoying the sunshine and catching up on what had happened both in Lusaka and in the Copper Belt over the past few days. Suzanne led the doctor back to her room, leaving Charlie to doze over her laptop.

Annette was tall and willowy, with dark auburn hair, glossy and made all the more distinguished by the few silver streaks beginning to show at her temples. She was obviously a strong woman; how else could she have allowed herself to love—and marry—a black African farmer, in those days pre-independence and the transition of Northern Rhodesia into Zambia. Suzanne found it hard to imagine the sort of reaction their union would have sparked in the colonial drawing rooms, but when she tried to ask her about this, Annette just smiled and shrugged her shoulders.

'We loved each other; that's all there was to it. Nothing anyone said could have had any effect on us.' She shook her head. 'But what man could not put asunder, disease snatched away just a few years later. I was a widow with a tiny baby and a burgeoning farm to look after.' She related how she'd handed the running of the farm over to her husband's uncle, awaiting the time when Nathan would be old enough to take over; and she returned to her interrupted education and trained as a doctor. Suzanne wondered if deep down Annette blamed herself for not recognising her husband's illness in time and was trying to make reparation by saving other people's husbands and fathers instead.

'Well, there doesn't seem to have been any lasting damage,' Annette said, folding up her stethoscope and stowing it in her old leather bag. 'Do you need any more of those sleeping pills?'

'I slept like a log,' Suzanne said, shaking her head, 'I shouldn't think I'll need them at all.'

'Hmmm,' was the cautious reply, 'you were exhausted last night, so I'm not surprised you slept, but once your body makes up for your lost sleep, you may find your mind starts reliving some of your recent experiences.' Annette patted her hand. 'Just keep them by you for a little while, okay?' She stood up and stretched, before turning to face her patient. 'Right, that's me off duty for the rest of the day. How about we pick up Charlie and I give you folks that tour of the farm before we have lunch.' And with her Dr Harawa hat firmly replaced with her dowager landowner hat, Annette led the way back to the terrace, where they found Charlie fast asleep with her legs on a chair and her laptop forgotten on the ground.

'The property covers around one hundred acres,' Annette said a while later as they strolled across the formal lawn, past the acacia trees where she told them she often entertained other local landowners and their wives to tea and cakes; across the little bridge over the ornamental lake—shaped exactly like a miniature Lake Victoria—and through the white picket fence into the farmyard. In the distance, they could see the glasshouses where the roses were grown, together with the sheds where tobacco leaves were dried and prepared for sale. But right in front of them was a stable block. Charlie and Suzanne glanced at each other in delight and headed for the nearest loose box.

'You like horses?' Annette asked.

'We love them,' Suzanne replied. 'We always wanted one when we were growing up, but there was no room— and frankly not enough money—for us to have one at home.'

'One of our friends at school had a couple,' chimed in Charlie, 'and she was happy for us to spend time with them.'

'So you can ride?'

'Charlie can; she's a natural,' said Suzanne, 'but I've always been a bit frightened of being up on their backs, to be honest. I was happy to look after them, talk to them, feed them—in fact I helped deliver a foal once when I was about fifteen—but I tend to leave the riding to Charlie.'

'Well,' said Annette, 'these are working animals. We use them to get around the farm. I'm sure Nathan would be happy to take you riding when he gets back, Charlie. And he knows their natures very well, so if you fancy having a go, Suzanne, he'll pick out a docile one for you.' Suzanne nodded, wondering if her fear of being on the back of such a high, unstable-feeling creature could be overcome for the opportunity to spend more time with Nathan Harawa.

After they'd fed and patted all the horses in the stables, made a fuss of the dogs milling around their legs and admired the small herd of cattle in the pen behind the buildings, Annette pulled a key from her pocket and gestured to a small golf buggy parked in the corner of the yard.

'Come on, let's go and look at the roses,' she said. But just then, they heard the sound of hooves galloping on beaten earth and into the yard came a magnificent black stallion, ridden by what Suzanne thought was a child in her early teens. She gave Annette a cheery wave as her horse clattered to a halt. A stable lad grabbed the reins, and the girl threw her leg over the horse's neck and slid elegantly to the ground. She ran over and threw her arms wide.

'Auntie Annie, I didn't know you'd be here today; how are you?' Annette hugged the girl before turning to Suzanne and Charlie with a smile.

'Ladies, can I introduce my favourite niece—and Nathan's best friend—Lily Harawa. It was Lily's grandfather who ran the farm after Marcus died.'

'Your niece?' Charlie said, looking as confused as Suzanne felt. Annette laughed.

'Well, strictly speaking, she's my late husband's first cousin once removed, but niece is much easier to say.'

The girl shook hands with the sisters and Suzanne realised with a shock that although she was tiny, slim and obviously very fit, given the huge horse she had handled with such ease, Lily Harawa was by no means a young girl. She was at least in her late twenties, if not older.

'Did you have a good ride? Was Prancer behaving himself?' Annette went on.

'I know he's big, but he's an old sweetie once you get to know him,' Lily said, 'and yes, I had a lovely ride. Although I found some of the fencing out on the perimeter has been damaged. Can you tell Nathan he'll need to get it repaired or he'll have the rose rustlers in again?'

'Well, why don't you stay to lunch and you can tell him yourself? He's out on business this morning, but he was hoping to be back in time to join us.'

Lily's face lit up and she readily agreed to this suggestion. Annette told her to go and freshen up while she finished conducting the tour for her 'English visitors'. Suzanne watched the girl thoughtfully as she went off first to check that Prancer was properly looked after. She wondered if there was anything other than a distant blood relationship between Nathan and Lily—and then wondered with a start why she cared about the answer to that question. She noticed Charlie was also watching Lily speculatively.

'There was a time when I thought Nathan and Lily would get together,' said Annette, as they climbed into the buggy, seeming to read Suzanne's mind. 'He was very keen on her when they were teenagers. Then she went off to college and things petered out. But now she's back living here, who knows?' Then she turned on the engine and drove out of the yard at full speed, removing the necessity for either sister to respond.

They started with the tobacco drying huts. One of the workers who tended to the crop brought samples of the leaves at different stages of drying and explained the process. Suzanne and Charlie buried their noses in the fragrant material at the end of the line and said in one voice: 'Granddad's pipe drawer!'

'These days we're much less supportive of the tobacco industry,' Suzanne said, 'but there are some smells that take one straight back to childhood and this is one of them.' Charlie nodded and carried on the story.

'There was a drawer in the built-in cupboard right next to where our grandfather used to sit to watch television. It always smelt of the pipe tobacco he used.'

'And it always had odd chess pieces and pipe cleaners in there,' Suzanne added. Annette nodded her head.

'As a doctor, I'm obviously very ambivalent about the tobacco trade,' she said, 'and we're gradually phasing it out as the rose business grows, but it's what paid for our home and educated my son—and me—not to mention keeping whole families in work and housing, so we can't stop it until we find a viable alternative.'

Finally they moved to the rose-filled glasshouses, where every pane was shaded with white paint, to prevent the beating sun from scorching the plants. Each building housed hundreds of plants, with different varieties

133

arranged in blocks for ease of picking, since they all bloomed at different times of the year. The smell was overpowering in some houses, more subtle in others, and Suzanne and Charlie wandered among the rows, stroking the velvety petals occasionally and inhaling the wonderful perfume.

'And this is my favourite,' said Annette as she led them into the last glasshouse. 'Nathan had this variety, *Annette's Golden Pleasure*, bred especially for my fiftieth birthday.' The flower was a dark orange, rather than gold, with an irregular white slash occasionally across the petals. It reminded Suzanne of Annette's hair and she thought it a perfect present. Looking at the older woman, she realised she might be a doctor and the owner of an extensive farm in Zambia, but she was, above all, a very proud and grateful mother; a mother who would do anything to bring her son happiness.

By the time the three women had returned to the farmhouse, Suzanne was hot and sticky; so she was relieved when Annette looked at her watch and said there was time for a shower before lunch. Washed, changed and feeling a little less hot and bothered, she joined Charlie on the landing and the two made their way downstairs and out on to the terrace where Annette and Lily were sipping colourless drinks. They stopped talking when the sisters appeared and Annette held up her glass to them.

'A little G and T while we wait for the men?' she said. 'Or there's white wine or fruit juice if you'd prefer it.' Charlie opted for the gin, but Suzanne took a fruit juice. She didn't feel completely comfortable in Lily's company and wanted to keep a clear head. They chatted about the morning's visit and Lily's job in Lusaka for half an hour or so, before one of the maids slipped quietly onto the terrace and whispered in Annette's ear.

'I think we should go in to lunch,' she said. 'Maisie is concerned the food will spoil if we leave it much longer. The men will just have to make the best of it when they get back.'

The four women moved into the dining room, cooler than the terrace, and very dim with shutters closed against the burning midday heat. They were served delicate chicken broth with warm home-made bread rolls and salty, pale yellow butter in tiny pats embossed with a rose. Annette smiled at the sight of this.

'Maisie loves to pull out all the stops when I'm here for lunch,' she said. 'She came to work for us when Marcus and I were first married and has been here ever since—nearly forty years.'

'You don't live here all the time, then?' asked Charlie.

'No, I live above my surgery most of the time,' the older woman replied. 'It's more convenient for my patients—they always know where to find me, even if I'm not on duty.' She pulled apart a soft white roll and spread butter thinly across it. 'Besides, this is Nathan's home now—and one day soon I hope he'll be sharing it with a family of his own.' She looked pointedly at Lily, who didn't respond to her aunt's comments and appeared to be concentrating on her soup. But Suzanne, looking at her closely, thought she detected the hint of a smile playing at the girl's mouth. *I suspect someone else shares the same hopes*, she thought. She hadn't forgotten the way Lily's face had lit up at the invitation to stay and have lunch with them—and the chance to talk to Nathan about the broken fence.

Suddenly the two ridgebacks lying snoozing in a patch of sunshine, which had sneaked through a hole in the shutters, came alert and sat up. They looked towards the doorway.

'That will be Nathan,' said Annette. The others all looked towards the door too. 'Oh, you won't be able to hear them yet. The car's probably only just turned into the gate—or it might still be on the approach road. These dogs can hear things a lot better than we can.'

It was another five minutes before Suzanne heard a car pull up outside the house. The front door opened and

135

closed; heavy footsteps crossed the hall and Nathan and WB appeared in the doorway. *Now we'll see how Lily behaves*, thought Suzanne. But one look at the men's faces was enough to brush all thoughts of a relationship between Lily and Nathan right out of her mind. The two new arrivals hadn't stopped to remove their jackets or freshen up before coming into the dining room. They appeared to have news—and from the looks on their faces, it didn't look like that news was going to be good.

# 21: ZAMBIA; DEC 2004

Nathan clicked his fingers to the maid who was standing beside the doorway waiting to serve the diners with more food.

'Water,' he croaked, 'bring a large jug of water—and three glasses.'

Annette jumped up from the table and ran to her son.

'Tell us,' she said. But her son just pressed his lips together and shook his head. She looked across at WB who was wiping his face with a large handkerchief, once snowy white, but now grey and covered in black smudges. He looked up at them and Suzanne saw with a jolt that there were unshed tears glistening in the big Ugandan's eyes.

'It's gone,' he whispered, 'it's all gone. They've done it again.'

'The factory…?'

'…is just a hole in the ground.'

'Why three glasses?' Charlie asked.

'I'll get him,' said WB, turning back towards the hall, 'he was too shy to come in straight away.' He returned a few seconds later with a small, very dirty boy in torn shorts and T-shirt, with grey streaks on his arms and legs. Tears made tracks through the grey on his face and he was snivelling, wiping his nose on the back of his arm. As six pairs of eyes stared at him, he turned as though to run away, but WB held his arm and wouldn't let him leave. 'Tell the ladies what happened,' he said. The boy struggled and looked up at WB, shaking his head violently. Annette gave a gasp.

'Oh, you poor young thing, what have they done to you?' At that point, the maid returned with the water and the doctor poured some out and gave it to the boy. Nathan and WB grabbed the other glasses, filling them and immediately emptying them in deep gulps. The boy sipped his and coughed. Annette took the glass gently from him, and turned, her Dr Harawa hat firmly back on her head.

'Okay, you two,' she pointed to Nathan and WB, 'go and have a shower.' Nathan opened his mouth and looked like he was going to object, but Annette shook her head. 'Whatever you've got to tell us can wait a short while. This poor boy is terrified. We're going to look after him while you freshen up.' Like naughty schoolchildren, Nathan and WB left the room and their footsteps could be heard climbing the stairs. 'You come with me,' Annette went on, looking down at the little boy. Then she tutted. 'They didn't even tell me your name. What are you called, child?'

'I'm Freedom, madam,' he whispered.

'Well, Freedom, you come with me and we'll get you cleaned up. Then you can tell us what happened.'

'We heard the explosions as we were driving out of here,' Nathan told the women when they reconvened in the dining room a while later. 'But we had no idea what it was, or where it came from. Otherwise we would have gone there first and maybe we could have helped.'

'So, if you didn't go to the factory straight away,' asked Suzanne, 'where did you go?' Nathan looked up at her, although his eyes were still unseeing and she wasn't sure he'd heard her question. Then he gave a sigh,

'We went to Kabwe's house first,' he said. 'We thought if we could find him on his home territory, rather than at the factory, we could catch him off guard and get him to tell us what's been going on.'

'And did you find him?'

'No, There was no-one there—and the house was completely empty! It's been cleared out. Not a stick of furniture left.'

'We asked some of the neighbours and they said he's had a van there for the past few days, loading boxes and furniture, and taking it away,' WB took up the story. 'So this seems to have been a planned getaway.' He paused, then gave a sigh and continued. 'So we drove to the factory, although we weren't hopeful would find him there. We saw the pall of smoke from a mile or so away and the closer we got, the more obvious the location was. But even then we didn't suspect...when we arrived, it was terrible...' WB stopped speaking, cleared his throat and started again. 'There was a crowd standing in the yard just staring at the ruins of the building. They were completely silent. Not one sound. It was the eeriest sight I've ever seen. They just stood and looked, then, when we arrived, they parted to let us pass.'

'And when we turned back to look at them, they'd gone,' said Nathan; 'the crowd had melted away like smoke in the morning air.'

'And Freedom? Where did you find him?' asked Annette.

'He was lying against the back wall, partly hidden by some packing cases. That's why no-one saw him until then. In fact, we almost missed him. We stopped to unchain the dog by the gate and he ran over to Freedom, whimpering and licking his face.'

'He seemed stunned but not hurt otherwise, and I thought it would be safer to bring him back here, Mother. I knew you'd be here and could look after him.'

Annette just nodded and put her arm around the little

boy.

'But how can you be sure it was deliberate?' asked Lily, who had been sitting silently since the men started telling their story. 'Could it have been a terrible accident?'

'We wondered that,' said WB, 'although they only made liquid products at Mazokapharm, so there should be nothing explosive stored there. But from what Freedom told us in the car, I don't think there's much doubt.' He walked over and squatted down in front of the child, taking the small hand and engulfing it with his own. He whispered gently to him.

'Son, I know it's really hard, but do you think you can tell us the whole story of what happened? Can you help us find the men who did this?'

Freedom swallowed hard then nodded his head, but he clung to Annette as he started speaking.

*My sister, Hope, was late for work this morning. She'd been out with the bad men again last night. She didn't think I knew about them, but I see lots more than she realises. I'm only small and so quiet that often people forget I'm there. Or sometimes I hide behind the door, or in the cupboard, and listen to what people say to her. I worry about her, you see. She's supposed to look after me. She's older than me, but I'm the man of the house, or I will be when I get older, so I try to look out for her too.*

*Because she was late, Hope ran out of the house without any breakfast and I knew she would be really hungry by dinnertime. So I made some food for her. Just bread and preserve—that's all we had in the cupboard—but it's what she always eats for dinner anyway. I carried it carefully to the factory, although I wasn't sure how I was going to be able to get it to her. Once the women go to work, they're not allowed out until the end of their shift. But I thought I'd be able to slip in at the back, through the warehouse. One of the men who shifts the boxes around, Wally his name is, he likes her very much and he sometimes lets me go and see her if the boss isn't around.*

*I don't like the boss very much. Mr Kabwe used to be my friend, but since the bad men came, he's not the same anymore. He frowns all the time and makes the women work long hours.*

*When I got to the factory, Mr Kabwe's car wasn't in the usual place outside, but I knew I still had to be careful. He doesn't always bring the car; sometimes he walks up the hill from the town. I hid behind the empty packing cases at the back of the plot and waited to see if Wally was working today. Then I heard a vehicle pull into the yard. It was a big grey van, with blacked-out windows and I guessed it was the bad men. The back of the van opened and they jumped out—more than I've ever seen there before. There were about nine of them I think. They were dropping barrels out of the van and rolling them towards the factory. They stood them against the wall and the sun was shining full on them. But that wasn't right! Usually, the drums are rolled straight into the warehouse to protect the contents from the heat. It's only the empty ones that can go out in the sun. They must have been in a real hurry, to leave them there. I wondered if Wally would let me help him roll them around to the loading bay. He does that sometimes—and then shares his dinner with me, or gives me a penny or two to spend as a reward. I always give them to Hope; she doesn't earn very much money and it all goes on food and paying the bills for the house, so she's always glad of some extra.*

*Anyway, I watched the men finish unloading the barrels and then one of them walked around to the back of the building, and went into the warehouse. There was a grinding noise and the big roller door came down and locked into place. I thought that was very strange too. The doors are never closed during the day. Then he came out of the side door with Wally, who looked really strange. He kept looking across at the other man and licking his lips as though he was really thirsty. The man pointed to the padlock on the small door. Wally shook his head—but the man shoved him in the shoulder and pointed again. I saw something in his hand; it flashed in the sunshine—I think it was a gun. Wally put the padlock in place and then the other man grabbed his arm and marched him across the yard and pushed him into the van. I wanted to run after them and shout 'let my friend go,' but I was too scared. So I just stayed where I was and watched what was going on.*

*I kept hoping Mr Kabwe would come back. He wouldn't let anything happen to Wally. They're old friends from schooldays.*

*Wally tells me sometimes about those days. He says Mr Kabwe was very funny, always laughing and playing jokes on people, before he had his accident. He's not like that now.*

*Once Wally was in the van, most of the other men climbed in after him. The driver got back in his cab. There was just one man left—the man who pushed Wally. He walked around, checking all the barrels; he seemed to be counting them. And he put little packages on the tops of some of them.* They really are going to get hot in this sunshine, *I thought. Then he locked the padlock on the outside door. So both doors were locked and I couldn't get in to see Hope. I knew there was a spare key somewhere; Mr Kabwe always has one hidden in case he forgets his, but no-one else knows where it is, apart from the boss himself and his secretary. The man lit a cigarette and threw the match through one of the windows into the factory. It was the room where they stored all the packaging materials, the cartons and labels, so I knew it would burn quickly. I had to do something to warn all the women. But I was too scared to move while the men were there. The man laughed then climbed into the van and it drove away.*

*I ran across the yard and banged on the door of the factory. I screamed for Hope and after a couple of minutes I heard one of the other women call back to me. I told her about the man and the match and told her they needed to put the fire out. I said I would run to Mr Kabwe's house and get him to bring the key so we could let everyone out. 'You're a good boy, Freedom,' she said. Then she ran to warn the others. But it was too late. There was a bang and a whoosh and a sheet of flame flew out of the window. The fire was too big for them to do anything about. They only had one little extinguisher. I could hear the women screaming and banging on the door. I didn't know whether I should go to find Mr Kabwe or stay and try to help them. Then the woman came back. 'Freedom,' she screamed, 'run down to the town, get help. We're going to try to climb out of the window at the back, but it's very small. Run quickly.' But I couldn't. My legs didn't seem to work. I just stood and watched the flames. They were licking out of the windows and reaching up to the tin roof. The women were still screaming and moaning. I couldn't tell where Hope was, whether she was okay or not; my sister can't speak, you see, but I knew she was in there. I could feel her presence.*

*I still didn't know what to do; to run into town or stay and help. Then there was a huge bang, followed by lots of others. The barrels just split apart. I watched as they went off, one after another, and then I tried to run away, but I left it too late! The ground shook, I felt myself picked up and flung across the yard and slammed into the wall at the other side. Then everything went black. By the time I woke up, the building was completely destroyed and the screaming had stopped.*

As the boy stopped speaking, no-one in the room moved or made a sound, and then...

'How many...?' whispered Suzanne.

'Ten women, we think,' Nathan said, her horror reflected in his face. 'The administration building was empty. We don't think there were any men in the place; only the warehouseman, Wally, was supposed to be there—and Freedom says he saw him driven away. But whether to safety or more danger, who knows?'

'How could anyone do this?' Charlie burst out suddenly, banging her fist on the table and making the cutlery jump and jangle in the forgotten soup bowls. 'My God, I thought what we did to each other in the Middle East was bad enough. But to let your own people burn alive like that. It's not human.'

Nathan and WB looked up in surprise at her outburst, but it was the small boy who spoke, pulling away from Annette as she led him from the room and turning to face them.

'Not only our own people,' he said, shaking his head vehemently. 'The man in charge wasn't one of our own people.'

'How do you know?' Suzanne asked.

'He had a funny accent. He talked like the Terminator. The bad man who burnt down the factory was white.' Then he flung himself into Annette's arms and began sobbing noisily. She picked him up and carried him upstairs.

143

Nathan and WB sat down at the table, just staring at the food in front of them. Neither man seemed to have any appetite. Charlie cleared her throat but said nothing.

Suzanne knew the likelihood of Kabwe being innocent was fading. She'd been hoping all along that this son of WB's old friend was just out of his depth, mixed up in something he didn't understand, even led astray a little— but always redeemable. But now it didn't look like this was very likely. If he had planned his getaway so carefully, it looked as though he knew exactly what was going on; which meant he must have known about the plans for the fire. Although she found it really hard to accept, it looked like he had either ordered the destruction of his own factory, or he'd at least known it was going to happen and wanted to be away from there before it did.

'I'm really sorry, Suzanne,' WB said, taking her hand in his, 'but it looks like the trail's gone cold and we're no nearer finding out who kidnapped you, or why, than we were when we went out this morning.'

## 22: KENYA; DEC 2004

The Honourable Walter Mukooyo hadn't shown much enthusiasm for the IHF campaign when they'd crossed swords at the Swaziland conference and Suzanne didn't really expect his attitude to change. But if there was a chance of getting support from him, it would add weight, not just in Kenya, but in neighbouring countries too. Chibesa had requested a follow-up discussion before Suzanne had even left London, but the long silence had convinced her their altercation was neither forgotten nor forgiven. However, she was wrong. And during her fourth day at the Harawa ranch, she got some good news.

'But I can make some excuse; tell them you have to get back to London—or you're still out of town,' Chibesa said during his nightly phone calls to Ndola, when he told Suzanne he'd finally heard back from the Minister's office and the answer was positive.

'No, don't do that,' she said. 'We don't want to risk upsetting him again. I'm feeling much better now—and although Nathan's a wonderful host, I think it's probably time his unexpected guests removed themselves and left him in peace to grow his roses.'

'But don't get your hopes up too much,' Chibesa said

when Suzanne complimented him on setting up the appointment. 'Walter Mukooyo is notoriously good at skipping out of meetings he doesn't want to take part in.'

As Suzanne, with Charlie and WB, left for the airport next morning, she looked back towards the place that had been her safe haven for the past five days and reflected on the kind young ranch owner who had taken her in and given her the respite she needed to recover from her ordeal. She had been drawn to him from that first moment in the hall when he caught her smelling the roses, and from his behaviour during the first couple of days, she'd suspected he was attracted to her. Then Lily's appearance had reminded her she was only a visitor in this world and Nathan had a life of his own. But she couldn't help feeling a little sad as the ranch disappeared from view.

After a couple of days in Lusaka, the team headed for the airport once more, bound for Kenya. Suzanne had questioned whether it was really necessary for all four of them to go, but her companions were adamant they weren't letting her out of their sight again, even if Charlie knew she would have to stay in the hotel while they went to the meeting at the Ministry.

Mukooyo was a powerful and influential man, not just in his own country, but also in the whole of Southern Africa. There was talk of him taking a more regional role once his term of office in Kenya was finished. Something in the Common Market of Southern and Eastern Africa— or COMESA as Chibesa tended to call it—or maybe even a UN Ambassador.

'Although actually, I'd rather sit on the Board of the Olympics Committee or the African Football Association,' he'd joked once in an interview Suzanne watched on television. Mukooyo was well known for his love of sport and was often spotted in the VIP box at national and international sporting occasions.

When they arrived at Parliament House, the team was

shown into the Minister's office and they had been waiting nearly an hour for Walter Mukooyo to arrive.

'The Minister has been called away to an urgent meeting with the President,' said his PA—a 'traditionally built' African lady whose brightly coloured dress carried a picture of said President. 'But he asked me to make his apologies, give you tea and beg you to wait until he returns.'

Chibesa had already alerted them to the fact that the Regional Softball Championships were being held in the country at present and both the President and the Minister were big fans. They all suspected the urgent meeting, if it existed at all, would be taking place at the National Stadium.

'So, at that rate, we can expect the Minister to be back here in about half an hour,' Chibesa predicted now, as their desultory talk ran out and they all started looking at their watches. The office was decked out in white wooden furniture with gold hangings, curtain ties and door fittings. The chairs were upholstered in a black and white fake zebra fur, which took Suzanne right back again to their visit to Swaziland.

It was exactly thirty-three minutes later when the door opened and the Minister breezed in, full of apologies and calling for tea at the same time.

'Good meeting, Minister?' WB said as the two men shook hands and clasped arms like old friends. 'By the way, how's the softball going?'

Mukooyo, who was in the process of turning to shake Chibesa's hand, looked back at WB in surprise.

'I'm so sorry! I've been too busy to follow much of this week's sporting fixtures.' He gestured to his PA. 'I can get Esme to ring up and find out for you, if you like?' *Oh, he's good*, thought Suzanne, *he's very good*. There was barely a hesitation or a flicker in his eyes to give away the fact that he might be more up-to-date on the sports results than he would admit.

'Not a problem,' grinned WB, 'I was just making conversation.' The Minister nodded before taking a cup from his PA and joining the team at the seated area near the huge window overlooking the Nairobi suburbs with the game reserve on the horizon.

'Over there's our famous Game Park barbecue restaurant,' he said. 'Have you had a chance to enjoy it yet?'

'No, Minister,' Suzanne said somewhat frostily. She had been largely ignored while the Minister was greeting the two men, until WB pulled her forward and reminded Mukooyo she was the leader of the team. 'But we're hoping to get a reservation for tonight.'

The Minister clicked his fingers to his PA who was loitering in the background. 'Esme, ring the Game Park and tell them to give these good people my table for this evening. I won't be going there until the weekend.' The PA bowed and left the room. Mukooyo waved away their thanks.

'Okay, I've kept you waiting long enough,' he said; 'what can I do for you?' He addressed his question to WB, but it was Suzanne who replied. She brought him up to date on progress with the IHF project since they had all met in Swaziland. Following his own brief but tempestuous appearance, Mukooyo had left one of his juniors as a representative for the remainder of the conference.

'Have you seen his report yet, Minister?' she asked. But he was already shaking his head.

'No, I'm afraid not. We had a verbal debrief when he first returned, of course, but I've not seen anything in writing yet.' He turned once more to the PA, who had just returned and slipped a scrap of paper into Chibesa's hand. 'Please check with our delegate on when his report will be due.' He paused, and then went on: 'No, on second thoughts, set up a meeting for the beginning of next week. Then tell him I want the report by this Friday, so I can take it home and peruse it over the weekend.'

Suzanne would have been more impressed if the Minister had already been through this process without her having to prompt him. After all, the conference had been more than two months ago. Still, it was a start—and she also knew politicians like this, with several warring nations in the region, had other things to think about. She decided to put the memory of their confrontation in Swaziland behind her and have another go at convincing Walter Mukooyo to support them.

'We're really hoping you will agree to champion one of the pilot schemes here in Kenya,' she concluded. 'It would give great weight to the whole project if we had such an important national—and international—figure on board.'

'Miss Jones,' said Mukooyo, 'do you realise what a difficult job I have in this country? I've got a population of forty-five million souls. And the Good Lord, in his wisdom, has seen fit to give some three million or more serious illnesses. Unfortunately, the Good Lord has *not* seen fit to give my colleagues in the Finance Ministry any understanding of the problem and so they are less than generous when it comes to my budget. It's my responsibility to see that all those people—and anyone else who needs it—get the necessary medicine. Frankly, if some of the pills and potions we supply are produced unofficially by a low technology factory in Africa, rather than by the expensive methods used in some of your Western factories, I'm not sure what harm it does—and it certainly means I can supply more of my people's requirements.'

Suzanne was once again outraged by this response—and even more so by the self-satisfied expression on the face of the Minister as he looked around the room at his visitors. She wondered whether Mukooyo was alone in his opinions—or whether this was the prevailing view of other authorities in Africa. *Well, if it is*, she thought, *it's a view we're going to have to try to change.*

'But you're not supplying your people's needs—you're harming them. Why, in some cases, you're actually killing them—especially the young children.' But the Minister was shaking his head indulgently at her.

'Miss Jones, you are young, idealistic. I admire that. And in an ideal world, I would love to be able to agree with you. But we're living in the real world here. I just can't afford to look too closely at where my supplies come from.'

'And the deaths of children?' she asked again.

'Miss Jones, this is Africa. Children die every day—from disease, from malnutrition, from violence. Who's to say that the ones who die because of counterfeit drugs, even if we could prove that was the cause—who's to say they wouldn't have died anyway?'

'So you're not prepared to act as a champion for the pilot scheme here in Kenya?' she said, face burning and unshed tears not far from the surface. The Minister looked at her with a look of shock and surprise.

'I didn't say that. Of course I'm willing to back the campaign. I'm not a monster, Miss Jones. I would much prefer not to take a risk with the health of the people of Kenya. I'm just explaining why we can't solve the problem overnight. So, what do you want me to do?'

Needing time to recover from Mukooyo's abrupt change of direction, Suzanne indicated that WB should take over at this point and her Ugandan team member explained about training courses aimed at the pilot companies; the working party to try and equalise the regulations across the Continent; and the pressure being exerted on the customs authorities to crack down on illegal shipments of drugs.

'Of course, it's the suitcase merchants who'll be the hardest to find,' he said, referring to the individuals who crossed the borders with just a few packs of drugs in briefcases or other hand baggage. 'But if we can make a start on the major dealers, hopefully we can shut down some of the supply routes.'

The group spent the next fifteen minutes discussing tactical points; then the Minister's PA arrived at his elbow, pointing to her watch. Mukooyo stood up and held out his hand to Suzanne.

'I'm sorry; I have to go now. I have another meeting in just a few minutes time—and no, WB, it is NOT at the softball arena. Miss Jones, I wish you good luck with your project.' He paused as she raised her eyebrow at him and then went on with a smile, 'I'm sorry, I mean our project; and I'll get some of my team to work on the pilot scheme first thing in the morning. I'll be in touch.'

As they filed out of the office, Mukooyo called after them: 'and don't forget to let me know how you enjoy the restaurant tonight. Do try the crocodile: it's very tasty, like a fishy kind of chicken.' They could hear him chuckling as they walked down the corridor to the elevator.

## 23: KENYA; DEC 2004

When Suzanne and Charlie arrived in the back of Chibesa's beaten up old saloon, WB was waiting for them outside the Game Park restaurant.

Charlie had been appalled by the sights they'd seen as they drove through the streets of Nairobi, and although Suzanne had been there before, she too was horrified. Soon after they'd left their hotel, the elegant shops, smart town houses and villas gave way to a shanty town of broken down huts: corrugated roofing perched precariously atop lopsided walls of breeze block or wooden panelling. Light was provided by cables with occasional bulbs, strung across the narrow lanes between the buildings, like neglected Christmas tree decorations in which failed bulbs had not been replaced. Adverts in garish colours jostled for elbow room with lines of washing. And every space was crowded; mainly with women and children—many, many children. 'We have to succeed,' Suzanne had said as she looked into the eyes of a young child gazing up out of the mud and the filth to watch the car go by, 'these are the victims. We can't fail them.'

Now, as they climbed from the car, the surroundings changed again. They were on the hilltop Walter Mukooyo had pointed out earlier in the day, overlooking the city. The sprawl of the slums gave way to the skyscrapers in the distance. But here, they were surrounded by bush land: trees and shrubs growing lush and barely held in check by barbed wire fences. Suzanne felt the energy in the game park just metres from where they stood and fancied she could see the animals watching them from their hiding places in the undergrowth. The occasional roar, snarl, creak and howl confirmed that they were not alone—and were not far from nature in the raw.

WB bowed to Suzanne and offered her his arm. Chibesa similarly paired up with Charlie and the four strolled through the artfully-arranged screen of pampas grass—over two metres high and in full bloom with creamy fronds of froth bending gently in the evening breeze—into a scene of epic proportions. The restaurant area was open to the sky; diners sat at circular tables under thatched canopies, illuminated by floating tea lights in glass dishes. Their chairs were covered in zebra-patterned material, so soft to the touch that Suzanne suspected it was made from real pelts. Waiters, wearing similarly black and white striped aprons, and straw boaters, flitted from table to table, dispensing drinks, taking orders or delivering food.

The barbecue pits and ovens were in the centre of the restaurant, set in a massive square and attended on each side by three or four chefs. Even from the distance, the heat was palpable and the chefs frequently mopped their brows with the cloths tucked in their waistbands. Meats in many shapes and sizes, from tiny chicken hearts and liver to haunches of zebra and giraffe, were roasting on the racks above and in front of the charcoal filled pits. Waiters carried the cooked meats, still on skewers like miniature swords, around the restaurant. To one side, there was a huge, circular bar and at the other end, the fake market trolleys of a salad table.

Chibesa bet Charlie she couldn't manage a piece of

every meat on the menu—and she accepted the challenge. They sat at the table wrangling in a friendly manner and egging each other on to try even more of the tempting treats on offer. Suzanne, never a big meat eater at the best of times, decided to play it safe and only choose meat she recognised, but Charlie was much more adventurous.

'Hey, sis, you MUST try this crocodile. It tastes…'

'…just like chicken?'

'Well, actually, I was going to say a cross between chicken and prawn, but if it'll make you happier, then yes, it tastes just like chicken.'

They all agreed some of the meats were more palatable than others; those reared specifically for eating—chicken, beef and goat—had more familiar flavours, whereas the wild animals that had grown up naturally in the bush, were more gamey—a little bit musty in some ways.

'I suppose that's only to be expected when you're eating carnivores,' said WB; 'the herbivores have a much healthier lifestyle and their meat tastes better as a result.'

As she joined WB at the salad table, Suzanne suddenly felt as though she was being watched and turned slowly in a circle, casually scanning the crowded tables. She nearly missed her. She was so tiny and was seated partly hidden behind a plant pot overflowing with ferns, but by shifting sideways to get a clearer view, Suzanne was certain. It was Lily Harawa from Ndola. Her companion was sitting with his back to Suzanne and she was surprised to feel herself flushing at the possibility of meeting up with Nathan once more. Then, as Lily leaned forward to whisper urgently in his ear, he turned and glanced over his shoulder, looking straight at Suzanne. And it wasn't Nathan. Same build, same height, same slightly long curly hair, but the face was sharper, crueller somehow, and there was certainly no smile for her. Suzanne shivered and tried to straighten out her thoughts. She was glad Lily wasn't here with Nathan; she was sorry Nathan wasn't here, although there was no reason why he should be; she was disappointed for Nathan if Lily was seeing someone else—she'd come to the reluctant conclusion that he still had feelings for his young relative—and she'd thought they were reciprocated. But most of all, she was disturbed to feel the girl's eyes on her in this way. She'd been quite friendly when they first met at the rose farm, but somewhere along the line, the friendly manner had disappeared and all Suzanne could sense now was hostility. She wondered whether she should say anything to WB, and was turning towards him when Charlie called to her from their table.

'Hey, come on, sis; you can't come to a great barbecue place like this and eat salad, for Pete's sake!' Suzanne suspected her sister had drunk rather more of the strong rum punches than was good for her. She hurried back to the table to try and quieten her down, although in the hubbub of this busy restaurant, very few people would have been able to hear her. When she looked back at the other side of the room a few minutes later, the table in the corner was empty and there was no sign of either Lily or her stern-looking companion.

Throughout the meal, a steady stream of waiters brought choice cuts of meat to the table. Every time Suzanne managed to clear her plate another metal spike would appear over her shoulder, held by a waiter wielding a long knife with which a succulent slice would be carved from the joint.

'I don't think I can eat much more,' she whispered to WB, watching Charlie and Chibesa accepting yet more food.

'Don't worry,' he said, winking at her. 'I know how to turn off the tap.' And reaching to the centre of the table, he picked up a cotton reel from a basket hidden behind a vase of flowers. 'Here, put this beside your plate, red end up.' Suzanne realised the cotton reel was a simple traffic light system, painted red at one end and green at the other. With a little red marker next to her plate, the waiters knew, without having to ask, that this guest had eaten enough—

at least for the time being.

'Shouldn't we tell the other two about the traffic lights?' she asked WB but he grinned wickedly at her and shook his head.

'It's a lesson best learnt the hard way,' he said, 'and it's funnier for the rest of us if we don't. Someone did it to me on my first visit here—and everyone at the table thought it was hilarious.'

Suzanne wasn't sure about that, but decided to trust WB and go with the joke. It had been a hard two weeks for all of them, not least for her, and she wanted to relax for a little while, throw off the mantle of responsibility and just have some fun. There was time enough to start behaving sensibly again when they got back to Lusaka or she and Charlie returned to London.

They finally relented and told Charlie about the cotton reel twenty minutes later when she was almost weeping at the fact that she couldn't stop the waiters from giving her food. Chibesa had spotted the scheme a short while before and was smugly sitting with an empty plate while she was still struggling to finish what was on hers.

'You can't possibly waste any of that meat,' he laughed at her. 'Just think of all the little kids in this city who don't have enough to eat. They would kill for a plate like that.'

'And probably do, in some cases,' said WB, a sobering thought that instantly extinguished the grins around the table.

As they filed out of the restaurant, Suzanne glanced again at the scrubland and bush just the other side of the fence and silently saluted the animals that had given their lives so she and her friends could eat.

Charlie and Chibesa continued their friendly banter in the car back to the hotel, he driving and she sitting in the passenger seat beside him. Suzanne was curious about the easy relationship that had built up so quickly between her sister and this young man from Zambia. Was it because he had no interest in Charlie as a potential partner and just wanted a friend? Was it because he completely understood her sexual preferences and did not judge her in any way—as so many young men and women had judged her, and hurt her, in the past? Or was it just that the extra rum punches had broken down both their barriers? Suzanne wasn't sure which it was, but was just happy to see her sister relaxed and laughing.

WB had gone back to the hotel in his own vehicle, so Suzanne was alone in the back of the car. Thoughts about her sister's friendships and relationships led almost effortlessly to those of her own and she found herself thinking once more about Nathan Harawa. At that first meeting, he had seemed kind and sympathetic to her plight, and although that would have been a natural reaction from most people who saw her in the state she was in after her rescue, she had sensed a connection between them and would have welcomed the opportunity to get to know him better. Then she met Lily and found out that Annette wanted the young girl as Nathan's wife; so Suzanne had stepped back, albeit regretfully. Nathan had seemed to withdraw from her too and she wondered if he regretted allowing her to recuperate in his house. She'd not heard from him since they left Ndola and she doubted if she would see him before she and Charlie flew home the following week. It was a pity, but maybe it was for the best; a long distance relationship was not something she was looking for. She had enough difficulty keeping up with all her friends back home, given the amount of travelling she was doing. Goodness only knows how she would have managed to keep any sort of friendship going across two continents and several oceans.

When they got back to the hotel, Charlie and Chibesa headed off to the bar for one last nightcap—although Charlie promised faithfully it would be a rock shandy rather than a rum punch—but Suzanne was exhausted and said goodnight to the pair in the lobby.

The elevator took a long time to arrive. Suzanne

watched the numbers on the digital display as they slowly moved down from 9 to 0, stopping for several seconds on each floor in between. When it finally arrived, it was empty. She wondered if there was a party on floor 9 and all the guests were going back to their rooms. She couldn't think of any other reason why an elevator should stop at every floor when there was no-one in it.

Pressing the button for floor 8, she sagged back against the wall as the lift rose majestically. Her energy levels had hit rock bottom. Was it the stress of the past two weeks? Or an excess of food? Or another reason? Perhaps she was sickening for something.

The corridor was deserted when she arrived at her floor and she walked swiftly to her door. Even though it was well-lit, she found it eerie and lonely up there on her own.

As the door swung open, she was concerned to find the lights were on, but then she remembered she'd forgotten to put her usual 'Do Not Disturb' notice on the door handle before she left for the restaurant. So the maid would have been in to service the room. Sure enough, the bed was turned down, the lamps were all lit and the radio was playing softly in the background. As she threw her bag on the table and kicked off her shoes, she heard a slight noise in the bathroom.

'Is anyone there?' she called out, moving towards the phone as she did so. Her nerves were on edge and she didn't want to risk being taken prisoner again. The bathroom door opened and a uniformed maid walked out, carrying some folded towels in her arms.

'Sorry, madam, did I startle you?' she asked. 'I was just freshening up your supplies.' She wasn't one of the women Suzanne had seen before, but she knew it was unlikely she would recognise all the staff in such a large hotel. 'Good night, madam,' said the maid and let herself quietly out of the room, closing the door with a gentle click behind her.

Suzanne ran into the bathroom, checked behind the shower curtain, returned to the bedroom, checked behind all the curtains and in the wardrobe. Then, finally convinced that she was safe and alone, she locked the door, put the safety chain across, dropped her clothes on the floor by the wardrobe and climbed into bed.

It was only as she was dropping off to sleep a while later that a thought wound its way into her consciousness: if the maid really was just freshening up the room, where was her service trolley? The corridor had been completely empty when Suzanne came up to bed.

# 24: KENYA; DEC 2004

Suzanne sat bolt upright and hit the light switch above the bedside table. Jumping out of bed, she prowled the room, looking desperately for signs of what the maid had really been doing. The bin under the desk was empty. But then, it would have been emptied when the room was properly serviced earlier in the day; and she couldn't remember whether she'd thrown anything into it before she went out to the restaurant. In the bathroom, the towels were dry and carefully folded on the rail. And she'd had a shower earlier that evening, so certainly the towels had been changed. The end of the toilet roll had been folded into that annoying little triangle so beloved of hotel staff. She took a deep breath and looked at herself in the mirror, shaking her head at the flushed and worried face she saw looking out at her.

'You've got to calm down and stop seeing drama everywhere,' she told herself.

She went over to the wardrobe to check the safe was still locked. It was. But as she turned away and was about to close the door once more, something caught the corner of her eye. A flash of fluorescent pink in the dim light. She grabbed her suitcase and pulled it out of the bottom of the wardrobe and onto the bed. Suzanne had often been accused by her sister of being 'a touch OCD' but she saw it as merely being tidy. One of the habits she'd developed during her travels was keeping her dirty clothes tidily in her suitcase at the bottom of the wardrobe. She had no problem with the idea that hotel staff would be making her bed, cleaning the shower or the loo, or even seeing how many packets of crisps or nuts she'd eaten from the mini bar. But she did not want them going through her dirty clothes. So although, as now, she often dropped them untidily on the floor before she climbed into bed, she always made a point of folding and stowing them in her case before she left for work the next morning. She also found it made packing at the end of the trip much easier as well. So she was disturbed to see the sleeve of a blouse she'd worn earlier in the week sticking out from the side of the case. Opening the lid with trembling hands, she found to her disgust that someone had indeed been going through her clothes. They were rumpled and stuffed in any old how, as though someone had tipped them out on to the bed and then shoved them back in without taking care to replace them as they'd originally been packed. So someone had definitely been going through her things—and they didn't seem particularly worried if that fact was found out. 'Either an amateur or a very confident professional without any fear of discovery,' she said out loud.

She looked again around the room and noticed things that had passed her by the first time. The papers and magazines on the desk were in a less tidy pile than she had left them—and the folder on the top was not the one she'd been looking at last. Then she remembered her briefcase and looked around in a panic. Where was it? She'd left it under the desk when she came back from the factory that day. She knew it had been there—against the inside of the left leg, just as it always was. But now it wasn't there. After scrabbling around in a panic for a few seconds, she found it under the bed. Clicking it open, she confirmed everything was still in its place, although the corners of the papers were bent and dog-eared; not in the perfect condition in which she had left them.

Now she was definitely getting spooked. There was no getting away from the fact that someone had been in her room; whether it was the maid she'd surprised in the bathroom or someone else, she couldn't tell at this point. But whoever it was wanted to frighten her. There was just enough going on to scare her, without giving her any explanation of why they had been there or what they were looking for.

Suzanne returned to the wardrobe and looked speculatively at the safe. It was locked, that was for sure. She'd checked it earlier and she checked it again now. But had it been disturbed? Sighing, she keyed in the six digit code—the day she'd got her first pet back when she was a teenager—and pulled open the door.

Breathing a sigh of relief, she confirmed that the contents were untouched. Her passport, a copy of her visas, her wallet with the extra cash she'd brought for emergencies, and the envelope of notes she'd made on the case so far—including some of the details from Sara's story. Whoever had been in her room hadn't been through this stuff. 'Unless they were able to open it, take the details they wanted, and then replace everything carefully to put me off the scent,' she mused now. Then she smiled and shook her head. 'No, I'd have been able to spot that. They're much too untidy and careless to do it that well.'

She relocked the safe, pushed her suitcase on the floor to repack in the morning, climbed back into bed and switched off the light once more. But it was a long time before she could get to sleep.

At breakfast the next morning, she told WB of her disturbed night, her suspicions about the maid, and the fact that someone had been through her room. Neither

Charlie nor Chibesa had put in an appearance yet and Suzanne assumed they were sleeping off last night's rum punches.

'Would you like me to talk to the hotel manager?' WB asked. Suzanne smiled at him.

'Don't tell me—you know him from your days back in school?'

'University, actually, but yes, I know him and he owes me a favour.'

'Well, it might be a good idea to have a chat with him, although I've not got much proof and it seems a bit weak now, in the cold light of day, to say my dirty underwear looked as though it had been rifled and my papers were in a different order. Most people would assume I was imagining things.' But WB put his hand over hers on the breakfast table and smiled at her gently.

'However, I'm not "most people", Suzanne,' he said, 'and I know you better than that.' He stood up and threw his napkin on the table. 'Come on; let's go and see Henry now.'

They walked back across the lobby and through the discreet door to the side of the reception area.

'Sir, you can't go in there,' squeaked a boy who barely looked old enough to be out of school, let alone manning the reception desk in one of Nairobi's best hotels. But WB just waved a lazy hand in his direction.

'It's okay, lad,' he said, 'I'm an old friend of Lord Booth. We're just going to say hello.' Suzanne looked back over her shoulder at the boy; from his expression, he didn't seem to know whether he should be surprised, indignant or respectful. In the end, he just shrugged and turned back to the businessman who was waiting to check out.

At the end of the corridor, a door was marked 'Hotel Manager'. WB rapped sharply on the panels and on hearing an invitation to 'come', pushed open the door and poked his head around it.

'Henry, me old mate, how the devil are you?' Suzanne giggled at the fake cockney accent coming from the mouth of the huge Ugandan. She heard someone swear in surprise and then the sound of a chair being pushed back.

'Wilberforce, my God, I thought you were dead!' The voice was deep, rich, plummy—and very definitely British upper class. WB turned back to her and held the door open, gesturing for her to precede him. She walked into the office and found herself looking downwards at a tiny, rotund white man in a brightly coloured waistcoat and matching bow tie. 'Wowser, who have we here then, Wilberforce?' he said, looking back up at Suzanne.

'Suzanne, allow me to introduce the Honourable Henry Fortesque Williams, 5th Earl of Branchester, manager of this hotel, but better known to me, at least, as my old mate Henry.' Then, turning to his friend, 'Henry, this is Miss Suzanne Jones. She's with the British government.' Henry looked a bit concerned at this news—and Suzanne wondered if she should correct the misapprehension, but WB went on and it was too late to say anything. 'She's in Kenya on official pharmaceutical business.'

'Well, Miss Jones, I'm delighted to meet you,' the hotel manager said, pointing to a seating area in the corner of the office away from his desk, 'sit down, both of you. Can I get you some coffee?' They both declined and WB rested his hand on the other man's shoulder.

'Henry, this isn't a social call, I'm afraid. We can have dinner tonight if you're free and I can bring you up to date on all the news, but I'm afraid we're here because Miss Jones believes there was someone in her room yesterday evening, going through her things.'

Suzanne had never seen such a change come over someone so quickly. In an instant, the colourful clown was gone, replaced by a serious professional hotel manager.

'Tell me,' was all he said. Haltingly at first, then with more confidence as she realised neither man was looking sceptical, Suzanne told her story once more. 'And you're absolutely sure the safe was untouched?' he asked when she'd finished her story. She nodded her head.

'Yes, I'm sure. The necklace I'd been wearing the previous night was lying on top of my travel folder, just where I put it before I left for the Ministry meeting yesterday morning.'

'Hmmm, I wonder...' he said, staring into space for a few minutes. 'Miss Jones, I think we'd better go up to your room straight away, if you don't mind.' He reached into his desk drawer and pulled out a large bunch of keys. 'I have a suspicion I know what's going on—but I hope I'm wrong.'

As the three arrived at the eighth floor, it was a hive of activity. Trolleys were lined up along the corridor and laughter and chatter came from open doors as maids serviced the rooms already vacated by business people on their way to meetings or the airport. As they passed one of the rooms, a young girl walked out to collect supplies from the trolley. She jumped back with a smile when she saw Suzanne and the two men striding along the corridor.

'Good morning, madam, sirs,' she said.

'Hello, Daisy, nice to see you back,' called Fortesque Williams, not breaking stride. Suzanne hurried after him and as they stopped outside her room, she felt herself going very warm and guessed her face was bright pink.

'That's her,' she said. 'That's the girl I was suspicious of.'

'Who, Daisy? She's one of my best members of staff. She's been with me for years—just got back from a family wedding in Mombasa.'

'Oh dear,' said Suzanne, 'I have a horrible feeling I might have been letting my feelings run away with me. I think this might be a bit of a wild goose chase.' But WB put his hand on her arm and shook his head.

'With your recent experiences, you have every right to be a little jumpy. If there's nothing to worry about, then so much the better, but we'll just check everything through for you, anyway.' He looked across at his old friend. 'I'll explain everything later, Henry. Let's just say Miss Jones has not been seeing Africa at its best recently. Now, Suzanne, if you wouldn't mind...' and he indicated the door.

As soon as she walked into the room, Suzanne knew her fears were justified. The maids hadn't been in yet and the bed was untouched, but the curtains, which she'd left closed, were wide open, as was the wardrobe door and the safe. WB strode across and peered inside.

'All gone, I'm afraid, Suzanne. The safe is completely empty.' Suzanne sat down with a bump on the bed, clutching her capacious handbag to her chest.

'I was rather afraid of that,' said Fortesque Williams. He walked over to the safe and ran his fingers across the key pad. 'It's a trick I've heard used once or twice in the past. Did you notice anything strange about this keypad when you opened the safe last night?' he asked Suzanne. She shook her head and looked at him in a puzzled way as he continued speaking. 'Have you ever heard of gangs robbing hole in the wall machines back home?' She nodded her head.

'Something about stealing numbers when they're being used by customers?'

'Yes, that's right. There are two ways it can be done. One is to have a person lurking or a camera positioned to observe the numbers when they're keyed into the pad by a user. But the other is to insert a device into the keypad which steals the information as it's keyed in.'

'And you think this sort of technology has been used here?' asked WB.

'Almost certainly. Just think: why would someone go to the trouble of breaking into a room, taking nothing, but leaving such obvious signs to tell the occupant they've been in there?'

'To make them suspicious—' began WB.

'—and to make them go and check the safe,' concluded Suzanne.

'Yes, I'm afraid you were set up, Miss Jones. They knew if you were suspicious, you would check out the contents of the safe.'

'Which I did straight away. Oh, how could I have been so stupid?' exclaimed Suzanne.

'Don't blame yourself, Miss Jones,' said the hotel manager, 'it's the natural reaction—which is exactly what they were relying on.'

'So do we know which method they used?' asked WB. Suzanne didn't want to think about this. The possibility there was an illicit camera spying on her in her hotel room was just too much to contemplate. Fortesque Williams glanced around and then looked back at her with a smile, seeming to read her mind.

'I'll get my security people to have a look around,' he said, 'but I don't think it was a camera. There's a rough patch on the side of the keypad that suggests it's been tampered with. I think your privacy is safe, Miss Jones.'

'If not your valuables,' growled WB.

'Come back to my office and let's get this reported. I don't think we'll be able to find them, but the security tapes might give us some idea.'

'And I'd like another room, please,' said Suzanne.

'Of course; I'll get it sorted straight away and get the maid to move your luggage.'

'No!' Suzanne's voice came out more harshly than she'd intended and she swallowed hard as the men stared at her in surprise. 'No, thank you, but I'll pack and move my stuff myself. I've had enough of strangers going through my things lately.'

As the three went back down to the manager's office, they bumped into Chibesa and Charlie coming in through the revolving door into the foyer. They were dressed in running kit and seemed to have had a fair workout, judging by the sweat running down both faces and the dark patches under their armpits.

By the time they'd been brought up to speed, the

break-in reported and the security tapes had confirmed this was a professional job with no slip ups, it was close on midday. WB made arrangements to meet Fortesque Williams for dinner that evening and then the four friends went into the hotel restaurant for lunch. And only then, sitting out on the lawn under the trees, with no-one else within earshot, did Suzanne feel comfortable enough to admit to her friends that although her room had been broken into and her safe broken open, she had not, in fact, lost all her documents. As she hugged her bag to her chest once more, she confessed that after her concerns of the previous night, she had emptied everything out of the safe before she went to bed and transferred it all to her handbag. And even then, she couldn't explain why she hadn't felt safe enough to make this confession in the hotel manager's office—or indeed in her room when the open safe was first discovered.

.

# 25: ZAMBIA; DEC 2004

'Mini-bar; can I service the mini-bar, madam?'

The knock at the door of her hotel room came just as Suzanne was putting the finishing touches to her make-up. The team had returned from Nairobi that afternoon and they were having dinner together with Sara Matsebula before Suzanne and Charlie flew home for Christmas.

She inspected her caller through the spyglass in the door. She couldn't see the man's face, as he was bent over a trolley full of miniature bottles, bags of nuts and tins of crisps, writing on a clipboard. She unlocked the door and headed back into the bathroom, calling over her shoulder:

'Help yourself; could I have some extra bottles of water please?'

When there was no reply, she poked her head out of the bathroom. 'I said, could I have some...' but the words died in her mouth as she realised the person standing just inside her room, in the process of closing and locking the door with his left hand, was no mini-bar waiter. In fact he wasn't even a member of the hotel staff. Even before she saw his face, she knew who it was, from the strange angle at which he held his right arm. It was Kabwe Mazoka.

She gasped and looked around wildly for her mobile,

cursing herself under her breath when she realised she'd left it in her bag—on the other side of the room. And how could she have been so easily fooled? No wonder Charlie said she needed looking after. She remembered the house phone, on the desk just around the corner from the bathroom door and wondered if she could make it before Kabwe did. He must have seen her glance and read her mind. He put a hand out to her and spoke quietly.

'No, Mrs Suzanne, please don't. I need to talk to you.'

'Well, I have no wish to talk to you!' she cried, 'How dare you come here—after what you did!' He was shaking his head, but she carried on, her fear and anger making her voice shrill and loud. 'You had me kidnapped, you burnt down your own factory with all the women in it, you've killed God knows how many with your fake drugs.'

'I didn't know what they were going to do,' he said. 'I'd never have got involved if I'd known.'

'Am I expected to believe that?' Her voice was still unlike her normal one and she swallowed, trying to bring it back under control.

'It's true,' he said, 'please believe me! I know I'm a bad man—and I know I'm going to pay for that—but I never thought it would go this far.' He took a step towards her, but she walked backwards, away from him, desperately scanning the room for a weapon she could use if he tried to attack her—as she assumed he would, sooner or later.

Kabwe stopped following her and walked towards the window. They were on floor 15 and she hadn't pulled the curtains yet. He stared out in silence at the lights of the city as the night took over from the day.

'It wasn't for me, you know,' he said finally, turning with a sigh to face her once more. 'It was for my mother. She was very ill—needed medicines, but I couldn't afford them, not when father died. And all those women, they would have lost their jobs if we'd shut the factory down.'

'Instead of which, they lost their lives,' Suzanne said coldly.

Kabwe nodded and echoed her words. 'Instead of which, they lost their lives. Mrs Suzanne, I swear to you—' But she had heard enough.

'Kabwe, what are you doing here? Why have you come? If you're planning to kill me, just get on with it.' He was looking out of the window once more and she moved suddenly towards the door, thinking maybe she could get into the corridor and then scream for help. But he must have seen her reflection moving in the glass; he ran to intercept her and grabbed her arm, holding her still.

'Please, Mrs Suzanne, wait! I'm so sorry. I want to explain it all to you,' he said, 'tell you everything. Then you can explain it to the authorities.' He released her arm and sat down on the sofa, wiping his hand across his eyes. 'Please, sit and listen to me,' he begged.

Suzanne was far from convinced by this show of penitence and remorse. Nevertheless, if he was speaking the truth and if he did have information that would help them bring down Banda, she didn't want to miss the opportunity. She walked across to the door, unlocked it, then turned and stood with her back pressed against it, as far away as possible from her unexpected visitor. Now she was a tiny step closer to safety.

'Okay, Kabwe,' she said, 'I'm listening.'

*The men first came to see me just a couple of weeks after my father, God rest his soul, passed. They talked about the responsibilities I had to the workers, to my family, to my mother—and reminded me I needed another contract to replace the one we'd lost, if the company was to survive.*

*At first, much of the work was legitimate, with the occasional order for drugs to go into cartons with foreign names and overseas addresses. And even if the packaging wasn't right, I knew the contents were safe. We still followed all the rules and checked the batches before we packed them.*

*As time went on, the number of 'special' orders increased and for the past year or so, we've done nothing but make fake lotions and cough mixtures. I knew it was wrong, but I didn't know how to get out of it. Every time I tried to argue with them, they reminded me of my sick mother and once they threatened to make her even sicker, if I didn't do as I was told.*

*A couple of months ago, things started to go badly wrong. I knew there was something up, from the way they were talking. They'd always been edgy, but now they were extra-cautious about everything. It was after your conference in Swaziland.*

*Then I had a letter from Dr Businge, asking me if we would take part in the pilot scheme and informing me you were going to visit Ndola and inspect the factory. They wanted me to say no, but I couldn't work out how to do that without making you all suspicious. So we arranged for your visit. And one of the bosses came over from Ukraine to keep an eye on you; Nico, his name was; Nico Mladov.*

*As soon as you saw the labels and started asking for contact names in the multinationals, I knew we were in trouble. Their guy told me they would take care of it—hide you away for a couple of days while we moved to safety. We'd spent the previous week packing up my house—my mother passed recently, so I was planning to move to somewhere smaller anyway, somewhere with fewer memories. And they told me we needed to shut the factory down for a little while— just until the spotlight had moved on to somewhere else. I was worried about the workers, but they told me not to be—they would look after them.*

*So that afternoon, when you visited the factory, they told me they were sending an alternative car for you—and to make up a story so you would get in to it, rather than waiting for your own driver. When that broken down vehicle arrived, I didn't think you were going to get in—and part of me hoped you wouldn't—but then you drove away, just before the real driver arrived. And I thought that was it. A couple of days of discomfort—just to let us sort out the factory and then we could all disappear for a while.*

*But then when they took me away to hide, I realised they were just going to leave you there—and I couldn't let that happen. I managed to slip away from them when we stopped for coffee and made that call to Lusaka. Again, I thought that was it—the end of the problem. It was only days later when I heard about the fire, the death of all those poor women, who trusted me, and I realised I had to be brave—do what is right, no matter what the consequences for me.*

*Most of them remained nameless and didn't give much away, but over the months and years, I managed to pick up some pieces of information. The members of Banda that I met were mostly local; but the gang bosses are white. They come from Eastern Europe, Ukraine I think, or maybe Poland. But I don't think the operation is controlled even from there. I've heard them mention 'the Brit' as the controller of all the money—and I've also heard them refer to that person as 'she'.*

*That is all I know, and all I can tell you. But I, Kabwe Mazoka, swear this to be the whole truth, so help me God.*

As he finished speaking, Kabwe stood up and walked towards her, reaching into his pocket with his left hand. Suzanne flinched, expecting to see a knife or a gun, but all he brought out was a small brown envelope which he held out to her.

'My statement, plus the names and any other facts I've managed to uncover, are in this envelope. I've also sent a copy to Dr Businge and Mr Desai.'

There was a sharp knock at the door. Kabwe jumped, looking startled. Suzanne, shocked and distressed by what she'd heard, took the envelope from him and turned to the door.

'It's probably only Charlie,' she said, but mindful of the previous time she'd let someone in without properly checking, she put her eye to the spy hole. Her sister was standing just outside. 'Yes, it is; I'll talk to her and then we'll decide how to go on from here.'

Pulling the door open, Suzanne saw Charlie's eyes widen as she caught sight of Kabwe standing across the room. She'd never met him, but she'd seen his picture often enough since the kidnapping.

'What the hell's he doing here—are you okay?' She tried to push her way into the room, but Suzanne grabbed her sister by the arm and stepped out into the corridor to join her.

'Yes, I'm fine, don't panic. He came to offer his help catching Banda.'

'And you believe him? You actually let him into your room! Are you crazy?'

'Hush, Charlie and listen to me,' Suzanne urged. In a few sentences, she brought her sister up to date. 'And he thinks the financial controller is British and female,' she finished.

'Well, I'm still not convinced, given what's happened so far,' Charlie said, 'but if he really is willing to help, maybe we can use him to find out more about her. The more evidence we have, the better.'

'I don't think he knows more than he's already told me; but let's call the others up here. We can read his statement and ask Kabwe for more details as we go along.'

Suzanne turned and went back through the door, followed by her sister. But the room was empty and the door to the balcony was wide open. From the street fifteen floors below came the sound of squealing brakes and blaring horns. Then someone started to scream.

# 26: ZAMBIA; DEC 2004

As the last person to see Kabwe alive, and the one to receive his confession and information about members of Banda, Suzanne was told she had to stick around for the police investigation. So she and Charlie cancelled their plans for Christmas in London and postponed their flight home. Two days later, they met in Chibesa's office with WB and Sara for their own review of events.

'The police have rounded up a couple of guys who were living here in Lusaka,' Suzanne told them, 'and they're working with police in Ndola, so they're quite hopeful about catching the ones who live in the Copper Belt. But they're not optimistic of catching the foreign members of the gang. They'll be long gone; probably back in Eastern Europe by now.'

'Well, at least we've managed to interrupt the supply chain,' said Chibesa.

'But how long before the next one springs up?'

'Not too long, I suspect,' said WB, shaking his head. 'These were only the foot soldiers; we need to take out the generals if we're going to win the war, rather than just an occasional battle.'

'I'm hoping I might be able to help there.' Charlie

hadn't taken any part in the discussion so far; she had been tapping rapidly at her keyboard. They all looked at her expectantly. 'You remember our first meeting, when we talked about chasing the money?'

'Of course,' Chibesa said. 'You got so far and then lost the trail.'

'Well, I've been doing a bit more digging—'

'—and did you manage to get a name for the account?'

'Not yet, but I'm getting there. I'll let you know if I come up with anything.'

Later, back in the hotel, the sisters sat in the shade, sipping rock shandies. Charlie was chewing on her thumb nail.

'Okay, Charlie,' Suzanne said, putting down her drink and folding her arms, 'spit it out. There's something bugging you, isn't there? I could tell back in the office.'

'It's that account I was chasing. I did find a name, but it's so odd, I didn't want to say anything to the others until we'd had a chance to think about it.' She pulled open her laptop.

Suzanne looked over her sister's shoulder, but when she saw the name Charlie was pointing to, she laughed.

'Little Piggy M? Well, there's a coincidence. What with me seeing our own Little Piggy recently, after more than a decade. And fancy this one having those particular initials—' Then she stopped, jumped up from the table and looked at her sister in horror. She could see the same look reflected back at her. 'No, you don't think so, do you? It can't possibly be the same one.'

'No, I don't think so, not really. She was bit of a pain, but she was always honest, painfully so, in fact.'

'Though it might explain why she insisted on coming to my presentation—'

'—and if she managed to have a go at Sir Frederick, that would explain why he warned you off getting too close to Sara.'

'But why on earth would Francine Matheson be mixed

up in all this? She's Parliamentary Undersecretary in the Department for International Development, for goodness sake.'

'Exactly!' Charlie said. 'She's in the ideal position to influence things for Banda. And, let's face it, she wouldn't be the first dirty politician, either at home or here in Africa, now would she?' But Suzanne was shaking her head.

'Come on, there's a world of difference between fiddling a few work permits and profiting from counterfeit drugs sold to vulnerable people.'

'You're probably right,' Charlie said, 'and that's why I didn't say anything to the others, but let's keep an open mind on this. We need to find out a bit more about what Francine Matheson's been getting up to since you were sitting in the sixth form common room with her all those years ago.'

When the team weren't working on their theory that someone in the UK was funding the supply of counterfeit drugs, Charlie spent most of the time with Chibesa, either running before breakfast through the streets of Lusaka or helping him organise the Christmas festivities for the Aids orphans living in his house. Suzanne, on the other hand had been looking forward to the opportunity to chill out, and intended to spend most of the time lying by the hotel pool. But that was before she had a phone call from Nathan.

She hadn't heard from him since they'd left the Copper Belt and had decided to put the whole thing down to experience and move on. Now, at the sound of his voice, she felt herself moving into her boiled lobster impersonation and was very glad video phones hadn't reached Zambia yet.

'Suzanne, I'm coming into Lusaka tomorrow, on my way to Jo'burg. I was wondering if you would care to have dinner with me.' And just like that, her resolution disappeared and her time ceased to be her own. When she was not at the police station or in the IHF office, she was in the company of the elegant mixed-race ranch owner.

On the first evening, he arrived at the hotel five minutes early. She had wondered if he would come to her room to meet her, and whether she would object if he did. But in the event, the receptionist called her down to the foyer. Deciding to take the stairs rather than the ancient elevator, she had the opportunity to observe him unnoticed from the first floor balcony. He looked cool and relaxed in a smart casual kind of way. But when she walked down the final flight of stairs and he caught sight of her, his face lit up in a bright, excited smile. A smile she was sure was reflected on her face. He held out a bunch of proteus and jacaranda.

'For you,' he said, before turning to a messenger standing discreetly in the corner. 'Please put these flowers in water and take then to Madam's room.' Then he took her arm and steered her gently towards the door.

Suzanne had been anxious she would find it difficult to hide her attraction to Nathan—and that would be tongue-tied in his presence. But there was no need to worry.

'You've had quite a time of it over the past few days, I understand,' he said. So, she was able to recap everything that had happened since they returned to Lusaka. By the time they had exhausted that subject and moved on to more pleasant topics, she was completely relaxed. But there was one thing she felt she couldn't leave unspoken.

'How's Lily?'

'She's fine, as far as I know.' Nathan shrugged and pulled a wry face. 'I've not seen her very much lately. She's very tied up with her latest conquest and hasn't been out to the farm since you guys were there.'

'Her latest conquest…?'

'Yes. Some guy she met in an airport lounge somewhere. She was on the phone to Mother last week. Apparently it was Julius this… and Julius that…. It probably won't last—they never do!'

'Well they certainly looked close when I saw…' Too late, Suzanne regretted opening her mouth, but Nathan looked puzzled and so she went on, 'when we were in Kenya last week, I saw them in the distance at a restaurant.' He smiled and nodded.

'Yes, that would be right; she told mother she was spending a few days with him in Nairobi.'

'And you don't mind?'

'Mind? Why should I mind? It's nothing to do with me—and although she looks young and vulnerable…' He broke off and stared at her for a moment, then began to laugh. 'Oh, no! You've been listening to Mother's stories, haven't you?' Suzanne felt her face go warm.

'Well, when we were getting our tour of the farm, she did imply—'

'Suzanne, my mother's been matchmaking since I was old enough to shave! She's always had a soft spot for Lily and built this story around the possibility of us getting together. But it was never going to happen!'

'So there was nothing between you?'

'When we were teenagers, it was a useful device, especially for Lily. We would go off together, to a dance or the cinema, and we would come home together at the end of the night. But we never spent the evening together. Lily's great fun, but she's too much like my sister. We could never get together like that.'

'So why doesn't she like me?'

'What makes you think she doesn't like you?'

'Well, she didn't seem too pleased when we were staying at the farm.'

'Oh, that was nothing to do with you. She's the same when anyone else gets a bit of attention. Likes to be centre stage, does our Lily.' He reached across the table and squeezed her hand. 'Right, enough about Lily. I'm starving; let's order, shall we?'

Dinner lasted well into the small hours of the morning

and she was slightly disappointed when he dropped her back at the hotel, handed her out of the car, kissed her cheek and wished her sweet dreams. But as she walked away, he promised to call the next morning. And he did—at seven-thirty, as she was sipping her early morning tea, barely awake.

'I couldn't wait any longer,' he said. 'Have breakfast with me?' And when she walked out on to the terrace twenty minutes later, he was sitting waiting for her, squinting into the sun and sipping a glass of orange juice. Afterwards, he took her to visit Victoria Falls and they watched the sun go down over Lake Kariba. Their dinner took even longer that evening—and he didn't leave her at the door of the hotel this time.

Nathan kept a small penthouse in an apartment block in the centre of Lusaka. It was here they had dinner, here they shared their first passionate kiss, and here she woke next morning in a double bed, to the smell of coffee and bacon.

Suzanne went back to the hotel later that morning to change her clothes and to see Charlie. She was worried her sister might be concerned about her absence, especially considering what happened last time they lost touch overnight. But it turned out Nathan was as considerate of her sister as he was of her—and had texted her the previous evening to warn her. Suzanne didn't ask what time the text had arrived; she didn't want to find out how presumptuous he had been, but she was touched by the gesture.

The next three days went in a whirl and then it was over. The police announced they were satisfied with their investigations and would be prosecuting the members of Banda denounced by Kabwe. They were also satisfied that Suzanne was no more than an observer in his death—and she was free to go.

When she told Nathan she had to go home, he nodded.

'And I must continue my journey to Jo'burg,' he said.

Her English reserve prevented her from asking him whether she would ever see him again, but she suspected not. She had no more trips planned for the foreseeable future and it was a very long way from a ranch on the Copper Belt to Heathrow Airport and the city of London.

She refused to allow him to accompany her to the airport. 'I so hate goodbyes, don't you?' she said. And he agreed. In fact, she thought she sensed just a touch of relief in his face, although she might have been mistaken. He arranged to take the morning flight to South Africa. Their final evening was reflective, and a little sad. It was also New Year's Eve and they stood on his balcony in silence at midnight, watching fireworks rise from the city skyline. When she woke the next morning, he was gone, leaving a note on the pillow and the faint smell of his cologne in the air.

PART III

# 27: ENGLAND; MAR 2005

'Ms Matheson,' said the toffee-nosed PA into the telephone, 'there's a Ms Jones to see you. Ms Suzanne Jones.' There was a distinct sniff in her voice. 'She doesn't have an appointment. But she says you are old friends.'

After listening to her boss's response, she stood and walked from behind her desk, twisted her face into what probably passed for a smile in her case and pointed towards the oak panelled door to the inner office.

'Ms Matheson can just about fit you into her schedule, but she's very busy, so you're only going to be able to stay for about fifteen minutes,' she said.

It was more than two months since Suzanne and Charlie had returned to London after the traumatic trip to Africa.

On her first day back at work, Suzanne had briefed Sir Frederick on progress with the IHF project. She'd spent as much time as she could updating him on the factory visits, the company assessments and the pilot study they planned to commence over the coming year.

Then, quietly and calmly, she told him about the incidents surrounding her visit to Mazokapharm. He was visibly shocked, although whether by the loss of life at the factory, her imprisonment or Kabwe's suicide, she couldn't judge. She assured him she had suffered no lasting physical damage and persuaded him there was nothing he could have done to help then, or since.

He made her promise never to keep anything from him in the future—but it was a promise she immediately broke. He was already questioning her judgement in not reporting back as soon as her kidnap was over, and she didn't want to risk his further disapproval. So she didn't tell him about Charlie's trip to Africa. She didn't tell him about Sara Matsebula's presence in Lusaka. And she didn't tell him about their suspicions that Banda had been funded from Europe and probably from the UK.

Since then, the sisters had debated long and hard about their next step. Deep down, Suzanne still wasn't convinced Francine was involved in the counterfeiting but her sister was less certain; and they both agreed it was a 'line of enquiry', as Charlie kept calling it, that needed to be eliminated. They had finally agreed Suzanne should visit Francine and challenge her directly.

Suzanne had decided to arrive unannounced, hoping to catch the politician unawares. There was a risk, of course, that she couldn't, or wouldn't, see her, but it was worth taking if it allowed her to catch Francine on the hop, before she had a chance to destroy any evidence or get her story straight. Suzanne had seen her tackled in the House on difficult questions more than once, and knew she was able to think on her feet. She didn't want her to have that opportunity today if she really was hiding something.

The office door opened and Francine stepped out of her office, an apparent smile of welcome on her face.

'Suzanne, what a pleasant surprise,' she said, 'come on in.' As Suzanne passed her, Francine spoke to her PA. 'I think we'll bring elevenses forward a few minutes, Marjorie. Can we have it now, please? Suzanne, do you still drink Earl Grey with lemon?'

Taken aback that her old school friend—she'd only

slightly exaggerated their friendship to talk her way past the PA—had remembered a detail like that, Suzanne could only nod her thanks.

The two women chatted about inconsequential things until the tea was delivered. Then Suzanne looked at her watch.

'I know you haven't got long, Francine, but there's something I need to ask you—and I didn't want to do it by phone.'

'Well, that sounds intriguing,' Francine said with a laugh, 'and don't worry about Miss Snooty-Pants out there. Despite what she thinks, I still decide how I spend my time. Now, what can I do for you?' Suzanne swallowed.

'I wanted to ask how well you know Nico Mladov.' Francine sat up very straight and her cup rattled against the teaspoon as she dropped it back onto the saucer. She stared out of the window briefly and when she turned back to Suzanne, her cheeks were very red.

'You know, I really envied you when we were at school!'

'Me? Why, for goodness sake?'

'You had it all! You were bright—'

'Not as bright as you—I seem to remember you beating me in virtually every exam we did.'

'But do you know how hard I had to work to do that? I studied late into the night, every night, desperate to get a better score than you.'

'Why?' asked Suzanne again.

'Well, not only were you bright, you had friends, you were always the life and soul of every gathering—and you had Charlie too.'

'But you had friends as well, Francine.'

'Huh, only those kids who thought they could get something out of the poor little rich girl. That's the only thing I had more of than you—money. And it didn't get me anywhere, now did it?' Suzanne looked around the office, with its rich oak panelling, book-lined walls and a display of photos of Francine with leading politicians and other dignitaries from around the world.

'Well,' she said dryly, 'you don't seem to have done so badly for yourself.'

'But this is so transient,' was the bitter reply, 'and half the time, I don't feel I'm doing any good at all. We spend so long trying to get into Parliament—and then most of our time trying to stay here—that I'm not sure what the point is anymore.'

Suzanne realised with a jolt that the skilled politician at the other side of the desk was controlling the meeting pretty well. She'd asked a question, but Francine had neatly side-stepped it—and it still hadn't been answered.

'Nico Mladov,' she asked once again. 'Francine, I need to know if you know him or have had any dealings with him?'

'Never heard of him.' The professional politician was back again. 'I have no idea who he is or why you think I should have heard of him.'

'What about Mazokapharm?'

'No. Should I have?'

'No, not necessarily—but we think you have.'

'Well, I come across all sorts of companies in this job. And there are loads of little outfits in Africa. Why do you think I've come across this one in particular?'

'I can't tell you that, Francine,' Suzanne said, acutely aware she was on dodgy ground since her information had come from Charlie's illegal hacking activities. 'But I've seen evidence to suggest you've been in contact with them very recently and that what they're involved in is illegal.'

'If there's evidence, then you'd better show it to me.' Francine paused and looked closely at her. 'You can't, can you? The information's not kosher.' She sat back with a smile on her face. 'So, I think this meeting is at an end.'

Suzanne sighed, picked up her bag and walked to the door. As she reached out to turn the handle a thought struck her.

'A little outfit in Africa?'

'Pardon me?' said Francine. She was still sitting at her desk, leafing through papers, but her hands stilled at Suzanne's words.

'You said "a little outfit in Africa". But I didn't mention Africa—and I certainly didn't say what size the company is. How did you know, Francine?'

'Well, let me see,' Francine said, 'seeing as you're working on a major project to try to cut out counterfeit drugs in the Dark Continent, I would think that was an obvious guess. And seeing as it's not a company I've heard of, it's a safe bet that it's a small one. Also it's a figure of speech.' Francine resumed her perusal of the papers. 'Oh—and Mazoka is a Zambian name, from the Shona language. Very common in Southern Africa, but not well-known elsewhere. I did do a degree at the School of Oriental and African Studies, you know.' She looked up and gave Suzanne a dazzling smile, although her eyes signalled a different message. 'So glad you could drop in. We must do it again sometime. Goodbye, Suzanne.'

'Francine.' Suzanne nodded and headed out of the office. 'Well done, Ms Jones,' she hissed to herself as she waited for the elevator at the end of the plushly carpeted corridor. Despite Francine's flustered initial reaction, they weren't really any closer to knowing whether their suspicions were justified or whether it was just a coincidence in the name. And, far from catching Francine Matheson unawares and surprising a confession out of her, if she was tied up with Banda, Suzanne had succeeded in alerting her to their suspicions without getting her to admit anything.

Reluctant to return to the office and the pile of messages waiting for her to deal with, or to the flat and face Charlie, Suzanne turned right when she exited Portcullis House and strolled around the corner into Whitehall. They didn't seem to be getting anywhere with the investigations and every day they delayed meant more children at risk of death through fake drugs. Banda had been dismantled in Zambia, but Suzanne was under no illusions that this was any more than a small step towards stopping the whole dirty business. She desperately needed a breakthrough. Something that would allow her a step forward. She wandered aimlessly, turning right into Northumberland Place, and found herself a few minutes later back on the Embankment. She crossed the road under the railway bridge, where trains rattled continuously into Charing Cross or south-eastwards towards Kent.

In front of her was the tall dark mass of Cleopatra's Needle. She stared at the dirty, scarred lump of rock that must once, according to legend, have been gazed on by the great Egyptian queen herself. *What would you have done, Cleo?* she mused. *If you thought one of your politicians might be a dangerous criminal, but you had no real proof and no-one believed you. What would you do?* But she knew the answer to that. An adder in the bed, a drop of poison in a goblet of wine— and it would all have been over. The queen would mourn at the funeral, light the pyre herself—a great honour for an important man or woman—and then the affairs of state would move on. Suzanne grinned to herself as she toyed momentarily with the idea of surreptitiously wiping out a member of Her Majesty's government, and then shook her head. This wasn't ancient Egypt; the only place where that sort of thing happened these days was in a James Bond movie—and James Bond didn't exist, much as they'd like him to on occasion.

'Besides,' Suzanne said to herself, 'even if she is involved, I don't believe Francine is a major player. I suspect she's little more than an incidental. Taking her out won't help to bring down the rest of the network—and that's what we need to do.' But at the back of her mind, there was a tiny voice asking, what if she was wrong? What if Francine Matheson was a much bigger fish than they all realised?

When her phone buzzed, she didn't know whether to

be surprised, relieved or frightened to see she had received an email from the very person she'd been thinking about. There were just three words: 'daffodil bed, four'. Suzanne glanced at her watch. It was a quarter to three. She crossed back over the road and turned into a tiny café on the corner of Northumberland Avenue. She ordered Earl Grey with lemon and then sat, absentmindedly stirring the tea while her thoughts churned.

So Francine had remembered other things from school, as well as her tea-drinking habits. One of their games was to invent journeys around London, picking up clues as they went along. They weren't real journeys. They rarely got a chance to travel to London from their grammar school outside Exeter; and when they did, they were always chaperoned, never alone. But they had a large map of the capital, carefully drawn and illustrated as part of an old A Level project, years before. The map had ended up in the lower sixth common room and had formed a basic part of 'London Loiters'. Each term, one of the girls would design a journey, with codes, puzzles and red herrings, which all the others would try to solve. The winner took on the puzzle setting for the next term.

When Francine and Suzanne were in the lower sixth, Suzanne had won the game in the autumn term; narrowly beating Francine who was just one clue behind her at the final stage. Over the Christmas break, she and Charlie had spent every spare minute inventing fiendish clues to keep their schoolmates guessing. It had proved to be one of the most difficult—and the most popular—of the routes during their time at the school. At one point in the journey, the traveller had to visit the grave of a long dead poet, the opening of whose famous work was the only line of poetry most people could quote. So the question Suzanne had to ask herself was, why would Francine want to meet her at Wordsworth's Memorial in Westminster Abbey—and why was she being so mysterious?

'Well, there's only one way to find out,' she said aloud,

then drained her tea and left the bistro.

She arrived at Westminster Abbey with twenty minutes to spare. She wanted to be there before Francine, observe her arrival, check she wasn't being followed—and then decide whether she would talk to her or not.

*Although why I should be worried about talking to a government official in daylight, in the middle of London, I have no idea*, she thought. But she did know really. Since her ordeal in Africa, she was very wary about meeting anyone, anywhere. She had lost her trust in most people—and it was going to take some time for it to come back. She'd even had to steel herself to make the trip to visit Francine that morning.

Suzanne took up her position in a tiny side chapel near the resting place of four Tudor monarchs. On this late summer's afternoon, there were a lot of people around and she wondered, once again, about Francine's choice of meeting place. She watched in amusement as a party of schoolchildren, led by a harassed-sounding young teacher, stopped to look at the great man's tomb.

'What did William Wordsworth write?' the teacher asked. Several of the youngsters, who must have been about seven, put their hands up. One jumped up and down in her anxiety to be noticed, bumping into her neighbour, a tough looking little boy, who gave her a shove. 'Yes, Jenny?' said the teacher, pointing to the little girl who had stopped jumping up and down to push the boy back, but now turned to the front, her fight forgotten.

'Daffodils, sir, he wrote a poem about daffodils.'

'Well, he mentioned daffodils in the poem, certainly, although it's not the only thing in there, is it?' was the reply.

'But it's the only thing we all remember, isn't it, Suzanne?' said a quiet voice just behind her. Suzanne jumped. She'd been so intent on watching for Francine in the main body of the abbey, she'd forgotten to check in the recesses, like the chapel she was in. But if she had checked, she didn't think she would have recognised the woman next to her as the Parliamentary Under-Secretary she'd visited a couple of hours before. She was wearing an old black jogging suit with well-used trainers. Her hair was stuffed into an NYC baseball cap and she was wearing a pair of cheap plastic-framed sunglasses. She took Suzanne by the arm and led her towards the entrance to the crypt. 'Come on, there will be fewer prying eyes down here.'

## 28: ENGLAND; MAR 2005

As they walked down the steps to the dim interior, Suzanne's heart began to thud and her breath caught in her throat. She'd not been in any enclosed spaces like this since the hut in Zambia, and she wasn't sure this was a good idea. Supposing Francine was going to kidnap her; supposing she was going to kill her? *Oh, for goodness sake, pull yourself together*, she thought, *she's an old friend—well, an old schoolmate anyway. And we're in the middle of one of the best known and busiest buildings in London.* And yet, whispered the little voice in the back of her head, she's gone out of her way to hide who she is and she's taking you into a deserted part of the building. Suzanne decided to listen to both voices at once, so followed Francine down into the crypt, but stopped when she got to the bottom of the steps, with one hand on the rope banister, ready to run back up to the main body of the church if she got suspicious of the other woman's actions or words.

Francine walked a little way into the crypt then turned to look at Suzanne. She took off her baseball cap and shook out her blonde bob, making her instantly more recognisable—although the clothing was still disconcerting.

'I'm sorry for this little charade,' Francine began, 'but I couldn't afford to let them know I was talking to you—or anyone for that matter.'

'So you do know who they are?'

'Well, yes, I know Nico Mladov and I am aware of Mazokapharm, but I'm not sure how they are connected—and I have no idea why you might be interested in them.'

'I think you'd better tell me what you do know; start from the beginning.'

'Well, it all began after I got elected. You remember what it was like in 1997? Everyone was making a fuss of the new intake of women; and there were all sorts of opportunities flying around for a short while. Well, I managed to talk my way onto an overseas mission to Africa. We visited several different countries—even spent time in Seychelles and Mauritius. So many friends were envious, offered to carry my bags, come and keep me company. They all thought the life of a politician was really glamorous. If only they knew the half of it.'

'Yes, I guess no-one works as hard as you guys in Westminster.' Suzanne tried to keep the sarcasm from her voice, but Francine's wry smile told her she'd not succeeded.

'Our main reason for being there was a conference on International Aid in Lusaka. And that's where I met him.'

'Him?'

'I know it wasn't a smart move, Suzanne; I worked very hard for my constituents when I was on the back benches. And now I do everything I can to ease the plight of the people in the countries we're helping. I genuinely care. But it gets lonely sometimes—and what with all the stress of the election campaign, Gerry and I had been going through a bad patch back home.'

'Go on.'

'His name was Ernest. He was beautiful. Tall and slim; pale coffee-coloured skin and the most wonderful voice I've ever heard. He told me he was from Ndola—had come to Lusaka especially for the conference. He was funny, kind and very polite. We sat together during most of the sessions and afterwards, chatted for hours. We even talked about taking a drive to the Cheetah Park if we had any spare time. I'd not had much time for sightseeing—and I'd always wanted to get close to some of the big cats.'

Unbidden, a scene came back to Suzanne of a distraught Francine kneeling in the mud, cradling a bloody body to her, after the headmistress's cat had been run over. Francine went on, staring at the ground and fiddling with the cuff of her sweatshirt, her voice getting quieter.

'He was a perfect gentleman; throughout the five days of the conference. And not once did he try anything on, although I sensed he really liked me. And I really liked him too. And a small part of me wondered why he didn't want to take our friendship further. The part of me that was still a dumpy, unloved schoolgirl.

'Anyway, on the last evening, there was a knock on my bedroom door and there he was. Well, my guard was down and I was happy to see him. It was one of the craziest and most impulsive things I'd ever done.' Francine stopped and Suzanne realised with a shock that the cool politician was crying. Tears rolled down her cheeks and she brushed them angrily away with the back of her hand. Suzanne moved forward to comfort the other woman, but she shook her head and held a hand up to keep her away. 'Afterwards, we agreed it would have to be a one-off. When I awoke the next morning, he was gone. I never saw him again. And I never did get to see the cheetahs.

'The first envelope arrived later that day, addressed to me personally and handed in at the hotel reception. Another one was handed in at the British Embassy. Luckily, they both said 'Private and Confidential'. If we'd been back in London, one of the admin staff would probably have opened them, but when we're out travelling, they stay back home to run the office and we fend for ourselves.'

'What was in the envelopes, Francine?'

'Pictures—pictures of Ernest and me, compromising pictures. There must have been a camera set up in the bedroom.'

'So you think Ernest was in on the set-up?'

'Isn't it obvious? He must have planned the whole thing from the start. The bastard!'

But Suzanne could see her heart wasn't in the condemnation and guessed Francine still clung to a faint hope that her lover had been duped in the same way she had. Although it really didn't seem likely.

'Francine, that's an old trick; they used it all the time in Russia. Although it was usually a glamorous young Soviet girl and a middle-aged or elderly businessman who thought they'd got lucky.'

'Instead of a sad, lonely female who was fool enough to be led on by a handsome face,' said Francine. 'So that's how they caught me. Although there was no further contact during my trip to Africa, or when we got back to England. Gradually, I convinced myself it had all been a bad joke—or that they'd lost their nerve. After a year or so, I stopped being frightened of the daily post and even managed to put the whole thing out of my mind for months at a time. Until last year, when they finally made contact.'

'So what have they asked you to do?' said Suzanne quietly. 'Validate documentation for them? Let them win government tenders? Maybe even give them Overseas Aid grants...' But her voice petered out at the look of complete shock on Francine Matheson's face.

'Good God, what sort of a monster do you take me for? I may be a politician, but I have got some morals left!'

The vehemence of Francine's reply took Suzanne by surprise and seemed completely genuine. She sat down on the cold steps behind her and folded her arms.

'I think you'd better tell me the rest of the story,' she said. Francine swallowed and shook her head.

'Well, there's not a lot more to say. Back in the summer, I had a visit from your Mr Mladov. It was completely unexpected. And as he's Ukrainian, rather than African, I didn't suspect anything to begin with.'

'How did he get close to you?'

'He was part of a delegation that came to my office to talk about trade links and support. He was very charming to begin with.'

Suzanne thought back to that afternoon in her flat, the only occasion when she'd met him. She remembered how initially she'd been quite impressed with the man's suave manner; although Charlie had been uncertain about him from the beginning. And after the burglary in her flat and the tragedy at Mazokapharm, she knew her sister's instincts had been right. Francine continued.

'As they were leaving, he said to me quietly that he was a keen photographer and he would love to talk to me about the photographs I'd picked up during my first trip to Africa. I particularly remember the way he said "picked up". I thought it was a strange way of saying "took", but then I remembered I didn't take any pictures on that trip—my camera had been playing up and I hadn't had time to replace it—so he had to be talking about the ones of me and Ernest.'

'So what did you do?'

'I agreed to meet him again.' She glanced up at Suzanne's startled look and smiled sadly. 'What else could I do?'

'Call his bluff?'

'But at this point, I had no idea what his bluff was. Gerry and I have long since sorted out our difficulties and I didn't want to risk destroying my marriage, not to mention my reputation in Parliament, unnecessarily. I needed to find out what he was planning before I decided what to do.'

'And what was he planning?'

'To be honest, I have no idea. He came back to my

office one evening after work.'

'Wasn't that a bit risky?'

'Well, I thought it was safer than meeting him somewhere else—like the crypt of Westminster Abbey,' she said with a rueful grin. 'It's quite common for MPs to meet with constituents and other people in the evenings. And there are always plenty of people around. In fact, we had a drink in the Members Bar. I remember looking out across the Thames as he was talking to me and wondering whether it was worth calling his bluff and letting him do his worst. But I didn't want to lose everything I'd worked so hard to get—and, frankly, I don't want to have to deal with the humiliation. You do see that, don't you?'

'Francine,' Suzanne said patiently, 'you still haven't told me what he wanted you to do.'

'Nothing,' she said, 'it's that simple; at this point, he just wanted to remind me the pictures exist and to tell me they would be in touch if they needed a favour from me.' Suzanne stared at her in amazement.'

'So, nothing's actually happened so far?' she asked.

'Well, there's a little matter of compromising pictures of an MP and the attempted blackmail of a Parliamentary Undersecretary in Her Britannic Majesty's government— but yes, essentially nothing's happened.' She stopped and looked closely at Suzanne. 'Why, what did you think had happened?'

'I told you earlier—trade links, dodgy contracts and things like that.' But Francine was shaking her head adamantly.

'Suzanne, I thought you knew me better than that. I may be a coward who's scared to let the good people of this country know I've been taken in by a love rat, but I can assure you, if the story has to come out, so be it. There's no way I would let myself get pulled into anything like that. But I think it's more likely to be a simple case of blackmail.'

Suzanne sighed and stood up.

'Okay, Francine, I believe that's what you think is going on. But I suspect it's much more sinister than that.'

'Then I think you'd better fill me in on the details,' was the icy reply. The tears had gone and the calm politician was back in control.

'Well, I will,' Suzanne said, 'but I have one request. Let's get you out of that ridiculous outfit and go and have some dinner. There's nothing suspicious about two old school friends eating together, is there? Besides, it's getting very cold down here.'

# 29: ENGLAND; MAR 2005

Two hours later Suzanne and Charlie, together with The Honourable Francine Matheson, were sitting in the flat in Vauxhall, eating the takeaway they'd collected from Sanjay's. Francine had opted for Chicken Korma with Peshwari Nan, while the sisters ordered their customary Vindaloo. Francine and Suzanne ate off trays on their knees while Charlie sat cross-legged on the floor.

Charlie had been a little taken aback when Suzanne phoned her on the way from Westminster Abbey and warned her about their supper guest but had seemed willing to accept her sister's assurances that she knew what she was doing. The conversation so far had been light-hearted and general. But now Suzanne wiped her fingers on a paper napkin and sat back with a sigh.

'Well, I suppose we'd better get back to the real reason for this little get-together,' she said. In a few words, she brought Charlie up to date on what she'd learnt so far that day. She was pleased and surprised to see that Charlie didn't mock Francine for getting caught in a honey trap; in fact her sister was more sympathetic than she had been.

'When we met earlier,' Suzanne now said, 'your reactions made me suspect you knew Mladov and that was confirmed when we talked in the Abbey. But I also suspected you knew of Mazokapharm and Kabwe Mazoka. How did you come across them?'

'Didn't I say?' said Francine. 'That's where Ernest was working. He told me it was only a tiny company and I got the impression he wasn't going to be there very long, but he'd been picked to go to the conference as one of their representatives.'

'I don't remember anyone called Ernest at the plant when I visited it,' said Suzanne. 'And I thought I'd met, or at least been told about, everyone.'

'I've got a picture of him here,' said Francine. At the sisters' startled looks, she gave a grimace. 'What can I say? He may have turned out to be a bastard, but that week still meant a lot to me and I wanted to keep a souvenir. And before you ask, no it's not one of the ones taken in my hotel room.' She opened her handbag and took out her wallet. In the side pocket was a folded newspaper cutting; it was a report on the conference and included a standard photograph, with all the delegates lined up, smiling and looking as though they were all best friends, even if they had recently been at each other's throats. She pointed to a figure on the back row. 'There, that one at the end. That's Ernest.'

Suzanne took the photograph from Francine, stared at it silently and then handed it over to Charlie.'

'Shit, I don't believe it,' said her sister.

'Well, I think we can say the camera doesn't lie.'

'What is it?' said Francine. 'Do you recognise him? Is it Kabwe Mazoka?'

'Oh yes, we recognise him—and no it's not Kabwe,' said Suzanne.

Staring out at them through round glasses, looking as confident as they'd ever seen him, was Chibesa Desai!

'Shit!' said Charlie once more. Francine looked from one sister to the other, her puzzlement deepening.

'But this doesn't make any sense,' Suzanne said. 'He's

been as damaged as anyone by all this. He's never forgiven himself for George's death.'

'Well, it looks like he's a better actor than we thought,' was Charlie's tart reply.

'I still don't buy it.'

At that point, Francine stood up, put her hands on her hips and stamped her foot—bringing back to Suzanne's mind for an instant, the overweight teenager who'd had a tantrum on the rare occasions her exam results had been beaten by someone else in the class—usually Suzanne. But this wasn't about exam results; this was much more serious than that—and the schoolgirl was now a member of the Government and insisting on some answers. Suzanne patted the sofa next to her. 'Sit down, Francine. There's a lot more to this than you realise—and I think we need to tell you everything.'

Between them, the two sisters brought Francine up to date on everything they knew or suspected: about Mladov, about the lost suitcase, the ransacked and spied-upon flat; about Suzanne's ordeal in Zambia; and about Kabwe Mazoka's disappearance, reappearance and confession—and his subsequent suicide. They told her about the team that had been working with Suzanne on the counterfeiting project: the big powerful Ugandan from the pharmaceutical industry, WB Businge; and the soft-spoken logistics expert from Zambia, Chibesa Desai. Then they told her gently that Chibesa and Ernest were one and the same person. She refused to believe them at first, but when they'd showed her the pictures from the recent IHF conference in Swaziland, she had to accept it.

'And because anything else would be a coincidence way too big to be believed, we have to assume his involvement in Suzanne's team and his seduction of you are part of the same operation,' said Charlie.

'Charlie,' said Suzanne, 'I think we have to explain to Francine why we came after her in the first place.' Her sister went pale and bit her lip. 'It's okay; given the circumstances, I don't think she's in any position to report you, but,' turning to Francine, 'what we're about to tell you may be compromising for all my team, and Charlie in particular, so we're trusting you to handle the information sensitively.' Francine nodded impatiently and looked at Charlie, who took a deep breath.

'We needed to follow the money, to know who was talking to whom, so I did some fancy things with my computer.'

'By "fancy things", I take it you mean hacking,' said Francine icily.

'Oh, shit, sis, I told you this wasn't a good idea.' Charlie turned to Suzanne with a despairing look on her face. But her sister just put a hand on Francine's arm to quieten her and nodded for Charlie to continue. She pulled a face but then carried on speaking. 'We have reason to believe that Mazokapharm was involved in some heavy duty counterfeit manufacture. Suzanne can give you the evidence for that later on if you need to see it. And it seemed that most of their funding was coming from Mladov's gang, Banda.

'The money was obviously being hidden; it was quite tortuous to follow—and I almost lost it in the Cayman Islands. But finally I picked up the trail again—and it led me right back here to London and to a special account in your name.'

'In my name? That's impossible!' Francine jumped up and started striding around the room. 'I've not got any secret accounts, special or otherwise. Why would I have? I get sufficient money from my day job.'

'In my experience, few people would ever accept they had "sufficient money", no matter what their level of income,' said Charlie dryly. Francine glared at her and Suzanne realised the conversation could get out of hand if she didn't step in.

'Francine, the account wasn't actually in your name— but it did use that nickname we had for you at school—

back in the days of 'London Loiters'.'

'Not 'Little Piggy Matheson', said Francine with a laugh. 'I thought I'd got rid of that image, but some idiot from our old class was talking to a friend of hers in Fleet Street and gave him the details a few months back. There was a short burst of ridicule in the papers, and somehow they managed to find an old picture of me, back in the fourth form, but there's no crime in being plump.' At this Charlie snorted and Francine glared at her again before going on, 'Okay, maybe I was a little more than plump, but the fact remains that anyone in the country who reads that particular newspaper or watches *Have I Got News for You* knew about my old nickname. It was news for a couple of days, but then it went away. Frankly, I had more important things to worry about than this country's obsession with how a person looks.' But as she said this, Suzanne watched the other woman glance in the tall mirror on the back of the door and tuck her hair behind her ears. Francine was obviously more comfortable with her current self-image than she was with her fourteen-year-old one. 'So, this is the only evidence you have against me, is it?'

Charlie looked uncomfortable and licked her lips, apparently unsure what to say next. But Suzanne took up the story at that point.

'Well, it may not sound like much, Francine, but the fact remains that you do have links to Mazokapharm and Mladov has been threatening to blackmail you. So you're definitely part of this whole picture, even if we don't know why yet.' Francine threw herself back on the sofa and groaned.

'Yes, you're absolutely right. But I can tell you hand on heart that I had no idea about this account and I have never profited from any counterfeit drugs.' The two sisters stared at their old school friend, saying nothing, and then looked at each other. Charlie slowly nodded and smiled.

'Okay, Francine, we believe you,' Suzanne said. 'Now are you willing to help us sort out this mess and try to work out what's going on—and why they might want to involve you?'

'Of course I will. After all, it seems someone decided to involve me personally in all of this—although I still don't understand why—so it's as much in my interests as anyone else's.' She paused and looked at Charlie, pointing her finger. 'But I don't want to know about any more computer hacking, right?' Charlie grinned and held out her hand to shake Francine's.

'You've got a deal,' she said.

'Okay,' said Suzanne, standing and starting to pick up the dirty plates and empty curry cartons, 'we need a plan of action. Let's get this mess cleared up and then look again at everything we know.'

With Charlie taking notes on her laptop, the three women went back over every scrap of information and speculation they had so far, and tried to identify a pattern.

'One thought occurs to me, Charlie said at one point. 'If Chibesa's dirty—and it rather looks as though he might be—then what about WB? Do we need to worry about him too?'

Suzanne was still trying to get her head around the fact that the efficient Zambian, on whom she relied so much for the organisation of her trips, could be working for the other side. She couldn't bear it if WB was also found to be untrustworthy.

'I don't think so,' she said. 'He's proved himself to be very useful over the past few months, especially when it came to helping Sara get out of Swaziland.'

'Sara? Is that the woman who started all this for you?' Francine asked. 'The one you mentioned during your presentation?' The only thing the sisters hadn't mentioned so far to Francine was Sara Matsebula's involvement. Now, Suzanne glanced over at her sister and the pair had another of their silent communications.

'You do realise how unnerving that is for other people, don't you?' asked Francine.

'Definitely; why do you think we do it?' said Charlie with a grin. Then she turned to Suzanne. 'I think we need to give Francine the last piece of the jigsaw; otherwise, why should she trust anything we say?' Suzanne nodded.

'I think you're right.' She took a deep breath and explained to Francine exactly what role Sara Matsebula had played in getting the investigation going. Then she went on to talk about their fears when things started unravelling in London and how relieved they were to meet Sara in Zambia with WB.

'And if WB had meant to do Sara any harm, why would he have gone to all that trouble to smuggle her out of Swaziland? Wouldn't he just have walked her into the bush and got rid of her? No-one would ever have been any the wiser?'

'That sounds logical to me,' said Francine, while Charlie nodded her head. 'But if Chibesa,' she still seemed to be having difficulty saying that name and paused to swallow before going on, 'if Chibesa knows where WB is hiding her, isn't she still in danger?'

'Possibly, yes, although now that her information is more widely spread, and Banda's operations have been shut down, there's less to be gained by doing her any harm.'

'Unless it could be used to give a message to anyone else who thinks they should talk to the authorities,' Charlie chipped in.

'Good point. We'll talk to WB tomorrow and see if we can arrange for Sara to be moved somewhere safer. Francine, is there anything you can do to help, there?'

'Oh, I should think so; I've got some good contacts down there in the British Embassy,' their new partner replied with a grin.

'Francine, if I didn't know you better, I'd think you were enjoying all this cloak and dagger stuff,' said Charlie, picking up the wine bottle and pouring them all another drink. 'I'd better open another of these, sis; it looks like it could be a long night.'

# 30: ENGLAND; MAR 2005

'Well, I still don't believe it! Chibesa's not like that! He's completely honest.' Suzanne knew she was repeating herself, but she didn't care. It was after midnight; Francine had finally taken a taxi back to her apartment in Dolphin Square, but the sisters were still talking through everything they'd learnt that evening. Charlie sat on the sofa, saying nothing and watching as her sister went back over the arguments again. 'No, there's got to be a logical explanation.'

'Well, maybe there is, sis; but you have to admit it's not looking good—' But Suzanne wasn't in the mood to listen to that sort of comment.

'I'm sorry, Charlie, I just don't believe it.'

'Well, you could always ask him; see what he has to say for himself.'

Suzanne threw herself down on the sofa next to her sister and exhaled hard. Then she sat up and nodded.

'Yes, you're right, of course. That's what we need to do. But it's not going to work over the telephone. We're going to need to talk to him, face to face.'

'Well, that should be easy,' said Charlie, 'we'll just jump on the next plane and hightail it out to Zambia, shall we? I can't see Sir Frederick having a problem with that.'

'No, of course it's not going to be easy, but we need to think of something—and pretty damn quick, too.'

But when the solution to their problem arrived a few days later, it was from the last direction they might have suspected.

Suzanne was in her office, staring out of the window at the scene below her. It was late afternoon and the sun was starting to set. Looking down at the Thames, she watched barges and the occasional charter vessel meander along the river, sluggishly nosing through lazily lapping water turned pale gold in the setting sun. The trees along the embankment were still bare, but if she peered carefully, she could just make out buds starting to appear. Soon, they would be heavy with thick green foliage; blossom peeping shyly from behind leaves in the chestnut trees. She realised with a start that winter was over and spring was advancing. Then raising her eyes to the iconic building across the bridge from the hospital, she mused on the many people, famous faces and less well known ones, sheltering behind the ornate façade. She wondered if Francine was sitting across the river from her right now and, if so, whether she was still brooding on the whole Ernest/Chibesa episode. Last time they'd spoken, she had seemed rather depressed about the whole thing. *As well she might,* Suzanne thought. *She's supposed to be a smart, educated woman, yet she fell for the oldest trick in the book.* She sighed. They really did need to find some way of getting to talk to Chibesa. There were just too many unanswered questions.

It might have been fate that made the telephone ring just then—or it might have been pure coincidence. As a scientist, Suzanne didn't really believe in fate; but as a realist, she knew that apparent coincidences very rarely were such.

'Suzanne Jones speaking.'

'Mrs Suzanne, it's Mukooyo here.'

'I beg your pardon?'

'Mukooyo, Walter Mukooyo—from Kenya.' The voice sounded irritable, as though he was not used to repeating himself. Suzanne gave a start, and then stood up, as though the Minister was in the room or they were on a video phone.

'Minister, good afternoon. How lovely to hear your voice.'

'Hmm, I doubt that somehow, Mrs Suzanne.' There was now a hint of laughter in the voice and Suzanne felt herself blushing as she remembered the less than friendly atmosphere the first time they'd met, back in Swaziland. 'I believe you think me unhelpful and complacent.'

'Oh, I wouldn't say that, Minister,' she replied, feeling her face burning even more. 'Besides, I've learnt a lot in the short time I've been on this project.' A thought occurred to her. 'And I never had the opportunity to thank you for loaning us your table at the Game Park restaurant when we were in Nairobi. It was a most entertaining evening.' Looking back, it was more than that, but she didn't think the Minister would be interested in hearing about the burglary in her hotel room. 'What can I do for you, sir?'

'I was hoping you could do me a favour, Mrs Suzanne. Do you have anything to do with the guest list for next month's London shindig?'

'Which shindig? Oh, you mean the International Health Forum quarterly review meeting?'

'That's the one.'

'Well, that's mainly organised out of Sir Frederick's office. But the counterfeiting project is a major element of the upcoming meeting, so I'm having some input this time around.'

'Excellent, excellent.' Suzanne could almost see Mukooyo rubbing his hands together. 'Mrs Suzanne, could you get me on the list?' Suzanne was surprised by the request—and immediately suspicious. The Minister hadn't been too impressed with her project, so she didn't believe he would be willing to come all the way to London just to go to another meeting about it. What could be bringing him here? But before she had time to frame a diplomatic question, the answer came unprompted. 'I know Sir Frederick will be busy hosting all the delegates, but hopefully he'll have time to come to the world rifle championships with me. They're being held in the UK the week after the IHF meeting.'

So that was it; a sporting competition. Had the man no shame? She wished it was as easy for her to move people around the world when she needed to. And just like that, the solution to the Chibesa problem presented itself. She planted a smile on her face.

'Why, yes, Minister; I'm sure that could be arranged,' she said. 'But there is one tiny thing I'd like to ask you to do for me—call it payment in kind if you like.'

There was a pause on the line, and Suzanne wondered if she had pushed him too far; but then a bark of laughter burst across the airwaves.

'Go on then, Mrs Suzanne; name your price!'

It was the first time Chibesa had been to London and he gazed out of the taxi window with a look of pure glee on his face as they drove past Buckingham Palace and down The Mall. If he was surprised that The Honourable Walter Mukooyo, Minister of Health in the Kenyan government, had requested the company of a logistics expert from Lusaka on the trip to London, rather than one of his own minions from Nairobi, he didn't say anything. From the day Suzanne had emailed him to warn him of the Minister's 'suggestion', he had been nothing but enthusiastic and helpful in preparing for the trip.

Despite Francine's revelations and their suspicions, Suzanne had been genuinely pleased to see her erstwhile colleague when he walked out into the arrivals hall of Heathrow's Terminal 3. They had gone through a lot together in the past six months and she was still finding it very difficult to believe he was mixed up with Kabwe Mazoka and Banda. The women had arranged a little surprise for the next evening, which would hopefully shock the truth out of him; but for now she was just happy to be sharing a taxi with this smart young man once more. They had arranged for him to fly in to London a couple of days before the Minister, along with the rest of the delegates, was due to arrive.

'There are a few last minute arrangements to be worked on,' she'd said on the phone when he got in touch to confirm his itinerary, 'and it will also give us a chance to get up to date on the counterfeiting action plan.' He agreed without question and she'd felt guilty about the trick they were going to play on him.

'Come on! Given what happened to Francine, I don't think there's anything to feel guilty about,' said Charlie when she heard of Suzanne's qualms. Francine had not said anything at all, although she looked a little uncomfortable every time the upcoming trip was mentioned.

Now, as the taxi pulled up in front of the hotel, Chibesa turned and smiled at Suzanne. 'Makes a change, doesn't it?' he asked. 'For you to be delivering me to a hotel, rather than the other way around.'

'It certainly does, Chibesa.' She watched as the porter took charge of the bags and ushered the guest into the reception area. 'Right, I'm going to leave you to get some sleep; I'll pick you up in the morning at eight-thirty,' she said. As she walked away from the hotel and towards Vauxhall Bridge and home, she wondered if her friend would still be smiling at her this time tomorrow—or indeed if they would still be thinking of each other as friends at all.

## 31: ENGLAND; APR 2005

The three women had decided, after a lot of deliberation, to hold their confrontation meeting at Suzanne's flat.

'Is that wise?' Francine had asked. 'Suppose he turns violent?'

'Have you ever known Chibesa to be violent?' Charlie asked Suzanne. When her sister shook her head, she turned to Francine. 'And, Francine, did Ernest ever show any violent tendencies when he was with you?'

'Never; he was always gentle and considerate. At least, he seemed to be.'

'Well, I don't think he's likely to turn into a violent monster overnight, do you?' She grinned at the other two. 'And besides, I would think the three of us are well able to deal with one slim young man, are we not?'

So the next evening after work, Suzanne and Chibesa strolled along the embankment together in the twilight. Suzanne had found the day increasingly stressful as the time approached for them to tackle Chibesa and maybe find out that he had been working for the other side all along. Chibesa didn't seem to have noticed a problem, although he was quiet now. He yawned frequently and when Suzanne asked, he admitted he had not been able to sleep well in the hotel the previous night.

Charlie was waiting for them when they arrived. She seemed genuinely pleased to see Chibesa once more and Suzanne wondered if she was acting too. She had been more willing than the other two to accept that Chibesa might be 'dirty', but that didn't show in her grin or the hug she gave him. She seemed perfectly relaxed as she poured him a beer and steered him towards the sofa.

'We'll have a drink and a chat to start with; then we're going to ring down for some takeaway, if that's okay,' said Suzanne. 'I know you grew up with Indian food and it would be good to get your opinion on our favourite local place.' Her mouth felt dry and she found she was having difficulty getting her words out. She wasn't sure whether it was a sense of relief or a sense of impending disaster that hit her when the doorbell rang.

'I'll go,' said Charlie, darting out of the room and pulling the door to before Suzanne could open her mouth. Maybe her sister was more nervous than she looked, after all.

After what seemed like an interminable wait, but was probably only a few seconds in reality, the door to the lounge swung open and a short blonde woman, in business suit and high heels, walked in.

'Good evening, Ernest,' said Francine.

Chibesa jumped up, catching the coffee table with his foot as he did so. There was a crash as the table turned over, tipping his beer all over the pale green rug in front of the fireplace. No-one else seemed to notice and Suzanne knew it was the least of her worries just now.

'Francine, what are you doing here?'

'I live here! This is my city; my job is here—no thanks to you. Why wouldn't I be here?'

'But why here, in this flat?'

'These are my friends!' And as the words echoed around the room, Suzanne realised how true they were. Their early life might have been fraught with conflict and rivalry, but that was all a long time ago. And the issues they'd all been facing for the past few weeks had certainly brought them together.

'Well, it's a surprise, but a really nice one,' said Chibesa. 'I've been watching your career with interest.' There was a gasp, although Suzanne wasn't sure whether it came from Charlie or Francine. But she was sure which one of them took the next step. There was a blur as Francine covered the distance between herself and Chibesa, her arm rising through the air as she travelled. The crack as her hand contacted with his cheek was shockingly loud and seemed to ricochet around the small room.

'You bastard; you fucking bastard,' she spat through gritted teeth, before turning on her heel and striding out of the room. There was a bang as the front door closed.

Chibesa sank back onto the sofa, rubbing his cheek and blinking his eyes which shone brightly with unshed tears.

'What was all that about?' he asked. Suzanne wondered how she should answer this question. Either he genuinely didn't know—or he was a very good actor. But Charlie seemed to have no such doubts.

'Oh nothing very much,' she said, the sarcasm dripping off her tongue. 'I guess the Parliamentary Undersecretary for the Department of International Development doesn't appreciate being deceived, seduced and blackmailed, that's all. Funny that; you'd think she'd have more of a sense of humour, wouldn't you?'

'Who deceived her? And who's blackmailing her?'

'So you are happy to accept that you seduced her?'

'Well, I seem to remember it was a mutual agreement, based on the attraction between two consenting adults, but I guess some people might describe it as seduction, yes.' He raised his hands in a gesture of bewilderment and almost supplication. 'But I really don't know why she's so upset. We agreed it was a one-off and we said goodbye amicably.'

Suzanne thought back to her week with Nathan and

realised there were similarities in the two situations. She would think about that later. Now, she needed to find out exactly what Chibesa knew.

'Okay, Chibesa,' she said, sitting down on the sofa next to him. 'Why don't you go back to the beginning and tell us what happened when you met Francine in Lusaka. And then we'll fill you in on the details of why she's so upset.'

'So, how much has she told you?'

'Just assume we know nothing,' Charlie said, plonking herself down on one of the dining room chairs and folding her arms. 'Start from the beginning and tell us everything, even the little details you might think are irrelevant.'

*It was back in 1997, my last year at a student. I was taking Economics and Business Studies at the University of Zambia, in Lusaka. There was a big conference being held on campus during the autumn holidays; a Commonwealth Conference on International Aid. People were coming in from all over the world. And a call went out for volunteers to help with the organisation and hosting. It was a great opportunity, and we all jumped at it. I was given the job of welcoming delegates, handing out their documentation packs, that sort of thing.*

*And it was on the afternoon before the main event started that I first saw Francine. She strode into the foyer where the tables were set up, like a galleon in full sail! I thought she was magnificent! So smart! So self-assured! So strong! And not like the skinny models we see on television and in the magazines. This was one European who was comfortable being more 'traditionally built' as we call it in Africa.*

*Of course, she didn't notice me. Why should she? I was just one of the youths in T-shirts and baseball caps, handing out delegate packs and name badges. She went to the table next to mine, so I heard her give her name, take the pack, smile and turn to go. But that was enough. In just those few seconds, I knew I wanted to get to know Francine Matheson—but at the same time, I knew it was impossible.*

*But although Francine failed to notice me—and my interest in her*—someone else was watching—and decided to help me out.

'Would you like to get to know her?' asked a voice in my ear. I turned to see one of the other members of the British Delegation watching me with a quizzical look. 'Our Francine; would you like an introduction?'

'I certainly would, but it's not going to happen. We're under strict instructions not to engage the delegates in conversation. We're here as hosts, available when required, but otherwise invisible,' I said with a sigh.

'But how about if we were to convert you into a delegate for the next few days? You're a student, aren't you? What are you studying?'

'Economics and Business Studies.'

'Well then, wouldn't a seat in the auditorium be better for your career than sitting behind a desk out here?' He gave a sly smile. 'And it would probably bring you closer to the lovely Francine at the same time.'

Well, I wasn't going to argue with an opportunity like that, now was I? My new friend introduced me to Kabwe Mazoka. He was attending the conference on behalf of the Zambian Pharmaceutical Society and was supposed to be bringing his production manager with him, but he'd come down with a dose of malaria and had pulled out. So for the next week, I became Ernest Wishaw from Ndola, attending my first conference with my boss.

And it was a fascinating occasion. I heard all sorts of prominent people talk about the importance of aid: how it's raised; how it's spent; how it's monitored. It was certainly good material for my course. Some of my essay results after that week were truly impressive.

But more importantly, I was able to get close to Francine—and she actually noticed me and seemed to enjoy my company. She'd only just been elected to Parliament earlier that year and, as an unknown backbencher, seemed a little distant from the rest of the British delegation, although people who heard her comments, and the occasional question she asked during plenary sessions, were saying she had a sharp mind and would go far.

I sat down next to her in the main auditorium at the start of the first morning's session, and by the end of the day, we were firm friends—and I hoped we would become more than that. We spent every mealtime together and sat in the same seats for each of the presentations. In the evenings, we tended to get separated; she had a number of formal dinners to attend, whereas I was eating in my student accommodation. There weren't many dinner invitations for a relatively obscure delegate from the Copper Belt, especially one that didn't really exist anyway.

On the last day, Kabwe Mazoka was leaving for the airport to fly home—and I had to pretend I was leaving with him. So we said goodbye and I thought I would never see her again. I put back on my T-shirt and baseball cap and helped everyone get ready to leave. I got a couple of curious looks, but without my suit and tie, I managed to look very different, especially wearing my sunglasses. And it was right at the end, as the last people were leaving, when I saw my friend from the first day once more.

'How did you get on?' he asked?

'It was wonderful. I learnt so much; thank you so much for suggesting it.'

'Yes, yes,' he said impatiently, 'but did you have a good time with Francine?'

I nodded my head. 'Yes, of course; I was just sorry it all had to end when it did. I really enjoyed the last few days.'

'Only days? What about the nights?' he asked, raising an eyebrow at me. I felt myself go hot with embarrassment.

'I didn't…; I wouldn't…; that would be disrespectful…' I faltered to a halt; my companion was laughing at me and shaking his head.

'You idiot; she's a modern European woman. She would have jumped at the chance to spend the night with you.'

I didn't really believe him, but he took me for a beer in his hotel; that beer turned into supper—and a few more beers. And at the end of the evening, he steered me into the elevator and deposited me outside Francine's room. I knocked; there was a long pause during which time I nearly decided to run away, and then I heard footsteps on the other side of the door. When it opened, it was as though she was expecting me. She just held out her hand and pulled me into the room.

*Later, we both agreed it would be better if we left it at that. I was going back to college and to my real name. I didn't dare tell her I wasn't really a production manager, but merely an undergraduate. She was returning to the United Kingdom and soon afterwards, she was promoted and that was that. Until this evening, I never expected our paths to cross again.*

When Chibesa had finished his story of impersonation and infatuation, the Jones sisters sat in stunned silence. It sounded so plausible, and his demeanour was so open that Suzanne found it difficult to do other than believe him. But that didn't alter the fact that this strange episode and encounter between Chibesa and Francine had resulted in their politician friend being blackmailed, not to mention being implicated in the organisation of a counterfeiting gang in Africa.

She wondered if there was any chance of tracking down the mysterious benefactor who had been so conveniently on hand to present Chibesa with the opportunity to participate in the conference. It was seven years ago, but most public service employees she knew saw the civil service as a job for life. It was highly likely he was still around. She made a mental note to check if Francine still had a record of the other members of the delegation.

'Chibesa,' she asked, clearing her throat, 'have you ever met Nico Mladov?' Chibesa shook his head.

'No, I'd never heard of him until Kabwe Mazoka mentioned his involvement in the fire at Mazokapharm. Why would you think I knew him? He's European, isn't he, not African?'

'Yes, he's a Ukrainian. According to Charlie's investigations, he's the son of a big time gangster in Kharkov. But we met him here in London a few months back, just after I returned from the IHF conference in Swaziland.

'No, sorry, can't help you. Why is he so important?'

'We know he's connected to Banda.' Charlie took up

the story. 'Even before the fire in Ndola, we were concerned about him. He returned Suzanne's suitcase after it went missing in Heathrow Airport, pretending to be an airport official. But we think he was just casing the joint—the following day I disturbed an intruder in here, ransacking the place.'

'We think he was looking for Sara Matsebula's evidence,' Suzanne chipped in. 'But more significant than that, it was Mladov who threatened Francine with blackmail.'

'Yes, you mentioned blackmail before. Why was he blackmailing her—and with what?' His question was asked in such a straightforward manner, that Suzanne once again had the strong feeling he was telling the truth; he really didn't seem to have any idea of what was going on. But she needed to see his reaction to the next piece of news. She gestured to Charlie, inviting her to take up the story once more so she could concentrate on observing Chibesa.

'Last summer, a Ukrainian delegation visited London on a trade mission. One of their meetings was with a group of MPs in Westminster. Mladov was one of the delegates.'

'So he's a businessman?'

'Maybe, we are not really sure; as I said, I've been doing some digging and he has definite connections to organised crime in Ukraine. But it doesn't matter—he was on the delegation.' Charlie was sounding impatient now. 'And he asked to speak to Francine privately about the photographs she'd acquired in Africa.'

'What photographs?'

'You really don't know, do you?' Suzanne broke in, unable to keep quiet. 'On the morning she was leaving Lusaka for London, an envelope was delivered to her at the hotel. It contained several photographs of you and her, taken in her bedroom.'

'What? You mean...?'

'Yes, Chibesa—or should I say "Ernest".' Charlie was

back on the war path again. 'Let's just say they were rather compromising—and leave it at that.'

'Francine didn't take her camera on that trip in 1997,' Suzanne continued, 'so when Mladov mentioned photographs from Africa, she knew what he was referring to—and she agreed to meet with him in the bar of the Palace of Westminster after the rest of the delegation had gone.'

'And what did he want?'

'Well, that's one of the stranger parts of the whole thing. He didn't want anything.'

'Nothing? Not even any money?'

'That's right. But he did say they would be back in touch when they needed a favour. '

'And have they been back in touch?'

'No. That was the last she saw or heard of him—until we brought her into the discussions about Banda and we realised she recognised his name.'

Chibesa rubbed his hands over his face and exhaled sharply.

'Poor Francine. No wonder she's so mad at me. But I really didn't know anything about this. I had no idea any photographs were being taken. And I certainly would never get involved in any blackmail schemes.'

There was something about this story that was worrying Suzanne; something she thought they were missing, but she couldn't put her finger on it. She shook her head, and decided to come back to that. She would go through Chibesa's story again later on and see if anything jogged her mind. In the meantime, she stood and picked up the phone.

'Right, I think it's about time we had something to eat. I'll just go and get the number.' She walked out into the hall then after a few seconds called out:

'Charlie, have you moved the menu for Sanjay's place? I can't find the phone number.'

Charlie poked her head out of the lounge, looking

puzzled.

'But it's number five on speed—'

She didn't get any further, as Suzanne grabbed her sleeve and dragged her out into the hall and through to the kitchen.

'Hush,' she hissed, 'I just wanted a quick word with you alone. What do you think? Is he telling the truth?' Charlie pulled a face and shrugged her shoulders.

'I really don't know, sis. I want to believe him; and he certainly seemed shocked to hear about the blackmail. And he didn't seem to know about the photographs; but it's all a bit unlikely isn't it?'

'And there's something niggling at the back of my mind—but I can't work out what it is.' Suzanne gave a sigh. 'Look, Charlie, he's supposed to be a friend of ours. He was a great help with the project when we were in Africa. How about we give him the benefit of the doubt?'

Charlie pursed her lips and Suzanne held her breath until her sister nodded—and then, pointing to the telephone, said with a grin:

'So are we really going to eat? I am starving—and I should imagine our guest will be too.'

The two women returned to the lounge where Chibesa was still sitting on the sofa, looking as though he'd not stirred while they were out of the room.

'Right, Chibesa,' Suzanne said, 'let's get some food ordered and then we can think about how we're going to get Francine back here.'

'You may have convinced us you're an innocent bystander in all of this,' said Charlie, 'but I suspect she's going to be a much harder nut to crack.'

## 32: ENGLAND; APR 2005

In the end, they didn't have to think of a way to bring Francine back. While Charlie and Chibesa were across the street collecting the takeaway food, the doorbell rang. Suzanne was pleased to see their friend standing in the hall.

'I was sitting in the car trying to calm down,' she explained, 'and saw the other two head over to Sanjay's. So I thought I'd come and talk to you before they came back. What did he have to say for himself?'

'Well, it's a convoluted story, but I think I believe his reason for taking on a different *persona*. He certainly seemed shocked when we told him about the photographs and the suggestion of blackmail. Unless he's an even better actor than either you or Charlie, I think he's telling the truth. Although there is still something I can't work out. Something that's worrying me. But it will come to me, I'm sure of it.'

Francine walked up and down in front of the fireplace, hands behind her back, and a fierce look of concentration on her face. Then she stopped and turned to Suzanne.

'I want to believe him; I really do. But I was so hurt when I saw the pictures…'

Suzanne put her arm around Francine's shoulders and steered her to a chair.

'Look, the others will be back in a few minutes. We've over-ordered as usual, so why not have some supper with us and decide for yourself whether Chibesa is telling the truth or not?'

When the front door banged shut and Charlie called out from the hall, Suzanne went out to meet them.

'Chibesa,' she said, 'Francine has come back.' He looked with a start at the door of the lounge. Suzanne went on. 'It's okay; she's calmed down and I've brought her up to date on everything you told us. I think you're safe from further assault.'

'Unless she finds out you're lying, that is,' said Charlie. Suzanne frowned at her.

'That's enough, Charlie; don't tease him. He's had quite an evening of it so far.' Then she turned back to the young African man who looked like he was deciding whether to run away or not. 'We'll set the food out. You make your peace with Francine.' He hung back, but she gave him a gentle push towards the lounge. 'Go on, she's not going to hit you—again!'

The sisters took their time setting out the plates and opening the boxes before Suzanne poked her head around the door of the lounge.

Francine was sitting on the sofa with her arms folded. Chibesa was standing by the window, staring out across the Thames to the lights of Pimlico. There was silence in the room. But it was a comfortable silence, and Suzanne breathed a sigh of relief.

'Food's ready,' she said. 'We've set it out in the kitchen. Come and get it.'

It was later that evening, just as Francine was getting ready to leave, having offered Chibesa a lift back to his hotel, that the niggle at the back of Suzanne's mind finally fell into place.

'Kabwe! Kabwe Mazoka!' The others all looked at her in surprise. She rounded on Chibesa and threw her hands wide in question. 'You said it was Kabwe who sneaked you in to the conference. Kabwe who gave you the papers for his delegate, Ernest Wishaw.'

'Yes, that's right.'

'So why did you never mention this before, Chibesa?' Charlie and Francine swung round and stared at him as well as the meaning of Suzanne's words started to sink in. 'All the time we were planning my itinerary; afterwards when you heard about my being kidnapped. For goodness sake, when the man killed himself! All that time, Chibesa, you never once mentioned you knew him. What the hell is going on?'

For a minute it looked as though Chibesa would refuse to reply. A range of emotions passed across his face and Suzanne suspected he was contemplating just keeping on walking—out of the lounge, down the corridor and through the front door. And a part of her wondered if maybe that would be the best possible thing. She had been through so many emotions in relation to this man: she thought he was her friend; he tried to discourage her from getting involved with Sara Matsebula; then, after George's death, he became a wholehearted supporter of everything she was trying to do. Then she saw Francine's picture and thought he was one of the enemy. But this evening he had managed to make them trust him again and believe he was an innocent dupe in all this. And now, there seemed to be yet another twist in the tale. She was not sure she could handle it. But Charlie also seemed to sense the thoughts going through Chibesa's mind; she jumped to the door, slammed it shut and stood with her back against it.

'Oh no you don't,' she growled. 'I want to hear your answer to Suzanne's question.' Francine didn't say anything. She just went very white and stood staring at Chibesa, a look of betrayal once more on her face.

Chibesa closed his eyes and shook his head then

opened them, took off his glasses and polished them on the bottom of his highly coloured embroidered shirt.

'I tried to tell you,' he said in a voice so quiet they all leaned forward to catch his words. 'When we were in the office planning your trip to Ndola, I mentioned I'd met Kabwe once before.'

'Yes, but you gave me to believe it was a chance meeting, years before.'

'It was. At least it was more than seven years before, and I only met him at the conference. We never communicated after that.' He sighed and looked around at the three of them. 'May we sit down again, ladies; this may take a while.'

Suzanne sat at one end of the sofa, while Chibesa took his former seat at the other end. Francine chose a hard-backed chair as far away from Chibesa as she could. Charlie didn't move from her position guarding the door. The young man continued to talk in his quiet tones. Suzanne realised she had never heard him raise his voice to anyone.

'To tell you the truth'—at this point, Charlie snorted, but Chibesa ignored her and carried on talking—'I was embarrassed about the deception I'd taken part in—and I was also very fearful for my job. Work's scarce in Zambia these days and those of us lucky enough to have a job are very careful not to do anything to risk getting fired.'

'But, as you say, Chibesa,' interjected Suzanne, 'this all took place years ago. Why should it affect your position now?'

'There is always someone snapping at your heels, eager to get you into trouble and then profit from your misfortune.'

'But why would you be in trouble?'

'Because I impersonated someone else; I tricked my way into the conference. And afterwards, I used some of the experience and some of the knowledge I gained that week to enrich my essays and push up my marks. It could be suggested I cheated my way to my degree.'

'That's all a bit convoluted, isn't it?' It was the first time Francine had spoken.

'It may seem so to you, Francine, but believe me, I've seen it happen before,' he said, smiling ruefully at her. But this time, she didn't return his smile. He turned back to Suzanne, maybe sensing she was currently the best opportunity he had for an ally. 'Besides, it was a big thing to me, but it was probably something Kabwe didn't even remember. And Dr Businge was an old friend who knew his father. It didn't seem relevant that I'd met him once. And then after he killed himself, there didn't seem to be anything to be gained by speaking up. And the longer I left it, the harder it became to say anything.'

'But this would explain why you didn't want to come with me to Ndola. I wondered at the time whether the reason you gave for staying in Lusaka was nothing but a ruse.'

'Well, I did think it was better to "let sleeping dogs lie". Although when you were kidnapped, I was horrified. If only I'd been there, it might never have happened."' Suzanne didn't want to think about her interlude in the isolated hut; it was an episode she had managed—almost—to exorcise from her mind. She waved her hand at him.

'Or on the other hand, we could both have been kidnapped—or worse. There's nothing to be gained from regretting decisions made in the past.'

'Okay, Chibesa,' Charlie said from the doorway, 'I can understand why you might have kept quiet about having met Kabwe Mazoka. But why on earth didn't you tell us about knowing Francine? You were unmarried, even if Francine wasn't, and you didn't indulge in anything other than a bit of rumpy-pumpy.' Francine frowned at this dismissal of their passionate encounter in this way, but said nothing. 'You weren't spying or anything like that. What was there to lose?'

Chibesa looked puzzled for a while then said, 'But I didn't know anything about Francine's involvement in all this until tonight. You never mentioned anything about her when you were in Zambia.'

Suzanne thought back to the evening when their suspicions had been aroused. Not knowing who they could trust, the sisters had decided the best policy was to 'trust no-one'—except each other, of course—until they had come back to England and put some of their theories to the test.

'He's right, Charlie,' she said. 'We only discussed that aspect when we were alone. There's no way Chibesa could have known about our suspicions.' She stared at the young African man, searching for any hint of deception in his eyes. Then she stood up and walked over to pat his shoulder.

'Okay, Chibesa, I believe you.' She looked around at her sister and their old school friend. 'What about you two?'

There was a long silence and she was beginning to think the problem was not going to be resolved, but finally Charlie smiled and nodded her head.

'If you trust him, that's good enough for me, sis,' and, then pointing at Chibesa she went on, 'but we need to be sure you're completely open with us in future. Is that clear?'

Chibesa didn't say anything, but he nodded his head wordlessly and Suzanne thought she saw the hint of a tear in his eye. Francine sighed and shook her head.

'I'm sorry, ladies, but I'm going to reserve judgement for the moment. There's a lot to take in—and frankly, it all sounds a little far-fetched to me.'

'That's understandable,' said Suzanne. 'I'm going to vouch for Chibesa, so if anything goes wrong, you'll be able to blame me, won't you?'

'Hmm, not sure that's much of a consolation, but I guess it will have to do for the time being,' was the politician's reply. 'Right, are you ready to go, Chibesa?'

'You're still happy to give me a lift?' he asked 'You trust me that much.'

'You haven't seen the size of her driver,' said Charlie with a grin.

'Well before we leave, there is one other thing,' he said. 'Ever since you told me about Francine being blackmailed, I've been trying to work out how it happened.'

'But that's obvious, isn't it?' Francine snapped. 'Someone set me up. There was a camera hidden somewhere in the room. From the angle of the photos, it looked like it could have been in the wardrobe.'

'Yes, but why you? There were a couple of hundred delegates staying at the hotel. You weren't the most senior person attending. Why did they choose you?'

'And how did they know you would be providing them with anything to film anyway?' said Charlie.

Chibesa started counting things off on his fingers: 'If I hadn't been given the opportunity to attend the conference; if you and I hadn't got on so well; if I hadn't met my benefactor on the last evening of the conference and agreed to have supper with him; if I hadn't followed his suggestion and knocked on your door; if you'd been out—or hadn't been willing to let me in—there would have been nothing to film.'

'So either the cameras were set up in other rooms as well, just in case...,' said Suzanne.

'...or someone went to a lot of trouble to make sure everything went to plan,' finished Francine. Chibesa nodded.

'And that's why I think it's important I tell you a little more about my benefactor—the man who seems to have engineered all of these situations. He's someone else I've kept track of over the past few years. He's doing a different job today and he has a fancy title attached to his name. I'm sorry to have to tell you, ladies, but the guy who set me up with Francine is Sir Frederick Michaels, Director

General of the IHF. When I knew him, everyone just called him Fred. He was a senior civil servant, working in the Department of Health and Social Security. He seemed to know Africa pretty well and was confident in his dealings with everyone, at whatever level. We all looked up to him—but it's beginning to look as though he was playing us all along, isn't it?'

Suzanne and Charlie looked at each other in stunned silence. Suzanne found it impossible to believe her boss could be implicated in any way in Banda's schemes.

The silence was split suddenly—and shockingly—by laughter. Francine Matheson sat with tears of mirth rolling down her cheeks and shaking her head. 'Oh Chibesa, I've just remembered why I liked you so much. You were always making people laugh with your outrageous stories. But even for you, this one's a bit over the top.' She stood, smoothed down her skirt and picked up her bag and coat. 'Okay, ladies, I think we've had enough trauma for tonight. I've got an early meeting in the morning, so I'm going to take Chibesa back to his hotel and then head straight to Dolphin Square. We'll talk about this again tomorrow evening.' And as she swept out of the flat, followed by a rather crestfallen-looking Chibesa, she was still chuckling to herself.

## 33: ENGLAND; APR 2005

Suzanne couldn't pinpoint when the three women started to take seriously Chibesa's comments about her boss. It might have been when she talked about how he'd tried to warn her off getting involved with Sara Matsebula after her first IHF presentation. Or maybe it was Francine's comment about him being the one who introduced her to Mladov during the Ukrainian visit. Or it might even have been when Charlie made a throwaway remark about the sort of lifestyle he could expect once his much-heralded retirement arrived later that month. But suddenly all three of them seemed to be talking about Sir Frederick Michaels—and the more they talked, the more their suspicions grew.

They went back through their notes, looked at them from a different angle—and all at once, everything fell into place. The one common factor in all the links of the chain was the soon-to-be-retired Director of IHF.

'But this is ridiculous,' said Suzanne. 'The man's been knighted; he was a respected civil servant before he took on the IHF role. He's met the Queen, for goodness sake!'

'So did Antony Blunt,' said Francine dryly. 'I'm sorry, Suzanne, but I think it all makes sense.'

'And someone's obviously tried to frame Francine,' Charlie chipped in, head bent over her laptop and fingers flying across the keyboard. 'And I'll tell you something really strange.' The other two looked askance at her until she glanced up with a puzzled face. 'He seems to have been born in his mid-twenties!'

'I beg your pardon?' said Francine.

'There's huge amounts of stuff on here about his career, his marriage, even a bit about him winning a medal for shooting while he was a mature student at university,' Suzanne's mind flew back to his comments about shooting with Walter Mukooyo, 'but nothing before the age of twenty-seven.'

'But doesn't that just mean it's pre-internet days?' asked Suzanne.

'Not really; if you look up other people with his sort of profile, there's always something about childhood, schools attended and the like.'

'Maybe he was brought up abroad?' suggested Francine.

'Possibly, but I still think it's suspicious. I'll keep searching,' said Charlie.

The women spent the next few evenings rehashing the same ground, desperately searching for something that would confirm their suspicions—or lay them to rest for good. Although Suzanne knew if that happened, they'd be back to square one and yet more children could die.

At the beginning of the following week, Suzanne's mobile rang while she was sitting at her desk waiting for her laptop to power up. It was Francine, apologising for phoning so early.

'The Prime Minister's throwing a quiet little dinner party for Sir Frederick next Wednesday—and I've been invited. Are you going?'

'No, not to that one; I don't think anyone from IHF's been invited. We're all going to the general bash the day before, but I understand this one's just for very special guests. It's being hosted by the PM himself, isn't it?'

'That's right; I hoped you'd be there too. Looks like I'm going to have to do this alone.' Suzanne thought she detected a note of excitement in Francine's voice and that worried her.

'Do what alone?'

'Why, tackle him, of course. Accuse him right out and see what he says.'

'That doesn't sound like a very sensible approach, Francine,' cautioned Suzanne.

'No, it doesn't, does it?' came the amused reply. 'A bit like bursting into my office and accusing me of financing Banda.' Suzanne felt herself blushing.

'Fair point.'

'Besides, what's he going to do? It's at Number 10 for Pete's sake. The place will be bristling with security men. The guest of honour's not going to risk losing his comfortable retirement at the last minute, now is he?'

It wasn't the first time Francine had gone to the Prime Minister's residence in Downing Street. Once before she'd walked along the pavement under the eyes of the press, to hear what position she was being offered in the new government. Then she'd made the short journey from Westminster on foot. Now she was driven in her official car. And her Armani dress and elegant accessories were a little different from the everyday work suit she'd been wearing last time. But once again she had butterflies racing around inside her stomach and she wondered if she was going to be sick. She took a deep breath before stepping out of the car; smiling at the policeman on duty, she walked through one of the most famous doors in the world where the evening's host and the guest of honour were waiting to greet her.

Francine wanted to judge her approach carefully. Too early in the evening and Sir Frederick would probably find it easy to evade her questions. She knew he was adept at avoiding the issue if he needed to—it took one to know one, as her mother used to say. On the other hand, if she left it until after he'd had too much to drink, his reaction could be unpredictable.

Her opportunity came at the end of the fish course. An aide came in and whispered discreetly in Sir Frederick's ear. He nodded, dropped his napkin on the table, excused himself to the Prime Minister, and followed the aide out of the room. As the plates were collected and white wine glasses replaced with larger vessels for the Bordeaux accompanying the main course, Francine murmured apologies to her neighbour, the deputy leader of the opposition party, and slipped out of the room herself. She could see her target sitting in a small alcove off the main hall, talking earnestly into the telephone. Francine went into the ladies restroom, counted to one hundred and then walked out again. Sir Frederick was just completing his call.

'I'm willing to bet you won't miss that side of the job, Sir Frederick,' she said, making the man jump as she crept up behind him on the tips of her Jimmy Choos. 'Surely not a work emergency at this time of night?'

'No, no,' he said with a quick smile. 'Just a query regarding my travel plans.' Francine raised an eyebrow.

'It seems very late for a travel agent to still be at their desk,' she said. 'I thought maybe it was one of your pals in Zambia, or Ukraine maybe. How is Mr Mladov these days?'

'Mladov, Mladov? Do I know…oh, of course, he's the guy from the Ukrainian delegation, isn't he? Why would he be phoning me?' *Give him his due*, thought Francine, *this man is smooth*. 'Although I seem to remember he was very taken with you. Kept insisting on a personal introduction.'

'Well, there was a reason for that, wasn't there, Sir Frederick?' said Francine through gritted teeth. 'Did you have a good laugh about the pictures before he came to see me?'

'Pictures, my dear? What pictures?' He shrugged his shoulders. 'I'm afraid I have no idea what you're talking about.' He pointed back towards the dining room. 'Shall we rejoin our host?'

Francine marched back to her place, fuming that she had failed to get anywhere in her goading of Sir Frederick. She sat and glared at him for the next few minutes before manners, good breeding and pure common sense took over and she turned back to her neighbour, resuming their conversation from a few minutes ago.

Throughout the rest of the evening, she felt Sir Frederick's eyes on her more than once; but each time she glanced across, he was busy talking to the Prime Minister or the senior member of the House of Lords who was sitting on the other side of him. Then just as coffee was being served, another opportunity presented itself. The Prime Minister cleared his throat, tapped on his glass with a spoon and smiled across at the guest of honour.

'Friends,' he said, 'Sir Frederick asked that this dinner be informal without any long speeches. Of course, I told him I don't do short ones, but he insisted.' Polite titters greeted this attempt at humour. 'But I do want to mention one piece of good news that came across my desk this afternoon. I've been informed by the British Ambassador to Zambia that agreement was reached at yesterday's COMESA meeting to mount a multinational campaign across Africa against counterfeiters.' There was a murmur of pleasure around the table and a smattering of applause. The Prime Minister paused for the silence to return. 'As you all know, Sir Frederick has spearheaded the campaign for the past eighteen months and so it is a fitting tribute to the work of him and his team that we have reached this point now. A lot of drugs will be much safer in Africa as a result.'

Francine stared at Sir Frederick meaningfully, as he acknowledged the applause of the room. When his eyes met hers, his smile slipped a little, before falling back into place.

'Francine,' the Prime Minister's voice caught her unawares, 'as the senior representative here from the Overseas Development department, is there anything you would like to add?' She began to shake her head—then changed her mind; Suzanne or Charlie would not let a chance like this slip by, so she must take the opportunity presented.

'Thank you, Prime Minister,' she said, rising to her feet and glancing around the small table at the dozen or so faces looking up at her. 'We've heard about the IHF campaign, and the breakthrough in the African government forum. But I want to remind you that this isn't about major campaigns or parliamentary decisions; ultimately, it's about people.' She went on to tell the guests about Sara Matsebula and the loss of her sister; about Freedom's sister and her colleagues who died in the fire at Mazokapharm; and about Kabwe whose conscience eventually got the better of him and led to him taking his own life. 'We've got some of the culprits already—and we're close to getting the people at the top of the tree. It will take time, but we'll get there.' She turned to the guest of honour with a smile. 'I just want to assure Sir Frederick that his departure will not interfere with our endeavours and that his project is safe in our hands.' In the ensuing applause, Francine continued watching Sir Frederick, who was staring at her without smiling, a dull red flush spreading across his face. She bowed ironically towards him and then turned to shake the Prime Minister's hand and thank him for a most enjoyable evening.

'Francine, do you have your car here?' Sir Frederick's voice cut across what she was saying to their host, and she turned towards him.

'Yes, my driver's waiting for my call.'

'I wonder if I might beg a lift from you? My wife's promised to pick me up, but she's spent the evening with a

237

friend over near Victoria and it would be easier for me to meet her there. I believe you live in the same direction, don't you?'

'Certainly, Sir Frederick, I'd be glad to,' Francine said, unable to think of any way of refusing. Besides, she would be in a government car, driven by a government driver; the Prime Minister knew she was giving Sir Frederick a lift; and they would be driving a short distance across the city. What could possibly go wrong? Yet she couldn't suppress a shudder of fear as he stood back to let her through the door, then followed her into the night.

The journey was uneventful; Sir Frederick could be good company and their conversation steered clear of any controversial topics. Then as they pulled up in front of the modern apartment block where the IHF boss was meeting his wife, he reached across and gripped her arm with fingers that did not for one minute feel like those of a desk-bound public servant.

'You know, Francine, politics is a very dirty game in some countries, even here in the UK at times, You've been very clever, my dear, to reach your current position without a hint of scandal attaching itself to you. It would be a pity if that situation were to change. Do take care that you don't leave yourself open to any risks.'

'Oh, I think it's too late for that,' Francine said. 'Tell me, Sir Frederick, why me? Why did you feel it necessary to set me up in that way? I was a new MP, I wasn't important; I might never have left the back benches for all you know.'

'Oh, I think you're being too modest,' he said. 'I never had any doubt about your ability. It was obvious from the start you would become a very useful member of the team.' He leaned forward and kissed her on the cheek. 'Goodbye, my dear; thank you for your company and for the lift. I doubt if we will meet again.' And then he was gone. But the memory of his grip remained with Francine for the rest of the journey home.

# 34: ENGLAND; APR 2005

'Sir Frederick, your wife's on line two.' Phoebe's voice cut across his reverie and he gave a start. It had been a long week of farewells, at Downing Street, at Westminster and here in the IHF office. He was glad it was all coming to an end. The sun had gone behind the tower of Big Ben and lights were beginning to appear at some of the windows in the Palace of Westminster, just across the river. He wondered how long he'd been staring out of the window. 'Sir Frederick? Do you want me to say you're in a meeting?' Phoebe sounded concerned, in that genteel manner that had moved her up from the admin office to the General Director's office within a few weeks of IHF being established. He was going to miss her.

'No thanks, Phoebe. I'll take it,' he said. As he stretched out to pick up the receiver, he looked up and smiled at her. 'That will be all. You can head off now.' As he pushed the button connecting him to his wife, he felt, as usual, the iron overcoat snap into place.

'Frederick, where are you?' were her opening words. He guessed this was a rhetorical question, since even the silly woman he'd been saddled with for so many years should have been able to work out his location, since she was calling him on his landline. 'I thought you were coming home early today.' He forced a smile onto his face, believing this would find its way through to his voice. He couldn't afford to upset her now.

'I'm sorry, Popsy,' he said when her whine had come to an end, 'I got pulled into another surprise farewell—and it went on a bit longer than I anticipated. But I'm nearly finished; I'll be away from here in an hour or so.'

'But we're supposed to be at Carlina's by seven! You'll never get home in time. It's really too bad, Frederick—you know how much I've looked forward to this evening. And Carlina's put so much effort into this dinner party.' He closed his eyes and took a deep but silent breath. Then he smiled again—a genuine smile this time, as he realised with a jolt this might be the last conversation he ever had with Pauline—and that he wasn't going to have to sit through another of his daughter's stress-ridden dinner parties.

'Popsy, why don't you go on over yourself? I'll get Hodges to pick you up. He's not assigned to me any longer, but I'm sure he won't mind doing me one last favour. It's not a black tie do, and I've got my car here, so I can come direct from the office and meet you there. How does that sound?'

There was a silence at the other end of the phone then his wife spoke again.

'Well, so long as you promise to leave as soon as you can,' she said. He could hear the struggle in her voice: to continue moaning at him, or to accept the offer of a chauffeur-driven car one last time.

'And just remember, Popsy,' he went on, 'this is the end of it. After this evening, we'll never have one of these conversations again. Tomorrow is the start...'

'...of the rest of our lives,' she completed the sentence for him, her voice softening. After she'd rung off, he stared at the receiver for a long time before shaking his head and exhaling sharply. Then he did a final round of the office, checking every drawer was empty of personal effects and papers. He ran his hand under the desk, pulled out a small key, opened, emptied and relocked the hidden panel disguised in the leg of the hand-made bookcase. The only thing in there was a cream, embossed envelope addressed to his wife, which he dropped into his briefcase before snapping it shut. With a final look around the room where he'd spent so much time in the past five years, he clicked off the light and pulled the door sharply closed behind him.

The journey out of London was the usual Thursday night stop-start crawl. He pulled over just once, to drop the cream envelope into a post box on the Commercial Road. Then, once he got through the Blackwall Tunnel and reached the A2, the traffic eased off and he was able to put his foot down. He glanced in the mirror occasionally, checking there were no police cars on his tail. Getting a speeding ticket at this point was fairly irrelevant, but he didn't want to risk being delayed. He had an appointment to keep.

When he reached the end of the M2, he pulled off the motorway and took the Margate road. By the time he'd passed the airfield, the traffic was much lighter and his was the only car to turn off towards Dumpton Gap. It was quite dark by now, but he wanted to make absolutely sure he was on his own. Nothing and nobody was going to get in his way tonight. He parked the car in the last car park—deserted apart from a Ford Mondeo and one old Mini that looked like it had been dumped. *It certainly isn't going to be moving anywhere on just three wheels*, he thought as he drove past. He switched off the lights and sat in the darkness for ten minutes, until he was certain he was completely alone.

Finally he left the car, collecting his briefcase and laptop from the back seat, before locking the vehicle and dropping the key over the sea wall. Shivering in the cool spring air, he took off his jacket, folded it neatly and placed it on the bench overlooking the bay; he slipped off his highly-polished loafers and left them on the bench as well, placing his briefcase, laptop and mobile on top of them. Then Sir Frederick Michaels, recently retired Director of the International Health Forum turned and, in his stockinged feet, walked away.

His disappearance might have gone unremarked for hours if it wasn't for Deirdre and Mikey, a courting couple, driven out into the night by two large noisy families, and seeking some peace and quiet in the 'Love Shack' as the abandoned Mini had come to be known by the local teenagers. When they arrived, they were too wrapped up in each other to notice the Rover parked on the other side of the car park, but once their passion abated, they became curious. Who would be walking on the beach at this time of night, especially as the tide was nearly full and the strip of accessible sand was shrinking by the minute? They tiptoed across the car-park, poised to run if the vehicle was occupied or if anything seemed amiss.

Finding the briefcase and clothing was not what they expected, and Mikey made a crack about 'maybe someone's topped themselves'.

'You don't think…, Mikey, you don't really think it's someone who's gone over the edge, do you?' whispered Deidre, gripping her boyfriend's arm. He cleared his throat and shook his head, although he kept casting glances to the sea wall, against which the waves were pounding in the darkness. At that precise moment the mobile phone on the bench started to ring, making them both jump. Deirdre nudged Mikey in the ribs.

'Go on,' she said, 'answer it!'

'Not likely,' he said, backing away. 'It might be a trap.'

'A trap? How could it be a trap?'

'Well, it might be someone who's set this up to see how honest people are—you know, like that *You've Been Framed* programme on the telly.'

'Out here? At night? Don't be daft.' But the phone had

stopped ringing by then.

'Look,' said Mikey, 'let's head back into town and see if your Joey's in the pub. He'll know what to do.' The phone started ringing again, its shrill tone cutting across the darkness and making them jump once more. Fifteen minutes later, they found Deirdre's brother, Joey, enjoying a quiet pint in the Flying Catfish.

It had been a bit of a shock to the family when Joey decided to join the Force, and there were some conversations his siblings just couldn't have with him these days, but PCSO Joey Lynch was doing well since he'd joined up six months ago. And, although he didn't realise it when his sister walked through the door of the pub, he was about to get involved in the largest case his division had seen in a long time.

Pauline, Lady Frederick Michaels, was beginning to regret the second vodka and tonic her son-in-law had served her—but that didn't stop her accepting a third one, although she put it down untouched when her daughter came back in from the kitchen.

'I'm so sorry, Carlina darling,' she said, 'I have no idea where he's got to. I am *so* angry with him!' She screwed a tissue into a tiny ball between her hands and bit her lip to stop herself from crying. Carlina was looking very cross— and she didn't like it when her daughter got cross—she was so like her father in many ways. Carlina glanced at the clock on the mantelpiece and then back at her mother.

'It really is too bad of him, Ma, I spent bloody ages preparing that beef Wellington—and it's going to be ruined.' She glanced across at her husband who was mixing himself another drink. 'Paul, if Dad's not here in ten minutes, we're starting without him. Can you call the others in?'

'Sweetheart, it's your father's retirement dinner party; you can't possibly...' But maybe recognising the fixed position of his wife's lips, he shrugged and strolled over to the French doors where the remaining guests were shivering on the terrace, supposedly admiring the garden while letting the family members deal with the non-appearance of the guest of honour in private.

Two hours, five courses and some rather stilted conversations later, Pauline had had enough. She wasn't going to sit and endure the pitying glances of the guests any longer.

'Darling, I think I'll go up, if that's okay,' she said, dropping her napkin on the table and retrieving her handbag from under her chair. 'Do excuse me, everyone, won't you?'

Everyone around the table looked at her and there was a chorus of reassurance beginning to roll her way, when her mobile rang—and things got a lot worse than even the evening's dinner party had suggested.

'Good morning, ladies and gentlemen, this is your captain speaking.' The clipped voice coming over the tannoy boomed slightly in the First Class cabin until the steward adjusted the volume. 'Welcome to flight 249 to Rio de Janeiro. I can confirm that all the luggage is loaded, the hold is closed and we're cleared for take-off. Once we've reached our cruising altitude, I'll tell you a bit more about the flight, but for now, I'll leave you in the capable hands of Senior Steward Rachel Moss and her team.'

The clean-shaven tall man with close-cropped hair, sitting in seat 1A, pulled his phone from his pocket and checked it was switched off. He knew no-one would be trying to reach him—certainly not on this number—but it was inconceivable to travel without one these days. He stroked the skin above his top lip with his thumb and first finger—in just the same way that men with moustaches do. The violet of his eyes was startling; in fact, when he'd first seen the contact lenses, he'd wondered if they were a little too bright, but he knew he would soon get used to them.

At check-in, they'd been surprised that he only had one small piece of hand luggage. His fellow passengers were mostly travelling with multiple bags, both in the hold and in the cabin. But he'd just shrugged and flashed a smile at the very attractive young woman behind the desk.

'I travel light,' he said. He might have gone on: 'That's the beauty of making a new start. You don't have to take any of your baggage with you.' But although he'd always believed in speaking his mind, this would have been too risky. There would be plenty of other young women to impress when he reached his destination.

'Mr Hawkins.' The steward was standing next to his seat with a bottle of champagne in her hand. 'Can I get you a top-up, sir?'

'I rather think you can, honey,' he replied, the faint Afrikaans burr coming easily to his lips, 'yes, you certainly can.'

And as the Boeing 777 made a final turn across the city of London before heading westward across the Atlantic, Michael Hawkins raised his glass and silently toasted the life he was leaving behind.

## 35: ENGLAND; APR 2005

As Charlie took her usual shortcut across the park at the end of her daily run, she was thinking about Sir Frederick and wondering how they were going to prove he was behind the counterfeiting operation; she was so engrossed, she didn't notice the slim dark-haired woman sitting on the bench until she stood up and softly said her name.

'Hello, Charlie.' Charlie stopped dead in surprise, then flung her arms wide.

'Annie; sweetie, it's great to see you.' She pulled the young woman into her arms and hugged her. 'I've missed you so much,' she whispered. 'How did you know where to find me?'

'I phoned Suzanne's office and she told me you would be heading back to the flat about now.'

Charlie pulled Annie even closer, but there was no response and she felt her girlfriend, her partner or ex-partner—she wasn't quite sure which it was—trembling.

'Annie, what's the matter?' she asked.

'How touching! I do love a good reconciliation scene.' The voice was sneering, menacing—and heavily accented. Charlie spun around to find Sandro standing behind the bench. He must have been hiding in the bushes waiting for her to arrive. But how had he known she would be there? She looked back at Annie, realising why she had been trembling. Annie's face crumpled and tears spilled down her cheeks.

'Charlie, I'm so sorry; he made me do it...' she whispered. Charlie shook her head and gave Annie another squeeze.

'Don't worry; it's not your fault, love. I'll sort this.' Then taking a deep breath, she turned once more and faced their former boss.

'Hello, Sandro,' she said. 'What a surprise. I'd like to say it's a pleasure to see you—but I'd be lying!'

'And you'd never lie to me, now would you, Charlie? Cheat me, steal from me, maybe, but lie to me—never.'

'It wasn't stealing! You owed us at least that amount in wages—and our passports belong to us.'

Sandro waved his hands dismissively.

'Maybe you're right—although you certainly robbed me of all my staff—and right in the middle of high season, too. But I'm not talking about money or your papers. There's something much more important that you've taken from me.'

Charlie wondered if bluffing would work.

'I've no idea what you're talking about, Sandro.' The Greek took a rapid step forward, grabbed Charlie by the neck and dragged her towards him across the bench. Annie gave a squeal of distress. *No*, Charlie thought, *bluffing wasn't going to work.*

'My book; I'm talking about the book you took from the safe—as you well know.'

'Oh, that tatty old notebook; I threw that away,' she said, gasping for breath as his fingers tightened around her windpipe.

'I don't think so! That's not what your little bitch told me!'

Charlie's heart sank. She hadn't mentioned the notebook to Annie, but she'd obviously seen her hide it

247

safely away in her rucksack on the train. Somewhere, in the distance, Charlie heard the church bells start to chime the quarter hour. She needed to gain time—just a little bit of time would do.

'Okay, Sandro, I admit I still have it—although what it means, I have no idea. It's all Greek to me, so to speak!' He obviously wasn't impressed with her humour, any more than her bluffing. 'Let me up and we can talk about this in a civilised manner.'

The pressure on her neck ceased immediately. Charlie wasn't surprised. In the two months they'd worked for Sandro, she'd heard him use his tongue to bully everyone he could—but she'd never seen him get physical with anyone. He'd always hinted that he had 'others to do that sort of thing for him!' She straightened up and deliberately brushed herself down, smoothing back her hair and giving Annie what she hoped was a reassuring smile.

'Thank you, Sandro. There's no reason why we can't be civilised about this, now is there?' Sandro stirred and took another step towards her. She shook her head but stepped backwards quickly. 'The thing is, I don't have the book, but I do know where it is,' she went on quickly, hoping to stall him. 'As I'm between homes at the moment, I gave it to a friend of mine to look after.'

'And where will we find this friend of yours?'

'Actually, I'm expecting her very soon. We're both visiting my sister Suzanne this evening. It's Friday night, curry night.' She crossed her fingers, hoping Annie hadn't told Sandro she was actually staying with Suzanne. 'Why don't we have a coffee while we're waiting—or maybe you'd prefer a drink, Sandro—it's just about ouzo time, isn't it. We could pop into the pub.'

But Sandro shook his head. 'We'll wait here!' he said and sat himself on the bench, folding his arms and staring at the two women. Charlie reached out for Annie's hand and squeezed her fingers gently. Initially there was no reaction, but then, to her relief, she felt a faint pressure in return. Annie looked up at her and smiled a watery smile.

It seemed like forever to Charlie, but eventually, a black Daimler turned into the street, nosed quietly along to the apartment block and stopped.

'Ah, here she is now,' said Charlie. 'And Suzanne's with her. Do come and meet them.' Pulling Annie along behind her and leaving Sandro to follow in their wake, Charlie ran across the road, just as Suzanne and Francine got out of the car. 'Hello, ladies. I've got an old friend from Greece I'd like you to meet. And, Francine, I think your friend in the driving seat would like to meet him too.'

Francine looked surprised, but then nodded and spoke quietly into the car. The driver's door opened and Little Andy got out. Charlie gave him a brief salute then turned back to Sandro.

'Okay, now this,' she said, pointing to Suzanne, 'is my sister. She works for the IHF—that's the International Health Forum. She's recently come back from single-handedly sorting out a major counterfeiting operation in Africa.' Suzanne looked like she was about to object to this exaggeration, but Charlie just winked at her and carried on, 'there's no need for modesty, sis.' Then she turned towards Francine. 'Now you probably recognise this lady, even from your short time in this country. No? Well you soon will. Let me introduce The Honourable Francine Matheson, Member of Parliament and Parliamentary Undersecretary in the Department for International Development. Going places, is our friend Francine.' She turned and indicated the driver 'and this good man is Little Andy. You can see we go in for a fair amount of irony in our nicknames over here.' She stretched up on tiptoes to pat the man on his massive shoulder. 'We reckon Andy here could give Sly Stallone a run for his money; a regular Rocky is our Little Andy in his spare time.' Finally she turned back to Sandro, whose mouth had dropped open at the sight of the car, and who was looking more uncomfortable by the minute.

'And this, ladies and gentleman, is Sandro. You may have heard me mention him. He's the little shit that we—and several other naive young women—worked for in Crete. He withheld our wages to stop us leaving his employment. He kept our passports in the safe to stop us leaving Greece. And now he's come over to our country, threatened my Annie and tried to attack me—in search of a little black book that he seems to think is important.'

'Not the black book that—' said Suzanne.

'Yes, that's right, Suzanne,' replied her sister, crossing her fingers once more and hoping Francine would realise where she was going with this, 'the black book I gave to our favourite MP for safe keeping.' There was a pause, and then Francine gave a start.

'Don't worry, Mr Sandro,' she said. 'I haven't looked at your book. It's locked safely away—and will remain there so long as nothing happens to make me take it out and examine it closely.'

'And by nothing happens, she means no harm coming to me, to Annie, to Kitty,' there was a hiss from Annie, and Charlie really wished she hadn't mentioned Kitty, 'or to any of the other girls that escaped that day.'

Sandro scowled at the women, but said nothing. Finally he nodded, bowed slightly and turned away. But Francine called him back.

'Mr Sandro,' she said, 'I'm very friendly with my opposite number in Athens. If there is any suspicion that you are up to your old tricks again, I won't hesitate to hand the book over to him. I'm sure it would make very interesting reading.'

Within seconds, Sandro was forgotten. Suzanne and Francine turned towards the apartment steps, while Little Andy got back in the Daimler and drove slowly away. Charlie turned to Annie who was standing to one side, biting her lip.

'Are you coming to join us?' she said. 'We're having a quick curry across the road in a little while. Afterwards, we could come back and talk...' Her voice trailed off as Annie shook her head.

'No, I don't want to do that, Charlie; it's too public,' she said.

'Well, how about I come over to your place?'

'No, you can't do that, either. I'm visiting my aunt this evening; she's in hospital and I promised.'

'Okay, I get the picture,' Charlie said, her shoulders slumping. 'I'll see you around.' She turned to follow the others into the building.

'Charlie,' the quiet voice called after her, 'I really am visiting my aunt; but I'll be free tomorrow evening. Why don't you come round for supper? We can talk then.'

Charlie ran back, hugged Annie hard and swung her around.

'That's great. Will seven o'clock be okay? And shall I bring my toothbrush?'

Annie pushed her way out of her arms and pulled a face. 'I said we could talk. Let's just see how it goes from there, shall we?' She reached up on tiptoes and kissed Charlie on the cheek. 'I have to go. See you tomorrow, then,' and turning, she walked away.

Charlie watched Annie cross the street and walk through the park gates. She had a good feeling about this. She was sure Annie wanted her back. And if she did, this time she wasn't going to screw it up.

There had been too many other Annies in the past; women she'd kept at a distance, in order to protect them. When they'd got too close, she'd either walked away or more often, given them a reason to leave. She was tired of living that way.

Sandro's little black book wasn't, as he thought, held safely in a government office. Charlie had passed it up the line on her return from Greece. What they did with it, she didn't need, or want, to know. As far as she was concerned, that project was now closed. And if tomorrow's dinner went well, she would tell them she wouldn't be doing any more.

Charlie felt relief wash over her. It was finished. Now she could tell Suzanne how she'd funded her trip to Africa, where she'd got the surveillance device from—and what had really happened when she was thrown out of army training camp all those years ago.'

Charlie was grinning to herself as she ran up the steps and through the front door. She took the stairs three at a time and caught up with the other two just as they reached the front door.

'Put the television on if you want to watch the news, Francine,' said Suzanne, as she headed towards her bedroom. 'I need to get out of this suit before we go across the road.' But Charlie grabbed her hand and pulled her back.

'It looks like I'll be out of your hair very soon, sis,' she said. 'I'm having supper with Annie tomorrow evening.'

'Oh, Charlie, that's wonderful,' her sister said, then as though realising how that might have sounded, 'oh, I mean, that's wonderful for you. I don't mean I'll be glad to see the back of you.' But Charlie waved away her protestations.

'It's okay, I know what you mean—although you must admit it would be nice to get your privacy back.'

'Charlie, you know you're welcome to stay here whenever and for as long as you like!'

'Yes, I know—and I'm very grateful—but there are some home comforts a sister just can't give you, if you know what I mean,' she said, giving Suzanne a saucy wink. From the lounge she heard the familiar signature tune for the six o'clock news. Then there was a screech from Francine.

'Suzanne, Charlie, get in here now!'

Francine was transfixed in front of the television where Sir Frederick Michaels's picture was emblazoned across the screen. The newsreader's voice could be heard in the background, talking about the eminent, recently retired public servant who went missing on the way home from the office on his final day.

'Sir Frederick has been missing for twenty-four hours, and police and family are concerned for his safety.' Charlie gave a snort of derision, but was shushed by the other two women. 'The police have so far declined to comment on the report from a member of the public that a car, believed to be the same make as that driven by Sir Frederick, was found abandoned in the car park at Dumpton Gap in Kent.'

# EPILOGUE

It was front page news for a few days, until other stories came to the fore and it slipped down the list. It had reached page five in the newspapers and number seven on the list of broadcast items before it was confirmed that the car did indeed belong to Sir Frederick Michaels, as did the pile of clothing found on the bench next to the sea wall. An extensive search of the surrounding countryside and shoreline resulted in no body being discovered. It would take a year or more for an official conclusion, but the unofficial consensus was that Sir Frederick had taken his own life. So-called friends and workplace pundits were interviewed on television, giving their views on whether the loss of status and purpose occasioned by the retirement from such a prominent position was likely to result in suicidal tendencies. His wife remained completely silent on the matter.

In June, Suzanne flew out to Zambia for a project update meeting. WB had returned to Kampala at the beginning of the year, taking Sara Matsebula with him to meet his family. But now they were back in Lusaka. With the exception of Charlie, who had stayed in UK, Suzanne's team of conspirators was reunited. On the first evening of her trip, she invited them to dinner at her hotel.

'So, Chibesa,' she said as they sipped their drinks on the terrace, 'what's the news on the ground? Any rumours of Banda setting up again?'

'Not as far as I can tell; not in Zambia anyway,' Chibesa replied. He took off his already spotless-looking glasses and polished them on the hem of his shirt. 'We know that after Kabwe Mazoka's confession, most of the local Banda members plus others in the region were rounded up and charged. Whether there will be any convictions is unclear, but at least they're off the streets and unable to cause any more harm for the time being.'

'And what about Nico Mladov?' said WB. 'Do we know for certain that he escaped back to Ukraine?'

'That's what the Zambian authorities believe; I understand they're working their way through the intricacies of extradition. But it could take years, so I wouldn't hold your breath on that.'

'Actually, I have some news on that front,' said Suzanne. 'Francine has been tipped off by someone in the British Embassy in Ukraine that a body was pulled out of the River Dnieper on the outskirts of Kiev last week. It was badly decomposed, but they're fairly certain it's Mladov. He seems to have fallen foul of someone, although on which side of the law that might be, isn't clear.'

'And probably best not to enquire too closely,' said Chibesa. 'So it looks like we can draw a line under Banda.'

'Well, it's a start,' said Suzanne. 'I'm not naive enough to think we've solved the whole problem, but, at least it's the first step.'

'Yes, but what about the man at the top?' asked Sara. 'Have they found his body yet?'

'No, they haven't, and we really don't think they ever will. Neither Francine nor I believe he would have killed himself. We suspect he had an escape route planned all along.'

'And the rather clumsy attempts to frame your MP friend;' WB said, 'why do you think he did that?' Suzanne shrugged.

'Probably a diversionary tactic to buy him some time,' she said. 'He must have known the stories wouldn't stand up to detailed examination, but there was just enough to slow us down and stop us going to the police.' She sighed and went on, 'But it's so frustrating. And not just for Charlie, Francine and me. I'm sure you'd like to see some closure too, Sara.'

'So is that it? Do we just give up?' Sara said.

'Absolutely not! Charlie never met him, but she's really taken personally the fact that this man was responsible for my kidnapping and trying to make Francine into a scapegoat; not to mention the deaths of Ruth, of George, of Hope and her workmates, plus however many have been killed by the fake drugs. She's carried on researching and she won't stop until she finds Sir Frederick Michaels again.'

The project meeting was upbeat; countries which already had drug regulations in place were starting to set up agencies to monitor both local production and the quality of imports. Other countries were working on getting the regulations in place. The Kenyan representative—not Walter Mukooyo himself, but this time a much more senior official than the one he left behind in Swaziland—volunteered to chair a liaison group of customs officers, aimed at tightening the border controls.

'But we all realise it's a tiny step in a huge journey,' WB said, as he and Suzanne strolled in the hotel gardens one evening. 'And it's not really the local operations we need to worry about. There's so much flooding in from India and China, the stuff supplied by Banda was just a drop in the ocean. So the fight goes on!'

'And what are your plans, WB? Are you going to start

again?'

'Yes, I think so. The fire at the factory wasn't as devastating as the initial reports would have us believe. We reckon we can be up and running again before the end of the year. And in the meantime, I'm going to do some work with the new agency, help train up their inspectors.'

'Is Sara going back with you?'

'No, not this time,' he said with a smile. 'I asked her, of course; she would have been a great asset to my company, and there's nothing for her to go back to in Swaziland. But, let's just say she seems to have other plans.'

On the day before she flew back to UK, Suzanne accepted Chibesa's invitation to eat at home with him and his family. As they sat in the garden, waiting for Hannah to call them to the table, Suzanne was amused to see a continual succession of young children peeking around corners at her, before disappearing with a giggle when she looked at them.

'How many children have you got staying here, Chibesa?' she asked. He shrugged and smiled ruefully.

'I think it's about twenty-three,' he said, 'but they tend to come and go, so we often lose count.'

'And they're all your relatives?'

'Most of them; although we get an occasional friend stopping over for a few weeks. They're all AIDS orphans, we've got the room, and they need the help, so...' He shrugged again.

Just then a group of three young boys walked into the garden. Chibesa beckoned them over.

'Suzanne, you remember Joey and Samuel, don't you?'

'Yes, of course I do,' she said. 'Hello, guys; how's it going?' and then, realising the identity of the third boy, she jumped up and held her arms wide open. 'Freedom! I nearly didn't recognise you.' She had helped Chibesa arrange for Hope's brother to be brought to Lusaka after the fire in Ndola, but the healthy looking boy who now returned her hug bore little resemblance to the dirty, frightened and undernourished child she'd met six months before.

Just then, Hannah called to say dinner was ready. As the children started appearing from all corners of the compound, heading for the main house, Suzanne caught Chibesa's arm and held him back.

'I was going to ask you to come and work in London,' she told him. 'We could really do with your local knowledge back in IHF headquarters.' She watched conflicting emotions running across his face. Then she shook her head. 'But I can't do that to them, can I? You're much too important to these kids, to your family.'

'But Hannah's here, and Silas,' he said. 'I wouldn't want to be away for too long, but there's nothing to stop me coming over there every so often, now is there?' He grabbed her hand. 'Come on, I'm ravenous—and you're going to love Hannah's cooking.'

As they entered the kitchen, Hannah was dishing up the mutton stew. A young woman stood with her back to them, draining a pot. And as Sara Matsebula turned from the sink to greet them, Suzanne suspected it wasn't just the children who would be keeping Chibesa anchored in Lusaka from now on.

It was three months later that Charlie invited Suzanne and Francine to meet her at Sanjay's for supper. She had moved back into Annie's flat three days after the showdown with Sandro and the couple seemed blissfully happy. However, on this occasion, Charlie was on her own when the others arrived. She was looking remarkably smug and could barely wait for their drinks to be delivered and their orders taken before she pulled open a folder and started to read from her notes.

'I've been doing a bit of research,' she began. 'The story starts back in 1955 when a young man called Michael Hawkins arrived in South Africa on the cargo freighter

Prince Albert, out of Liverpool. He was the youngest of seven from a poor family in Bradford, and he'd run away to sea at the age of fifteen.'

As their food arrived and the meal progressed, she told the others about the time Hawkins had spent in Africa, his growth in stature within the underworld in Cape Town and how he finally found things too hot for him over there.

'So one day, he just disappeared! He was seen boarding a boat bound for Europe, but when the ship docked there was no sign of him either on board or in the documentation.'

'This is fascinating,' said Francine, 'but why are you telling us all this, Charlie? What's so special about this young man?'

'Well, how about if I tell you the ship on which he disappeared was the same one that brought Frederick Michaels to England?'

'But that's just a coincidence, isn't it?' Suzanne asked?

'And if I tell you that there was no trace of Michaels getting on the ship in the first place? That he seemed to appear out of thin air just as Hawkins disappeared?'

'Sounds a bit too much of a coincidence to me,' agreed Francine, nodding her head.

'And,' Charlie drawled, obviously enjoying the element of suspense she was building up, 'how about if I tell you that on the evening of Thursday twentieth April this year, the very day that Sir Frederick Michaels was doing his disappearing act, someone called Michael Hawkins dropped a Ford Mondeo hire car off at Heathrow and checked into the Rose Bay guest house on the outskirts of the airport; and that the next morning, the same Michael Hawkins boarded a plane for Rio de Janeiro—and he was travelling on a one-way ticket.' She sat back, wiped her mouth before slinging the napkin down on the table.

'We've got him, ladies,' she said with a smirk, 'once we track down his final movements, we've got him!'

# ENJOYED THIS BOOK?

Reviews and recommendations are very important to an author and help contribute to a book's success. If you have enjoyed *Counterfeit!*, please recommend it to a friend. And please consider posting a review on Amazon, Goodreads or your preferred review site.

# ABOUT THE AUTHOR

Elizabeth Ducie was born and brought up in Birmingham. As a teenager, essays and poetry won her an overseas trip via a newspaper competition. Despite this, she took scientific and business qualifications and spent more than thirty years as a manufacturing consultant, business owner and technical writer before returning to creative writing in 2006. She has written short stories and poetry for competitions—and has had a few wins, several honourable mentions and some short-listing. She is published in several anthologies.

Under the Chudleigh Phoenix Publications imprint, she has published one collection of short stories and co-authored another two. She also writes non-fiction, including ebooks for writers running their own small business. Her debut novel, *Gorgito's Ice Rink*, was runner-up in the 2015 Self-Published Book of the Year awards.

Elizabeth is the editor of the Chudleigh Phoenix Community Magazine. She is a member of the Chudleigh Writers' Circle. Exeter Writers, West of England Authors and ALLi (The Alliance of Independent Authors).

For more information on Elizabeth, visit her website: www.elizabethducie.co.uk; follow her on Goodreads, Facebook, Twitter or Pinterest; or watch the trailers for her books on YouTube. To keep up to date with her writing plans, subscribe to her quarterly newsletter: elizabeth@elizabethducie.co.uk

# OTHER BOOKS BY ELIZABETH DUCIE

Gorgito's Ice Rink
Flashing on the Riviera
Parcels in the Rain and Other Writing
Sunshine and Sausages

**The Business of Writing series:**
Part One Business Start-Up (ebook only)
Part Two Finance Matters (ebook only)
Part Three Improving Effectiveness (ebook only)
The Business of Writing Parts One—Three (print only)

WRITTEN WITH SHARON COOK

Life is Not a Trifling Affair
Life is Not a Bed of Roses